Nell Grant

Summer Led to Autumn

This paperback edition published in 2024
© Nell Grant, 2024

Nell Grant has asserted her right under the Copyright, Designs and Patents Act, 1988, to be identified as the Author of this work.

Cover design by Dave Sneddon, Firehouse Design

All rights reserved. No part of this publication may be reproduced or transmitted in any form or by any means, electronic or mechanical, including photocopying, recording, or any information storage or retrieval system, without prior permission in writing from the author.

ISBN: 9798327777286

The author would like to express her sincere thanks to Rod Grant, Stewart Anderson, Maggie McQueen and to her grandmother who hailed from Pennyghael.

Chapter 1

The metal jaws of the ferry closed as the last car drove on. There was a serious threat of rain from the dark, swollen clouds overhead, and with this in mind, the passengers made their way to the comfort of the lounge inside. Edina stared down at the bubbling cauldron of sea water below her as she hung over the railings on the deserted upper deck. A few heavy raindrops splashed rhythmically behind her like an introductory drum roll for what was to follow. Any minute now, she would feel the full force of nature's wrath and she deserved every cold lash of it.

The travel time from the town of Oban, on the mainland, to the Island of Mull, was approximately forty-six minutes, in which time Edina planned to stand at the front of the vessel to suffer the onslaught. A distant rumble of thunder unnerved her, but she stood firm. Alas, the heavens above opened, sending sheets of torrential rainfall in her direction. It stung her flesh, chilling her to the marrow. Her chin became a drip tip for the falling water as it poured down her face, taking her mascara with it. The boat rose and fell as the waves crashed against the metal hull. Edina clung to the railings as though her life quite literally depended on it.

Relocating to the Island of Mull was a necessity, not a choice, and try as she might, she could not muster a speck of enthusiasm for the new life ahead of her. Of course, America or Australia would have been her preferred option, but her meagre savings would only take her a hundred-and-fifty-one miles from her home in Edinburgh.

In the beginning, she had searched for suitable jobs across Scotland, but there were no positions in her field. In desperation, she threw the net wider to cover *any* jobs in Scotland. The vacant post on the remote island of Mull suited her desire to disappear, and although she had no experience whatsoever in the hospitality industry, she simply embroidered a few tales in her C.V. to secure the position. After all, adjusting the facts of a story to suit was what she did best. Her career in journalism had been entirely based on a tapestry of skilled embroidery.

The rain horse-whipped her ruddy flesh from every direction.

Standing strong, holding tight, and lifting her face to the sky, she shouted, 'Bring it on! Is that the best you've got?'

Her cheeks smarted; her clothes drenched through. Squinting to open her eyes for a moment, she caught a welcome glimpse of land and thought, *Thank you, God.*

As the ferry approached the Island of Mull, the sky cleared, and the sun appeared to wink at her from behind a fast-moving cloud.

Heading below deck, she waited in turn as the passengers filed along to their cars. As good fortune would have it, she had been the first to drive on, which also meant she was the first to get off. Her sodden clothes stuck to the ribbed plastic of the driver's seat, her underwear felt cold and uncomfortable. She turned on the engine, raising the heater's dial to its hottest setting. The air from the vent blasted cold at first, causing her body to tremble wildly. Her teeth chattered together as she gripped the steering wheel. The creaking metal hinges of the boat's doors opened, and a ferry worker in a hi-vis jacket instructed her to drive out.

The air from the convector on the dashboard began to blow warmth over her face and body. It felt most welcome as she drove to the ferry car park to find a space facing the sea. She rummaged around for a white envelope from her handbag. Within the envelope was a letter containing the rental agreement for the cottage she had paid a deposit on the previous week. Reading the address of her new home aloud, she entered the details into her satellite navigation system on her phone. No signal. *Great,* she thought, as she glanced further down the sheet of paper. Fortunately, the cottage owner had pre-empted this dilemma and set out a series of clear directions that a young child could have followed. Memorising the first few instructions, she headed off to find the house.

After taking a left at the car park, she stayed on the road for seven-and-a-half miles, as instructed. It was impossible not to slow to a crawl as she admired the most incredible scenery around her. The wild, mountainous landscape, so unspoiled, unpopulated and, for Edina, uncomplicated.

Perhaps moving to Mull wasn't such a bad idea.

She looked around her in every direction.

No one knows me here. Therefore, no one hates me here.

In this new life that she had reluctantly carved out for herself, she was starting from zero with a squeaky-clean slate.

Driving on the winding, single-track road, she had to question why the creator of the road had found it necessary to meander it in a snake-like design. Would life not have been simpler if the road had been laid straight, enabling the traveller to see all that was ahead? Perhaps the quirkiness of the twisty road was more in keeping with the extraordinary landscape of the island. Anyway, who was she to question the infrastructure of Mull? She was nothing more than an interloper.

In the distance, she could see a large hump on the road approaching. A childhood memory flashed through her mind of her screeching in delight as her mum drove at speed over bumps in the road for her enjoyment.

Should I? Why not!

She put her foot flat on the accelerator, charging at full speed towards the small oncoming hump. Chuckling aloud to herself with the sheer devilment of the deed, she gripped the steering wheel, bracing herself for take-off. She faced the bump with her foot flat on the floor and the speedometer displaying a worryingly high number. When she reached it, a car on the other side came head-on to meet her. She swerved the wheel just as her car took off, which caused her to lose control of the vehicle completely. With her eyes tightly closed, all she could do was hope for the best.

The car flew, then nosedived, almost turning over. Edina peeked through her fingers to see where she had landed. There was a grassy field all around her, with traumatised cows retreating clumsily in all directions. Her first thought, as she stumbled out of the car, was one of concern for the other driver. Through the field's mud she trapsed towards the roadside. In the ditch on the far side, a white Audi sat lopsided. A yelp escaped her lips as she ran over to offer assistance.

Edina peered through the window of the driver's side of the car. There was, what appeared to be, a youngish-looking man sitting with his head resting on his hands. His white-knuckled fingers clung, vice-like, to the steering wheel.

Gently tapping on the driver's side window, she shouted slowly, 'Are you okay?'

The victim lifted his head, turning slowly to look at her. Their eyes met, and Edina made to smile, until she saw the look of unbridled fury on his face. The window of his car began to retract as he kept his narrowed eyes on her.

'What the hell were you thinking, going at that speed on a single-track road?'

She thought his nasty tone was uncalled for. After all, they had just shared a frightening, near-death experience together.

Her bottom lip trembled as she babbled, 'I was just trying to go fast over the humpback in the road.'

The second the words left her lips, she realised how ridiculous it sounded.

'Do you want to know something?' he asked rhetorically, 'that statement might actually be quite funny if you hadn't nearly killed us.' He then shifted the gears in an attempt to reverse his car out of the ditch.

'Do you want me to guide you out?' she asked, ignoring his unpleasant tone.

'No, I want you to get out of my sight and never cross my path again. Ever.'

The car revved into action. He reversed out onto the road, leaving her standing alone in a cloud of black fumes. The smell of burning rubber hung heavily in the air.

As always, Edina switched to her automatic response of giving the impression that she couldn't care less. The flippancy she adopted in such situations had, on occasions, even fooled herself.

So much for the clean slate where nobody hates me.

She shrugged her shoulders as she walked towards the field where her car sat at a jaunty angle. Releasing the driver's side door from the mud, she climbed in, starting the engine. The incident had actually given her quite a jolt.

It may be a good idea to sit for a moment before setting off, she decided. A tear fell onto the steering wheel, but she quickly brushed it off with her trembling hand.

Back on the road, she glanced at the directions laid out on the sheet beside her. If they were correct, she should be arriving at the town of Pennyghael in about two and a half miles. For the remainder of the short journey, she would take it slowly. One near miss was more than enough for her.

I think I should approach every bump on the road with the respect it deserves.

Ironically, the turning for her new home was on the left, just after the sign announcing 'Pennyghael Welcomes Careful Drivers'.

The road surface beneath her wheels took a considerable turn for the worse. Had Edina closed her eyes, she could easily have imagined herself driving across the surface of the moon. It would seem that there was more pothole than tarmac. She feared for the suspension of her car. At first, she made a brave attempt to avoid the craters, but she soon learned that it was fruitless. In order to dodge one hole, you drove into another, which tended to be bigger and more destructive.

The road came to an abrupt end, and Edina found herself facing dense woodland. She cast her eye down the directions page, looking for instruction number seven. It was important for her to know what happened when she reached the forest.

Surely, this journey doesn't end with a hike.

No, there was no hiking involved, according to the list.

7. Take a right turn when you reach the forest. The gate will be shut but not locked.

'Oh no,' Edina said aloud. 'What? No gateman!'

Carefully avoiding the cowpats underfoot, she headed over to open the gate. She had known some wealthy businesspeople in Edinburgh who lived in gated communities. If she had been left with any friends back home, she might have told them that she was now one of the gated community people. Sadly, there was no one to make that joke with because all friendship bridges had been burned on the mainland.

The knot in the rope that held the gate shut was difficult to untie. After wrestling with it for a short time, she adopted the strategy of wriggling it free. Sure enough, the gate was released. Edina marvelled at her own resourcefulness. The wood that formed the gate was now scrubbed colourless by years of changing weather conditions. Edina climbed up onto the middle spar thinking, in a moment of madness, that it may be fun to swing on the gate as it opened. A memory of the humpback debacle flashed into her mind, shaming her into climbing back down.

There has been enough silliness for one day.

The area behind the gate was surrounded by Scots pines. Tall indigenous trees that displayed decades of growth. A circular clearing lay in the middle of the copse of trees. Within the clearing, a quaint little cottage was neatly positioned.

Surveying the scene from the gate, Edina felt an instant connection with her new home. Perhaps connection was too strong a word. Fondness... maybe she felt a fondness.

City Girl Finds Refuge in Highland Hideaway.

She decided that would be an acceptable title had she been writing an article about herself.

Near the front of the house, gravel had been laid to map out two parking places for the occupant and one guest. She mused that they'd thought of everything as she parked the car in the farthest away space.

I'd better keep the other space free for my many visitors.

A common-sense idea entered her head for a moment when she looked at the spaces for parking.

It may have been a better idea to lay the gravel in some of the potholes on the road. Parking on the grass would be a small sacrifice.

Again, she decided that it was none of her business. She was a city slicker who knew nothing of the ways of country folks.

The final instruction in the landlord's letter informed her that the key was hidden under the large rock at the front door. Turning her eyes downward, she saw the strategically placed rock with the red keyring clearly visible at the side. However, the key was well hidden. Edina laughed out loud when she pulled the key from under the stone. If she heard that it had been the original prop key used in the making of the film, 'The Secret Garden', she would have believed it without question. This ornate yet ever so cumbersome key took both of Edina's hands and all her strength to turn.

Chapter 2

On opening the front door, she was immediately standing in the lounge. There was no luxury of a hallway. Once again, a smile arrived on her lips as she absorbed her surroundings. It seemed that the oversized furniture had been retrieved from a nearby castle or stately home, and although it was aged, there was still life left in it. The wing chair by the fire and the non-matching sofa had way too much grandeur for the living space of this small cottage. Both pieces of furniture were faded by wear and time, but any amateur detective could work out the original colour of the fabrics by looking deep within the folds.

Edina walked over towards the fireplace, which had been cleaned out, ready for the next fire. Peering up the chimney, she noticed two large hooks hanging over where the fire would be lit. This was a true indication of the age of the cottage, although Edina had no idea in what decade or century people cooked over their sitting room fire.

I guess calling out for pizza just wasn't an option back then. Actually, it probably isn't an option now.

A door at the back of the sitting room led directly into the kitchen. There were some obvious indicators that this area badly needed an upgrade. The flowery curtains on pieces of string that replaced the kitchen unit doors were the first tell-tale sign. The cracked linoleum was the second.

A white-painted door, which Edina presumed was a larder, was partially concealed behind yet another curtain, the pattern of which did not match the makeshift cupboard doors. She stared at the intriguing-looking latch.

This is probably a cold room for me to use instead of a fridge.

Lifting the latch, she was surprised to see that the door opened outward, revealing not a larder but a steep, narrow staircase.

The stairwell was unlit, with no sign of a light switch on the walls. The top of the stairs led onto a small landing with a bedroom on either side. Both rooms were identical in size and shape, but the front-facing room housed a chest of drawers, which led Edina to believe it was the master bedroom.

The letter from the landlord had described the house as sparsely furnished; this was a gross understatement. There was nothing of a decorative nature to be seen anywhere in the house. No pictures, mirrors, or photographs graced the whitewashed walls, no rugs adorned the floorboards. It was a basic rental, which was costing her around a tenth of the monthly rent she had been paying in Edinburgh.

Chapter 3

Edina's apartment in the city had been situated on the first floor of a Victorian townhouse. The view from the expansive bay window looked across to the First Minister for Scotland's official residence. A life in the city with all of its convenience suited her perfectly. She was a thrill seeker, a no rules, come and go as you please, unpredictable city girl. How many times back then had she planned to have a night in, donning her pyjamas and settling down in front of the television, only to get redressed an hour later to head out to a nightclub.

Oh, that feeling of walking into a busy bar where everyone knows you and all heads turn to look at you.

She reminisced with great fondness. But these days were well and truly over. It was another time, another place, and travelling back there in her mind was non-productive, dangerous even. This was the life she had ended up with and the life she deserved, far enough away from people.

Dragging her suitcase up the narrow stairs, she headed into her new bedroom to unpack her clothes. An airing cupboard in the hallway contained linen for the bed. The towels were folded on the shelf above. The metal-framed bed looked a lot more appealing by the time Edina had dressed it with the sheets provided. After plumping up the insufficiently filled pillows, she straightened the Candlewick bedspread. It was not what she was used to by any stretch, but it could have been worse. She wasn't quite sure how much worse it could have been, but she had to think positively if she were going to make a go of it.

In the kitchen, she found the kettle in the cupboard under the sink. Strangely, she was pleased when she saw that it was not of the electrical variety; but the type that sat on the stove, whistling when it boiled. A caddy containing tea bags had been supplied by the landlord, and behind one of the little curtains, she found an oversized white mug. As she stood waiting for the whistle of the kettle, she opened the bread bin and was met with the welcome sight of Rich Tea biscuits.

These will tide me over nicely for tonight. I'll go to the shops in the morning.

Armed with her tea and biscuit dinner, she headed through to sit on the wing chair beside the unlit fire. As she chewed on the Rich Tea biscuit, she realised why her spirits were so low; here she was alone in her antiquated cottage in the middle of the woods on a Saturday night. Anyone would feel depressed in her situation. The silence around her pressed heavily on her eardrums. She fought desperately not to think of the Saturday nightlife going on back home in Edinburgh. *This isn't so bad*, she reiterated to herself, but she knew that it was.

With no phone signal and no television set, it was clear that entertainment was at an all-time low. Then, to her surprise, she spotted a wireless radio on the shelf in the alcove. At least it was something that made a noise.

The large dial on the front of the radio needed to be turned slowly in order to tune into a station. Crackling static was intermittently halted by the sound of opera or heavy debating from experts. She continued to turn until she heard music, but the static soon took over again. With great precision, she turned the dial back to where she had heard singing. Ever so slowly and gently, barely turning it at all, she tweaked this way, then that, until she arrived at a station with a reasonable reception, playing a rendition of *Cheek to Cheek*.

The thirties-style décor in the room was appropriately lit by the two lamps of low-wattage bulbs, this scene, set to the background music from a bygone age, confirmed to Edina that life as she had known it was over. There was nothing else for it - she headed to the kitchen to whistle up the kettle for more tea.

Feeling thoroughly miserable and lonely, she rested her head against the wing of the chair, pulled the coarse tartan throw over her legs, and cried for the bright lights of the city of Edinburgh.

Her mind drifted back to happy times before all the unthinkable events happened. She pictured herself in her flat in the city centre, checking her outfit in the hall mirror before heading out for the night. George Street with its trendy bars and cosmopolitan feel, was where she was happiest. She entered every bar or club alone but was soon surrounded by people who knew her or wanted to know her. Bar staff warmly welcomed her with hugs and continental kisses. When she made her way home at the end of the evening, the early morning sun was making an appearance. She may have started the evening on her own but she rarely went home alone. If her mother had known of her lifestyle, she would have accused her of being cheap. Edina preferred to describe herself as a free-spirited girl who enjoyed free love. It had crossed her mind, on occasion, that she may have lived a previous life in the swinging sixties.

The Glenn Miller Band soon brought her back to reality as *In the Mood* travelled through the airwaves. Opening her eyes, she saw that she was back in her time capsule instead of living it up in the bustling city.

Things will get better.

Stuffing the fifth Rich Tea biscuit into her mouth, she tried to console herself.

Things have got to get better.

One of the lamps began to flicker furiously before going out.

Well, there you go. That just about sums my life up perfectly. My light has been flickering, and now it's been snuffed out.

The room fell fiercely silent when she turned off the wireless. A few animal screeches could be heard outside, but from which creature they came, she had no idea. After all, she was a city girl. Empty cup in hand, she walked through to the kitchen to the narrow staircase to which led to her bed. Her Saturday night had now come to an end.

Thank the Lord.

As she climbed each step, she assured herself over and over.

Things will get better. Things will get better.

Edina made the decision to wear her socks to bed. She stood for a moment contemplating whether she should put her cardigan on over her pyjamas; yes, it was a good idea. An unlived-in chill hung in the air of the room making the place unpleasantly cold. A loud rattle from the bedframe echoed around her when she tucked herself under the duvet. The sound of metal rattling continued with every movement she made, big or small. It seemed impossible to get comfortable on the flattened mattress as she could feel every spring from the frame on her back. The full moon shone through the window onto her face, but she was glad of the light. Outside, in the darkness, it was the waking hours for noisy nocturnal animals, who showed no respect for the sleeping diurnals among them.

Overall, it would be fair to say that it had been a miserable night, and Edina willed it to be over.

Chapter 4

By morning, Edina wasn't entirely sure whether or not she had slept. However, she did know that she was incredibly hungry as she had not consumed a proper meal in two days. There was nothing in the house to eat as she had been greedy with the rich tea biscuits the previous night. A trip into Tobermory was her plan for the day.

I'm going to buy so much food, these revolting little kitchen cupboards won't know what's hit them.

Getting undressed, she lifted her previous day's clothes from the bathroom floor. After giving them a shake, to oust any roaming spiders, she slipped the jeans and sweatshirt on. Catching sight of herself in the mirror over the sink, she noticed that her hair badly needed a wash.

Oh, who cares? Edina twisted her thick locks up in a hairband. *I don't give a jot what the bumpkins of this island think of me.*

She grabbed for her car keys on the coffee table and headed to the front door. The oversized key looked ridiculous sitting in the lock. The idea of locking the door behind her seemed pointless. The house was so remote and off the beaten track that no one would suspect that someone actually lived there. She herself found it difficult to believe.

I think I'll leave the door unlocked. Any crooked opportunists would soon discover that the potholed road wasn't built for a quick getaway.

Outside in the gravelled, so called carpark, she became aware of the stillness around. She inhaled deeply into her lungs. The pine-scented, highland air was something that she had never smelt before. Looking across at the surrounding woodland, she saw an early morning mist entwined around the tops of the trees while some unseen birds sang the sweetest of songs. For a few moments, she stood processing the scene, and to her surprise, an unfamiliar feeling glowed within her. It was something akin to happiness, no, not happiness, perhaps contentment. It somehow gave her a stamp of endorsement that no matter how miserable things seemed at the moment, she had been brought to the right place at the right time.

The scraping of hunger pangs soon coaxed her into the car to head off in search of a supermarket.

After hitting every crater on the single track, she reached the luxury of a real, honest-to-goodness, road. Never again was she going to take tarmac roads for granted. Ahead, she could see a signpost informing her that Tobermory was eighteen miles away. This was further than she had expected, but the scenery was extremely easy on the eye, and it was the best way to become acquainted with her new island home.

As she approached civilisation, she spotted, with delight, the large sign in the distance displaying the word TESCO. Indicating right, she slowed down to enter the empty car park. Undoing her seatbelt, she reached into the backseat for her reusable bags.

See what happens when you get an early start to the day? You beat the rush. I will be in and out in half an hour, no mess, no fuss, no queuing. Perfect.

She approached the automatic doors which failed to open. She waved her hand vigorously in the air in the direction of the sensor. Nothing. Pressing her face up against the glass, she tried to attract someone's attention. The place was deserted. Not a living soul in sight. The poster listing the opening times was at the side of the door. Reading the information, she saw that on Saturday, the store was open from 8.00am-9.00pm, Sunday - CLOSED.

She climbed back into the car to head further into Tobermory. The nearer she got to the town centre the more obvious it became that everything except the church was closed. There had been stories of everything coming to a halt on a Sunday in the Highlands and Islands, but she thought that had been decades before. In the town's main street, a newspaper wrapper from last night's fish supper blew across the road in front of her car. A seagull from the harbour wall followed it, pecking furiously at the salty morsels left inside. She sat stationary in the middle of the road to allow the bird to salvage its feast. The patience she showed towards the gull was not out of the goodness of her heart; the thing simply would not move while there were pickings to be had.

Eventually, the seagull flew back to the stone wall from whence it came. Its beady eyes watched in wait for another banquet to happen its way.

'You're welcome,' Edina shouted from her car window.

She continued on her quest for food, but it became ever more apparent that nowhere was open on the Sabbath. The road led her in the opposite direction of her country abode, so she decided just to follow it along the coast of the island. Across the water, she could see many tiny islands floating haphazardly on the wide expanse of sea. With her car window down, she could hear the yelps and caws of the circling sea birds. The sun had burned away the morning mist, and the ocean had turned marbled green. For the duration of her journey, she kept one eye on her driving, the other on the scenery. The speedometer on her dashboard was fixed on the speed limit; never let it be said that she didn't learn from her mistakes. This was the new Edina, the self-reflecting, ever-improving version of the old one.

The road continued for some time with no signs of civilisation. Mountains with flat tops were on her left, the sea was to her right. She laughed aloud when passing a small herd of highland cows paddling at the water's edge. Ahead, she could see the outline of a sign propped up against a rock. She slowed down to read the lettering which appeared handwritten in black paint.

FRESH, FREE-RANGE EGGS FOR SALE

Food.

Her foot hit the brake. There was a drawing of an arrow on the board which pointed to the road on the left leading to a farm. The detour could be the decider as to whether she would or wouldn't eat that night.

Leaving her car at the front of the farmhouse, she walked over to the door. The sound of her loud knocking awakened a multitude of dogs. She could hear everything from deep growling to high-pitched yapping. In the heat of the moment, she decided it would be best to run back to the car before the occupant of the house opened the door, allowing the mutts within to run riot. Once she was safely back in the car, she rolled down the window and waited.

A rotund, elderly lady with an apron tied under her bust appeared in the doorway with two Jack Russells at her side.

'Yes,' she said suspiciously.

'Hello, I saw your sign about the eggs, and I wondered if I could buy a dozen from you?'

'Do you realise it's Sunday, dear?' she said abruptly.

'Oh, yes, I'm sorry. I just arrived on the island yesterday, and I have no supplies. I didn't mean to be disrespectful. I was just desperate.'

She learned a few important life lessons in her many years as a journalist. The first thing to remember when you want something from someone is to be polite, respectful and, if necessary, to grovel. The sympathy angle was a good direction to come from when hoping to get what you wanted.

'It's okay,' Edina added. 'I'll just go and come back tomorrow. I wouldn't want you to compromise your beliefs. I've managed this long; I can wait another day.'

She started up the engine for effect, then counted, '1… 2… 3…'

'All right, just this once, but don't tell anyone.'

The lady bustled back into her house to fetch the eggs.

Works like a treat every time.

The farmer's wife appeared back outside five minutes later, carrying a box containing the edibles. She carried it towards the backseat of Edina's car, explaining that the box contained a dozen eggs, a homemade loaf, a tub of butter, and a jar of homemade blackcurrant jam.

Edina made a show of being overwhelmed by her generosity, telling her that her secret was safe. An exchange of a £10 note for the goods was agreed, before Edina went on her way, waving with a smile.

I've still got the old charm.

With her box full of goodies, she rejoined the coastal road, pressing her foot down hard on the accelerator.

Eventually, she saw a sign telling her that Pennyghael was five miles away. The route she had taken approached the town from the opposite direction. The next sign that happened her way was for Pennyghael Country House Hotel. Underneath the hotel name was the tagline in italics: A Little Bit of Heaven on Mull.

So, this is my new place of work, very nice indeed.

She pulled over to the side of the road to ponder whether to drive down along to take a look or to head home.

It would be good to know what to expect when I officially start tomorrow.

Curiosity got the better of her.

Oh, what the heck? There's no harm done.

Being an investigative journalist at heart meant she could never just drive on by.

The private road leading to the hotel was covered in fresh tarmac, the grass along the verge was neatly mown. The owner had taken great care to keep the grounds looking impeccable. The road meandered up a hill, ending with the car park in front of the grand house. There were three cars in the parking spaces, a Jaguar and two Mercedes. Edina veered in alongside the Jag, then stepped out to inspect the property. She took her phone from her handbag and photographed the main entrance, the side view, the turret against the blue sky, and the courtyard beside the trees. The hotel was considerably more impressive when she stood facing it than the photographs had shown online. Now that she had seen it, she found herself actually looking forward to starting work there. It was far from her dream job but something about the old place felt right. An unexpected smile formed on her lips as she drove back down the winding road.

Maybe coming here was not the worst decision I've made in my life. Oh no, I've made a hell of a lot of worse decisions than this.

Chapter 5

Edina's cottage sat only a mile along the road from Pennyghael House. Both properties shared the same woodland, making her wonder if it had all been part of one large estate owned by the same family at some point in history.

The hunger she was now experiencing was becoming painful. As soon as she entered her *gated* property, she parked in her personal parking space and took the box from the back seat of the car. On the short walk to the front door, a thought entered her head.

Maybe I should put up a sign saying reserved parking, permit holders only. You just can't be too careful these days.

Using her foot to shut the front door behind her, she headed straight to the kitchen, where her first task was to make herself some lunch.

When she cracked the eggs into the mixing bowl, she marvelled at the rich dark orange of the yolks.

These are not like any supermarket eggs I've ever had.

She whisked them furiously with a little milk before pouring the mixture into the frying pan. On a tray, behind the flowery, cupboard door curtains, there was a sharp kitchen knife, which pleased her greatly. The idea of hacking through an uncut loaf with a butter knife was not ideal. The serrated knife edge sliced with ease through the, crusty on the outside and deliciously soft on the inside, loaf. Scrambled eggs on toast would be her first course, bread and jam, the dessert. Her mouth watered with anticipation of the delights that lay ahead of her.

When the food was ready, she carried it through to the lounge, laying it out neatly on the coffee table. The slices of bread were arranged on a plate alongside two pots containing the butter and jam.

During her time in Edinburgh, she had dined in top-class restaurants, eating the finest cuisine, but nothing she had ever experienced excited her more than the feast she had just prepared for herself.

The way she devoured the first course of her meal would have been shocking to any onlooker. Crumbs and little pieces of scrambled egg lay on the yoke of her jumper, her lips were slimy with butter. Whilst she ate, she retrieved her phone from her bag to look at the photos she had taken earlier of Pennyghael House Hotel. Clicking on the colourful photos icon, she scrolled through until she found them. The first picture was of the front of the impressive building. She examined the characteristics of the country-style mansion. Although she was no expert, she guessed it was of the Scots baronial period. Several years before, she had written an interest piece for the newspaper, which involved researching the features of Edwardian, Victorian and Baronial buildings. From what she could remember on the subject, Pennyghael House possessed all the identifying hallmarks of this baronial period, such as conical turrets, a tower, and an asymmetric plan which was contrary to most Edwardian buildings.

While she analysed the architecture, something in the picture caught her eye. Intrigued, she brought her phone up close to her face. She could have sworn that when she took the photo, there was no one around, but there, on the front steps of the main entrance, was a dark shape resembling a person. After zooming in on the image, she saw that it was the outline of a child. The features of the face were difficult to decipher, but the black attire and hat led her to believe it was a little boy.

How strange.

She flicked on to the next photo, which was of the side view of the hotel. Expanding the image with her index finger and thumb, she could see that the small dark figure was visible again. The enlarged image showed clearly a boy posing for the camera. The fingers on his clasped hands were clearly defined as was the unsmiling, almost angry expression on his face. Flicking frantically, she moved to the next photo, which she had taken of the tower against the blue sky. He didn't appear to be in that photo, but there was a dark undefined shadow at the window of the tower. The final image was of the courtyard with a wooded area in the background. At first sight, there was no sign of the mysterious boy. Edina scanned all corners of the photo, taking her phone over to the window to shed more light on it.

Ah! There you are.

The child was there, standing in a pose at the edge of the wood. She could see the hat and dark suit clearly outlined. It was most definitely a person in the photos, the same person. A boy, she decided. Two things she knew for sure, he was not there when she was photographing the house, and he was not dressed like any child she had seen nowadays. Although intrigued by the mysterious apparition, she was also a little disturbed by the fact that he was posing for her.

Why her?

The discovery played over and over in her head. She wanted to research the families who had lived in Pennyghael House over the decades, but her laptop would not work without Wi-Fi.

I may well be making something out of nothing due to the lack of entertainment around here, but it might be possible that the boy in my photos is a spirit. If this is the case, what do I know about ghostly apparitions? Let me think... absolutely nothing. Wait a minute. In every ghost story I've watched on TV or read in a book, the spirit only appears when it is unhappy. It is usually seeking help from the living to lay its soul to rest once and for all. Do you actually hear yourself, Edina?

She was now questioning not only her logic but her sanity.

Far-fetched as it seemed, there was a child in every one of her photos who had not been there when she took them; this was an indisputable fact. Something in Edina's nature made her want to dig deeper. Perhaps the investigative journalist was still alive and well within her.

Old habits die hard. If nothing else, it'll take my mind off the reality of what my life has become.

Chapter 6

It was Sunday afternoon. Edina sat alone with no television, no phone, no laptop. There was nowhere to go, nothing to do, and no one to talk to. It was torture. Even if she had known anyone on the island, she would have been unable to contact them.

It's a good thing that I don't have any friends back home in Edinburgh because they may have been worried that I wasn't keeping in touch. There are definitely positives to be found in every negative situation.

Twiddling away at her thumbs, listening to the ear-splitting silence, she suddenly remembered that she had a large notebook upstairs in her suitcase.

Now that's something I can do to pass the time.

Since Edina had been a schoolgirl, she tended to pack a notepad and pencil wherever she went. It became her ritual to fill the pages with useless information about what she had seen or who had said what. Sometimes, when she couldn't be bothered writing anything, she would simply make little sketches, setting them out in the form of a storyboard. Perhaps destiny had always intended her to be a journalist.

When she did go on to follow the route of journalism, it became ingrained in her psyche to write information about certain events, such as times of an incident, names of people involved, and locations where it happened. When she was working for the newspaper, the editor, whose name physically hurt her to say, would reinforce to his team of journalists that everything must be written down.

'Never rely on your memory,' he reminded them daily. 'And always keep the information accurate.'

She made sure she followed that rule religiously unless it was absolutely necessary to play around with the truth a little.

Unfurling her legs from the chair, she ran upstairs to where her suitcase lay under her bed. Inside the case lay the boredom reliever. It was an A4 size notebook filled with unused lined paper. She headed back down to her faded wing chair at the fireside.

Now, let me see.

With the palm of her hand, she made a gesture of smoothing out the already smooth first page as she chewed on the end of the pen.

What shall I write? I've got it! I will start a journal all about my new life in Mull. I will note all the events of each day, starting with yesterday. Admittedly, it will be a dull read, but who knows, things may heat up after a few months.

Edina began to tell the journal all about the ferry crossing, followed by her arrival at the cottage. Nothing much had happened in the past couple of days, but she managed to fill four pages of her notebook, and better still, it killed two hours of her day.

The temperature in the room dropped as the sun moved behind the trees. Edina reached for her cardigan when an involuntary shiver crawled its way up her back. Glancing at the open fireplace beside her, she decided that she would bring wood in from the store outside to start a fire. After all, it would not only use up a bit more of her free time, but it would also give her good practice before the autumn arrived. The empty log basket lay on the hearth. She grabbed the wicker handle and headed to the front door to slip on her shoes.

When she stepped outside the house, she was stopped in her tracks by the peaceful stillness that fell all around her. The silence was disturbed only by a distant dove coo-cooing from somewhere in the trees. There was a faint smell of burning wood in the air, which led her to think that someone had hatched the same fire idea as she had.

The logs were thrown in two at a time, until she filled the basket to the brim. Splintered pieces of wood were balanced on top of the pile; they would be ideal for kindling.

Before long, Edina was sitting in her wing chair with her feet up on the coffee table. A warm fan of flames crackled beside her in the fireplace. It was a perfect little fire which had been delicately nurtured into life.

By teatime, she had rustled up an unsurprising meal of scrambled egg on toast, with bread and jam for dessert. It was a perfectly acceptable meal under the circumstances. As she ate, she reaffirmed to herself that things were going to get better. Tomorrow would bring a new day to her island life. Starting work at the hotel would hopefully move things up a gear. If she were busy all day, then she would be pleased to spend her evenings alone in the house. Her plan was to work hard and keep her head down. The less people knew about her, the better. She would be the first to admit she was a party girl, but things were different now. The islanders on Mull would only ever know the quietly reserved Edina, the girl who liked to spend her evenings alone, in her pyjamas.

After clearing the dirty dishes from the coffee table, she carried them through to the kitchen. Her next mission was to search behind the little curtain doors for an iron. She needed to get the creases out of her white shirt and black skirt, which was the standard required dress for her new job.

The fire was dwindling, which left Edina faced with a dilemma.

Should I put more wood on to keep it going or should I let it burn out?

Looking at her watch, she saw that it was almost eight o'clock.

I think I will just let it die, she thought. *No point in wasting good logs. What shall I do now?*

She began picking away at a tiny fleck of old nail varnish that she had missed when removing the rest. She then gave a stretch accompanied by an exaggerated yawn. As she did this, the wireless radio caught her eye.

Maybe I should search for some music. No, I don't think I'll bother. I found that old-fashioned music a little depressing, now that I think of it. I'll just leave the radio well alone.

I could have a shower and an early night, or I could...

She couldn't think of an alternative, so she headed up the narrow, concealed staircase to fetch a towel.

Darkness was slowly making an appearance when she rattled her way into bed. The curtains were left open on purpose as she enjoyed looking out at the multitude of stars. There was a noticeable difference between city and island sky, and she had to admit that it was the only thing she preferred about living on Mull. The sky was a dark, admiral blue, but she could see the beams of light from the moon beginning to appear as it slowly worked its way around to her window. Pulling the quilt up to her chin, she made a promise to herself.

I am going to give this new life in Mull everything I've got. I will make it work. In fact, I'll make it great.

Unsure whether she believed her own pledge or not, she had to stand by it because, in truth, she wasn't exactly plagued with better options.

Sleep seemed to be avoiding her as she lay looking out at the now inky black sky. A quote from Shakespeare entered her head, when Macbeth said, '…nor Heaven peep through the blanket of the dark.'

Is there anyone from Heaven peeping through the dark, looking down on me? Surely God must have turned his back on me for what I've done. A feeling of shame enveloped her, filling her with self-loathing. *Perhaps my mum is gazing down through one of the pinholes that appear as stars. She always loved me, even when I didn't deserve to be loved.*

Being alone in the night brought visits from unwelcome memories and bitter regrets. Why hadn't she given more of her time to her mum? She pushed that thought from her mind. It was too painful to think about it. Again, a Shakespeare quote came into her mind, 'What's done, is done'.

The past could not be changed, but with resolve, she could still learn from it.

As the small hours of the night ticked slowly by, Edina turned restlessly around in her bed, causing great creaking and rattling. It was impossible to get comfortable. Her mind was active. Thoughts were coming into her head from a past that she wasn't yet ready to face.

Suddenly, in the quiet of the room, an unidentifiable noise could be heard from downstairs. The sound caused Edina's body to stiffen with fear, her insides turned watery. If it were an intruder, she was done for. With no workable phone and no neighbours to hear her screams, she would die unaided. If it was an animal, such as a rat, then she was leaving the house tomorrow, never to return. More strange sounds occurred from the floor below her. She pulled the quilt down from her face to enable her to listen closely. It was a rustling of paper, followed by the sound of something being thrown.

Okay, I have to think logically here. Someone is downstairs in my house. They are making a fair amount of noise, so perhaps they don't know I'm here. What am I going to do about this?

Beads of sweat broke out across her forehead. She had to think fast in case whoever it was decided to come upstairs. In her favour was the fact that the staircase was concealed behind what appeared to be a larder door.

Come on, Edina, what is the best route to take in this situation, confront or hide?

From a very young age, Edina had always looked trouble fearlessly in the eyes. In many ways, this was what made her an excellent journalist with a blindingly bright future ahead of her. Running away from a difficult situation had never been an option for her. That said, was it not fear that provoked her into running away to a remote island in the Scottish Highlands? Now lying in her bed, frozen in terror, fretting over what to do, she decided that the hiding option was the most appealing. Facing her fears was one thing, confronting the unknown was another. After all, she wasn't a complete fool.

With the quilt over her head, she lay completely still. If the intruder climbed the stairs, she didn't want to know about it.

She prayed in her mind, with her hands respectfully clasped.

Dear God,

I am eternally sorry for what I have done. I am in trouble now, and although I don't deserve help from you, I'm going to ask, anyway. If you protect me here tonight from whatever is in my house, then I will make it up to you. I will put things right and be a better person. Please, please.

Amen

It felt like minutes later when Edina pulled the quilt down from her head. To her astonishment, she found the room flooded with sunlight. The great blanket of night had gone, and so had her fears. Somehow, through the terrifying events, she must have fallen asleep. Her hair was soaked in sweat from remaining in her airless hiding place all night. Staring up at the stark white ceiling, she thought over what had happened through the night.

Now I'm brave enough to go downstairs.

Edina tossed the quilt to one side.

On second thoughts, what if it's an animal, trapped, frightened, ready to attack?

She swung her legs over the side of the bed, tiptoeing to the top of the stairs.

'Hello, is there anybody there?'

No reply.

With the palm of her hand, she banged loudly on the wall, then stamped her feet. This was a desperate bid to frighten off whatever creature could be down there.
Silence.
Ever so lightly, she walked slowly downstairs to see if there was anything out of place.
The kitchen was exactly how she had left it, a little untidy but clean. She peered into the lounge. The aroma of the previous day's fire still hung in the air. Somehow it seemed to suit the character of the house. Everything at first glance was in its place and the glass in the windows was still intact. It was a relief to her that the house had not been trashed by an intruder but she had unanswered questions still encircling her mind.
What on earth happened last night? I know what I heard. I didn't imagine it.
Her freshly ironed uniform was hanging from the handle of the wardrobe. Sitting on her bed, she stared at it as she ran her fingers through her hair.
Why am I so nervous about starting a new job?
Butterflies flitted around in the pit of her stomach.
It's a cleaning job, for goodness sake. No skill involved. Anyone could do it. Get a grip of yourself, girl. What's gotten into you?
As a journalist, she entered unfamiliar territory nearly every day in order to sniff out a story. Presenting herself unannounced to politicians, corporate businessmen, and people in the public eye was commonplace for her. Nothing fazed her because she loved the thrill of the chase. By knowing how to work people and how to read a situation, she always tended to get exactly what she

was looking for, sometimes more. She could be a rottweiler or a pussycat, whatever the occasion called for. So why was she so nervous about starting a new job on Mull?

The whistle from the kettle she had previously placed on the stove, brought her downstairs for breakfast.

Now, let me think, what shall I have with my tea? How about bread and jam, just for a change.

When she looked in the bread bin, she realised that she had eaten the whole loaf and was now down to the crusty outside slices.

Loaves must be getting smaller these days. Fancy me eating the whole thing.

After a quick shower, she dressed in her black skirt and white blouse. She brushed her thick, blonde hair back, securing it into a neat, low ponytail. A smattering of makeup was all that was required for a cleaning job, she decided. After sliding her feet into her low-heeled shoes, she took a step back to take a look at herself in the mirror in the middle panel of the wardrobe.

I look absolutely nothing like me. But maybe that's a good thing. New look, new me.

When working with the newspaper, her skirts were short, her heels were high, her tops were low, but her daily objectives were completely different back then.

With her jacket and car keys in hand, she headed to the front door. Suddenly, she stopped abruptly to take in the scene that lay on the floor in front of her. It was her journal, lying there, ripped and scribbled upon.

So that was the rustling noise I heard downstairs. It can't have been an animal because animals can't hold a pen to scribble. It must have been an intruder, but who would do that and why?

The sight of her notebook lying there, defaced, really shook her up. It didn't make any sense.

It's just an innocent, and quite frankly, uninteresting little diary of events. How could it inspire such destruction in someone?

She felt quite tearful at the idea that someone had entered her home.

How did they get in?

The door was still shut and bolted. The lounge window was closed, but she tried pulling it up to check that it was locked shut. It would not budge, in fact, she could see quite clearly that the window had been painted shut, proving that it had not been opened in a long time.

She retrieved the book from the floor, straightened out the ripped pages, before laying it with the pen on the sideboard.

I'll need to report this to someone. But who the hell will I report it to? The police? 'Someone sneaked into my house and scribbled on my book!' Yeah, the police are going to love that.

As she drove along the road to the Pennyghael House Hotel, she thought of the break-in at her home. The only good thing to come out of this was that she was no longer nervous about starting her new job.

Chapter 7

An uncontrollable trembling began in Edina's knees as she walked up the stone steps of the hotel. On entering the reception area, she had to admit the décor was impressively tasteful. The air was filled with an aromatic scent, which she inhaled deeply as she walked across the highly polished floor. A circular walnut table stood elegantly in the middle of the large open area. A Chinese vase filled with varying shades of pink blossom made an excellent centrepiece. Unable to resist, she found herself sniffing the perfect blooms whilst running her fingertips over the almost-reflective surface of the varnished table.
Very nice, and highly pleasing to the eye.
A chandelier filled with teardrop glass beads hung above the table. Its fragments of light fell on the flowers and bounced off the polished wood of the table. Glancing around the room, she noticed that on every wall hung portraits of people from the past, presumably previous occupants of Pennyghael House. She smiled at the painting of an elegant lady in furs standing with a country gent, who held an erect rifle in one hand, a cluster of dead pheasants in the other.
'Can I help you?' a voice came from behind.
Turning swiftly, she answered. 'Yes, my name is Edina, and I start work with you today.'
'Ah, Edina, I'm really pleased to have you with us. My name is Struan, I run the hotel with my mum. I believe you have rented our little but and ben?'
'The cottage, yes, I wondered if it was part of the estate.'

He smiled. 'It's a bit basic, but feel free to do anything you like to it. Just make it your own. Is there anything you need there?'

A proper kitchen, a proper bed, a television, the list is endless.

Instead, she replied, 'I could be doing with wi-fi if it's at all possible.'

'I'll see what we can do. Now, follow me, and I'll show you around.'

They climbed the carpeted staircase to where the bedrooms were situated. Struan explained to Edina that each room was designed uniquely, with a variation of old and new furniture. All of the rooms had a two-colour theme. The wallpaper, bedding, and artwork all contained the room's two chosen colours. Edina listened as Struan talked.

He is incredibly attractive. I wonder if I should make a move on him. Perhaps if we are in a social setting together with a bit of alcohol thrown in, I'll seize the opportunity.

Struan continued to disclose all the details of the hotel's history and how they attempted to restore many of its original features. She stared at him as he was talking and smiling, nodding to show that she was completely engaged in what he was saying. Checking his finger subtly, she could see that he was not wearing a wedding ring.

Good, I'm going to assume he's single. That lonely little cottage would be a whole lot more homely with Struan popping around most nights.

'So, that completes your guided tour of Pennyghael House,' Struan told her, raising his hands in a gesture that suggested, all done. 'Now, your duties.'

Damn it!

For a moment, she had forgotten that she was actually employed there, so mesmerised had she been by Struan's captivating highland twang, and his unusual green eyes.

'The hotel isn't busy *yet*,' Struan said with optimism. 'So, we don't have many staff. You'll be a kind of Jack of all trades! Breakfast dishes, hoovering upstairs and down, changing the beds, cleaning the rooms when the guests leave, and setting up the dining room for dinner. Susie has worked here since we opened, so she will keep you on the right track. Any questions?'

'No, I don't think so. It all sounds perfectly straightforward,' she told him, concealing the feeling of dread from her voice.

'Oh, by the way,' Struan added. 'We all go out for a drink on a Friday night to a little bar called The Shell Seekers. There are quiz nights and live music. It's great.'

'Count me in!' she said.

Now that's more like it. I can start dangling my bait on Friday, and then I'll reel in my catch for the weekend.

'My girlfriend Marnie is the manager of The Shell Seekers. You'll really like her. She can fill you in on all the Mull gossip.'

The old Edina would have relished the challenge of going after a man who was married or in a relationship, but that had been a major part of her downfall. She accepted that Struan was spoken for, and she would no longer look at him with eyes full of covetous intention. She would simply set her cap elsewhere.

'Great, that will be something to look forward to,' she said genuinely. 'Right, I'll just go and get started then.'

'Edina!' he called after her. 'We're really glad to have you on board. By the way, that's a very unusual name. I've never heard it before. It's nice.'

'Thanks. It comes from mediaeval times; it means from Edinburgh.'

Starting down in the kitchen, she began loading all the dishes from the previous evening into the dishwasher. She washed the delicate glasses by hand in the deep ceramic sink. Then, looking around the L-shaped kitchen area, she decided that there were many things that were not in the best possible place to ensure the day-to-day smooth running of the housekeeping duties. Having a fairly ordered mind, she needed things to be set out as efficiently as possible. Starting with the staff table and chairs, she dragged them to the unused corner space at the far end. The cleaning products had been stored in a cupboard overhead.

This will just not do.

She retrieved all the containers from the cupboard then arranged them neatly into the storage area under the sink. There was a distinct lack of worktop area to stack up dirty dishes. To rectify the workspace issue, she carried the microwave, kettle and toaster over to the opposite side of the room, where electrical sockets were on the wall.

Having rearranged the kitchen to how she wanted it, she cleaned it to her own acceptable standard.

Before leaving the room, she looked around at her handiwork, nodding in pleasure.

Now that's more like it.

The heavy industrial hoover was kept in a cupboard off the hallway. She dragged it to the foot of the staircase then bumped it up every one of the stairs. Initially, she found it almost impossible to push the contraption backwards and forwards across the thick wool carpets, but she soon got the hang of it, adopting her own special system. It wasn't in her nature to only vacuum the areas of carpet that could be seen, so she moved the furniture around to reach unseen parts. As she hoovered, she noticed that the thick pile on the carpet looked tidier when the marks from the vacuum cleaner ran in the same direction, a bit like the stripes on a lawn. Favouring this new method, she consciously decided to achieve this effect on every carpet.

The beds were stripped of their dirty linen. The clean sheets were replaced, before Edina dressed the bed with a colour co-ordinated throw and large cushions. With a critical eye, she looked around the room, fixing anything that was not perfect. The seams on the lampshades were turned to the back, the curtains were drawn a quarter of the way over, and the complimentary toiletries were all lined up with their labels to the front. This attention to detail was replicated in each of the seven bedrooms that she worked on.

By the afternoon, she was ready to start in the dining room, which had fourteen tables, but only six were to be set for dinner. Having dined out in most of the top restaurants of Edinburgh, she was well equipped with the skills needed to lay the table with the right cutlery in the correct order. Using a pile of napkins from the cutlery station, she made pretty white fans for each place setting. How many times had she sat at the bar of Tiger Lily's, watching the staff work their magic with the napkins? Memories of her life back in Edinburgh desperately tried to push their way into her thoughts, but she shut the door on them all.

She reminded herself, again. *I have to stay strong. Look forward, not back.*

When the dining room was hoovered, she gave it one last check before leaving. The stained tablecloths were added to the trolley which was filled with dirty bedding and towels. Now, it was time to figure out the oversized washing machine. The laden trolley containing the mess of strangers, was pushed, with no great ease, down the slope leading to the kitchen. The misconception Edina had formed in her mind before she arrived in Mull was that hotel work was easy. That fallacy was now put to bed, never to rise again.

On entering the kitchen, she saw an elderly man in a tweed cap, standing by the sink. The absurdity of his overgrown eyebrows was the first thing to catch Edina's attention, the matching sideburns were the second.

Tipping his cap slightly at her, he said, 'Good afternoon to you.'

'Hi,' she said. 'I'm Edina. This is my first day here, but I'm getting into the swing of it.'

She reached her hand out to shake.

He reciprocated, shaking her hand firmly, even squeezing a little. Edina was comforted by this. Her mother had once told her many years ago never to trust a man who had a weak, floppy handshake. She never forgot that.

'My name's Cameron McKenzie, but I'm afraid I go by the name of Stan. I've always been a big Stanley Baxter fan, and one day, for that very reason, someone started calling me Stan. It stuck, now everyone calls me that. I haven't heard my real name being used in years. Edina, eh! From Edinburgh. Where *are* you from?' he asked.

'I *am* from Edinburgh,' she said, smiling. 'How did you know what my name meant? No one ever knows.'

'I am interested in all that is historical about Scotland. I read history books all the time. I could tell you a thing or two about Scotland's history. I once thought of going on Mastermind with historical Scotland as my specialist subject, but I would let myself down in the general knowledge round because I don't know much about anything outside Scotland. If I'm being totally honest with you Edina, I've never been anywhere but Scotland. I never wanted to. You see, when your own country can offer you everything you need in life, what's the use in going to look elsewhere, eh?'

'You may have a good point there, Stan. Anyway, I better get on. It was very nice to meet you, and I may pick your brains sometime about a historical issue that has arisen in my life since I arrived,' she told him, referring to the little boy in the photos. 'Would you like me to call you Mr McKenzie, Cameron, or Stan?'

'Call me Stan. Truth be told, I like it,' he said, smiling. 'Are you the lassie from the but and ben in the woods?'

'Yes, that's my own wee highland home now,' she replied, thinking how fast news travelled in these parts.

'If you see me around there this week, don't worry. Struan has asked me to cut the grass and tidy up the garden for you.'

'That would be great. Thanks, Stan.'

Edina continued with her work as she had an inkling that Stan would stand there talking all day if she were willing to listen. She shoved the dirty laundry into the washing machine, turning the dial to the 60-degree cycle. Tipping his cap once more to bid her goodbye, he took the hint, leaving her alone in the kitchen. She took her phone from her apron pocket and saw from the clock that she still had several hours before the end of her shift. Still, what else would she be doing? Sitting alone in the silence with the fear of another unwelcome visitor.

Chapter 8

After almost a week of hotel work, Edina could truthfully say that it was the most physical, full-on job she had ever done. The rewards of the labour were short-lived because the following day, she had to repeat it all over again. In the evening, she returned home to her cottage, exhausted. The upside was that she slept deeply, unaware of any strange noises that may have been happening in the house.

Each night, without fail, she wrote about her day in the journal before going to bed. By morning, she found it lying on the floor, torn and scored over. There was no explanation for this phenomenon. It was beyond her understanding. With no signs of a break-in and nothing else touched, she began to question whether she was sleepwalking and perhaps damaging the journal by herself. To test this theory, she had pushed the heavy wardrobe in front of the bedroom door. It remained in the same position in the morning. She was no expert, but she was pretty sure that a sleepwalker wouldn't have the presence of mind to push the wardrobe out of the way and then replace it in its previous position.

The torn pages could have been done by an animal, but that would offer no explanation for the scribblings. It had crossed her mind to take the journal upstairs with her at night, but her fear was that the destroyer would visit her bedroom.

Whoever was doing this, night after night, to her property was not harming her, so as long as she stayed tucked away in her bedroom, she felt safe enough.

It's not a normal situation, but I'm not scared, just intrigued.

A highly annoying tune entered Edina's dream, causing her great irritation. She writhed around in her sleep under the duvet. When the music continued repeating over and over, it dawned on her that it was the alarm on her phone. Groaning aloud, she threw one leg out from under her quilt.

I can't do it. I'm too tired and my body is too sore.

A sudden revelation occurred to her, inspiring her to sit up and throw the duvet back.

It's Friday, I'm getting a night out tonight. I won't be sitting in the house alone in my pyjamas. I'm going to have drinks and see people.

Adrenaline rushed through her body.

'Woo hoo!' she shouted, as she catapulted herself off the mattress and headed for the shower.

Under the trickling jets of lukewarm water, she sang her ringtone song at the top of her voice, swinging her hips to the rhythm. Her light had been hidden under a bushel for too long now, tonight she was going to let it shine. A song popped into her head that reflected her thoughts perfectly. The song she had been singing got tossed to one side as she picked up the reigns of the new one.

This little light of mine, I'm gonna let it shine. This little light of mine, I'm gonna let it shine.

She stood in front of the mirror buttoning up her white blouse before tucking it into her knee length skirt. The black tights with the flat comfortable shoes made her feel so dowdy. Admittedly, the shoes were a comfortable necessity but throughout the day, she avoided looking down at her feet.

I can't believe that I'm getting a chance to wear real clothes tonight. No waitress outfit, no pyjamas, no sir-ee!

It was incomprehensible that she was going out to a bar where there would be alcohol, music and lots of people. The original plan for her new life in Mull had been to keep herself to herself. If she avoided people, then she avoided trouble. But, for Edina, isolation was never going to be an achievable goal. Being in a social setting regenerated her batteries, which at this moment in time were at an all-time low.

On the short walk to her car, yet another song burst forth from her, ruining the quiet stillness of the morning.

'I'm goin' out, I'm goin' out. No more uniform, no more pyjamas. I'm dressin' up, I'm dressin' up and goin' out, and goin' out.'

Admittedly, it wasn't the best song in the world, but it was straight from the heart. The nonsense songs, the dancing and all the conversations with herself were a direct result of being cooped up friendless in a remote cottage in the woods.

When she arrived at the hotel's car park, she ran towards the front door, leaping up two stairs at a time. The anticipation of the big night out had quite literally given her a spring in her step. Struan was on a phone call at the reception desk, but he gave her a nod with a wave as she passed. Bending her knees and holding on to the edges of her skirt, she responded with a curtsy. Struan screwed up his face, showing a mystified look.

She felt a little embarrassed.

Why did I just do that? I've never made a curtsy in my life.

Unable to hide the bounce in her step, she headed straight to the broom cupboard where her good friend, the industrial hoover, resided.

'Come on big fella,' she coaxed, as she dragged the heavy piece of equipment out into the reception area.

Struan was now clicking away at the computer keyboard in front of him, engrossed in the information on the screen.

'Thank goodness it's Friday,' Edina shouted over to him for something to say.

The reality then dawned on her that this stock phrase didn't really work when it came to the hospitality industry. In general, the weekend was their busiest time. Getting the weekend off was a distant memory of the past.

Oh, I loved it when Friday came around. Drinks after work with the boys in the office, sometimes not getting home until the morning. I always said I'll go home after one more drink. It turned out to be one...after another.

Stop it, Edina. Those days are the past. That life is over. No more romantic reminiscing.

'Still on for tonight?' Struan shouted over.

'I wouldn't miss it!' she said. 'I feel like I'm getting out on parole for good behaviour. What's the plan then?'

'Go home and get changed after work, then come back here. Stan drives us there in the hotel minibus. Sometimes, if he feels neighbourly, he returns for us at midnight. If he's not waiting outside, then we just get a taxi or, occasionally, we walk. It is further than you think, though, so we try to avoid that option.'

'Great,' she replied. 'How many people from the hotel will be going with us?' she asked.

'Well, as I explained, we are understaffed as we are not terribly busy right now,' he told her, sounding slightly embarrassed by that fact. 'There will be Susie, who you've already met and Freddy, who's just turned eighteen. He's our dishwasher. He only comes in if we need him on busy nights. There will also be me and you.'

'Sounds good, I can't wait.'

It didn't exactly sound like the most thrilling crowd, but when you've chosen a life in no man's land, you join whatever tribe is willing to take you.

By the end of her working day, Edina raced to her car, and drove at top speed in the direction of home. Faced with the craters in the road in front of her, she decided she was in too big a hurry to avoid them. Instead of slowing down over the potholes, she sped up in the hope that the car would glide over the top. It didn't. Her face remained in a frozen grimace until she reached the gravel in front of her house.

What should I wear?

From the few items that she had brought, she picked out her red dress, which she referred to as her saloon girl dress. It seemed perfect for the occasion. The hook-fasteners at the front and the fact that it was tightly fitted flattered her shape. The double-frilled petticoat hem added a cutesy touch to the ensemble.

Back home in Edinburgh, whenever she wore it, she gleaned a multitude of compliments, often from complete strangers.

The final touch was her red shoes, which she bought to go with the dress. She then shook free her thick blonde locks before turning around to stare at herself in the full-length mirror.

Imagine me getting a chance to wear a dress like this on Mull. You look knockout, girl. It's time someone like me came along to shake up this Shell Seekers joint.

For some inexplicable reason, she suddenly came under fire from memories of the past. Her thoughts were taken back to the night she seduced the editor, whose name was too painful to say. She had never found him particularly handsome, but he had an unquantifiable something. As a boss, he was respectful, approachable, and always fair. Edina had never met his family, but from all the accounts she had heard from her colleagues, he was happy and very much in love. This was obvious to her in the way he conducted himself after work. Rarely did he join them for drinks, but if a successful newspaper story were being celebrated, he would come along, have one drink, and leave.

On the night in question, the office staff had been in high spirits. The newspaper had just broken the story that a leading politician had been involved in illegal practices. Edina was the first journalist to uncover the details. By interviewing many witnesses and working long hours, she eventually managed to secure the exclusive. It became the headline story on all the major news channels, after which the police became involved.

All the journalists from the newspaper agreed to meet in the cocktail bar, Tiger Lily's, after work to celebrate. The editor, whose name was too painful to say, was coaxed into joining them.

The bar was filled with Edina's colleagues when she arrived.

'Here comes the girl of the hour,' one of them shouted.

'Class A ball buster,' another joined in.

'Well done!' they all cheered, clapping.

'That's him well and truly fucked,' her closest workmate shouted, referring to the politician.

Feigning a little modesty, she gave a humble bow.

'Let me be the first to buy you a drink, Edina,' the assistant editor offered.

'The first of many drink offers, I hope. Hey boys, did you hear that Eddie is going to be the first to buy me a drink? Who's going to be the second?' she shouted across the room.

As she downed the drinks, which were by now lined up in front of her, she looked along to the end of the bar. Standing alone was the editor, whose name was too painful to say. She watched as he sipped on his pint of lager. Pouring drinks down the hatch was not his style.

The details of that night were engraved in her memory like an epitaph on a gravestone.

Did I even really want him back then, or was I seeking a challenge?

That evening in the bar, the behaviour of her colleagues was becoming rowdier by the moment. The editor, whose name was too painful to say, stood facing the bar with his back towards the crowd. Noticing that he only had a mouthful or two left of his lager and knowing he would not stay for a second drink, she knew she had to move fast.

She brazenly made her way to the end of the bar where her intended victim stood.

The memory of this made Edina cover her face with her hands in shame.

Why did I do that? I was such a selfish narcissist.

Tears of regret welled up in her eyes.

What made me such a ruthless person? And before you even think it, Edina, no, it wasn't the job that turned me that way. I was always a bitch.

Against her better judgement, she allowed herself to continue revisiting the events of that night. Like a film playing the scene over, she saw the editor, whose name was too painful to say, still wearing his raincoat as he stood at the bar. The last foamy dreg of beer was drunk before he reached for his briefcase, which sat at his feet.

'Hi,' she said, leaning on the bar beside him.

'Hi, Edina. Well done on the story. We couldn't have done it without your commitment. You're shaping up to be quite a journalist.'

'Oh, thanks, I can't tell you how much that means to me,' she said, dropping her eyes bashfully. 'How are you getting home?'

Might as well move fast. There's no time to lose.

'I'm just going to walk. I live quite near. I like the liveliness of the city at night.'

'I'm going to head off home too. I don't like it when everyone starts getting rowdy. Would you mind if I walked with you? My house is nearby.'

She stifled a smile at the irony of her own statement. In truth, rowdy was the way she liked it. She was always the last to leave.

'Yeah, sure. Let's go.'

They walked out of Tiger Lily's together before heading along George Street, full of high-spirited Friday night revellers. The conversation was all work-related. Nothing of their private lives was mentioned. Edina made him laugh with stories of her colleagues.

'I never get to hear any of that kind of stuff,' he told her, enjoying the banter. 'I'm stuck away in my office for most of the day. It's a lonely life at the top, you know.'

Moving closer to him as they walked, she said, 'It doesn't have to be.'

She had waited for a response, but none came.

Okay, enough is enough, she thought, pulling herself back to reality. *What is done is done. I can't change the past, but I can realign my future. Come on, give yourself a shake. You're getting a night out tonight.*

With her spirits badly in need of an uplift, she began singing the dreadful song she penned earlier in the day.

I'm goin' out, I'm goin' out,
Tonight, tonight, ...

Chapter 9

Edina drove into the hotel car park. Stan was already sitting at the wheel of the minibus. Parking alongside him, she locked her car and made her way over.

'You're first to arrive, lass, and don't you look like a real dandy tonight,' Stan said, watching as she held her dress and petticoat up to climb the stairs of the bus.

'Thank you... I think,' she replied, unsure if Stan's description of her was a compliment or not.

A dandy. Was that the look I was going for tonight? No, not really.

Freddy was the first to join her. Dressed casually in a white T-shirt and jeans, he introduced himself by saying he was the occasional dishwasher at the hotel.

He then asked, 'Hey, are you the one that sorted out the kitchen?'

'Yes, I hope it was okay with everyone. I'm a bit anal when it comes to the Feng Shui in a room.'

She laughed.

'The Feng what?' Freddy asked, looking at her blankly.

'Oh, nothing. I just like everything to be in the right place.'

'Well, it is now,' he told her, sitting in the seat across from her.

Susie then came running out of the hotel doors, looking harassed. Taking her seat on the bus, she exchanged greetings with everyone, then retrieved her hairbrush from her bag. She slipped off her jacket and attempted to tame her thick, curly hair.

Edina noticed that Susie was dressed in torn jeans with baseball boots on her feet.

Freddy then leaned in saying, 'Edina, are you going somewhere else tonight?'

'No,' she answered in surprise. 'I'm coming out with you guys to The Shell Seekers.'

'It's just that you look a bit overdressed to be coming out with us.'

He laughed.

Just as Stan started the engine and lifted his hand to honk on the horn, Struan came running out to the bus.

'Sorry guys, I got caught up with a phone call. My mum's there to take over things now, so hit the gas, Stan.'

'Yes, let's go,' came a shout from Susie.

'Seatbelts on, please!' Stan shouted officially to his passengers.

Struan, who was wearing a black shirt with jeans, looked Edina up and down saying, 'Where do you think you're going?'

Everybody laughed.

Edina felt embarrassed.

It took the minibus precisely seven minutes to arrive at the car park of The Shell Seekers. Struan didn't wait for the others. He ran on ahead, excited to see his girlfriend, Marnie.

As he approached the bar, he stood watching her as she leaned forward to hear the customers' requests. He managed to catch her eye through the crowd to let her know that he had arrived.

When she saw him, her face broke into the brightest of beaming smiles. Holding up her hand with fingers stretched out, she gestured to him that she would be with him in five minutes.

Nodding his response, he felt more than happy to watch and wait.

Standing at the end of the bustling bar, he was reminded of their first meeting. It had been almost two years since Marnie and her friends had rented his holiday house on the beach for two weeks. He found out later that she had been convalescing after a stay in hospital. It still filled him with anger to think of the trauma she must have suffered when her boyfriend at the time had violently attacked her. He looked at the features of her sweet face now as she served drinks to the locals.

Who could ever hurt her?

On that first day, he went to the beach house to leave the key for the new holidaymakers. Hiding the key under the plant pot near the door was normal practice. This way, he had no reason to make himself known to the guests. There was a contact number on the booking details if he was needed.

With the key tucked away in the prearranged spot, he headed back to his car. At that moment, the new tenants arrived early, driving up alongside him. The driver rolled down her window and introduced herself as 'Bee'.

'Hi Bee, I'm Struan. I hope you enjoy your stay here on Mull. How was the…'

Struan thought back to how distracted he became by the girl in the back seat. He could not finish his sentence about the ferry crossing.

His fascination for the raven-haired beauty behind the driver must have been obvious, as Bee then intervened, saying, 'Oh, and sitting in the back there is Marnie.'

Etched in his memory was the physical blow to the heart he had experienced when she gave him a melancholy smile, saying, 'Hi, Struan.'

He couldn't believe his luck when Bee, her husband, and Marnie came along to the quiz night at the pub. He had joined them for a drink after closing time. Then Marnie offered to stay on to help him clean and set up the bar for the following day. Walking her home along the single-track road with only moonlight to guide them had been the highlight of the evening. When she appeared with her friends the following night and every night thereafter, they fell into a comfortable routine, staying after hours, then walking together along the dark country road.

When it was time for her to leave the island, they had agreed to keep in touch. Struan had no idea how much he would miss her in the weeks that followed. She had moved permanently into his thoughts with no sign of leaving. He saw her beautiful face smiling at him as he fell asleep at night. Each morning, when he awoke, her face was still in his thoughts. He had to do something to bring her into his life for good.

Soon after, Struan, together with his mum, embarked on the venture of restoring the old Pennyghael House, turning it into a five-star country hotel. Struan believed that Marnie would be the perfect person to run the pub while they focused their attention on the new business.

He had been right. Marnie did an incredible job revamping the place, and Struan loved having her near him. She then sought permission from her new bosses to rename it The Shell Seekers, after her favourite book by Rosamunde Pilcher.

Countless times, Struan had gone to look for Marnie in her flat above the bar. He knew that if she weren't there, he would find her walking along the beach nearby, barefoot, looking for shells.

Struan ran his hand over the glass vase positioned at the end of the bar. He smiled at the volume of shells that lay within it. Every last one had been collected by Marnie on her solitary strolls along the water's edge. He watched as she served the customers with a smile.

I can't survive without that special girl. One day, she will be my wife.

Edina, Susie, and Freddy thanked Stan as they clambered off the bus. Edina told him not to worry about coming to get them if he were too tired.

'I hate the thought of you having to come out late at night just to take us home. It doesn't seem fair.'

In her experience, the reverse psychology approach always worked wonders.

A fix of adrenaline coursed through Edina as she heard the pulse of loud music coming from the bar. It had been so long since she had socialised, and she couldn't deny that she had missed it enormously. Pushing past her two companions, she was determined to be the first one to walk through the door.

It became apparent as she strutted confidently that many customers were staring at her. This was only natural in a small town, on a small island, when there was a stranger in town, she decided. Sitting at a long rectangular table in the back of the room, she saw a gathering of young men drinking pints, laughing uproariously. She glanced around at the rest of the clientele and realised the dress code was casual. Suddenly, her saloon girl attire felt fussy and ridiculous. A table of girls to her left was staring over at her, pointing. This made her feel self-conscious, an emotion completely alien to her.

As she headed to the bar, she heard one of the young men from the long table shout to his friends, 'I don't bloody believe it! That's the maniac I told you about that nearly killed me because she wanted to go fast on the humpback bridge.'

The whole table erupted with laughter. Then one of them hollered back, 'You didn't tell us she was hot!'

Another joined in by saying, 'She's definitely looking for a cowboy tonight in that dress!'

'Yee-hah!' another added.

The banter was relatively harmless, but Marnie marched with a purpose over to the table of boys. No one was going to feel uncomfortable when she was in charge.

'I am warning you all, if you are going to behave like that towards a customer, you are leaving. I won't even wait until you've finished your drinks. Everyone is here tonight to have a good time, so let's not spoil it. Do I have your word?'

'Yes, sorry, Marnie.'

'Sorry. We won't do it again.'

She looked at the others sitting round the table, 'What about the rest of you?'

'We'll behave.'

'Okay, I'll trust you, but I will be keeping my eye on you.'

The rowdy crowd settled down once Marnie had ticked them off. They were regulars at The Shell Seekers and they had a healthy respect for Marnie. They were well aware of the fact that if she barred them, they would struggle to find a substitute drinking establishment.

Meanwhile, Edina was smarting with embarrassment. This was not how she had pictured the night would play out. Instinct made her want to call a taxi to take her home, even if it were just to get changed.

Struan bought the first round of the evening for his staff. With the drinks all balanced on a silver tray, he headed over to the table that Marnie had reserved for them near the bar. Fortunately for Edina, the table was far enough away from her hecklers.

Marnie slipped her arm around Edina's waist.

'Don't worry, believe it or not, they are all nice guys. They're fishermen, and they've been at sea for several days. They go slightly mad once they get back on dry land.'

'Thanks,' Edina said. 'I just feel a bit stupid because I got off on the wrong foot with one of them when I arrived. I'm also embarrassed that I got the whole dress code so horribly wrong.'

'Don't be silly,' Marnie told her. 'You're dressed for a night out at the weekend. I wish everyone came dressed up for the occasion!'

Edina instantly liked Marnie, just as Struan had told her she would.

Marnie led her over to the table, explaining that there would be karaoke later in the night. 'You'll wish you had brought earplugs because we have some dreadful singers in here.' She laughed. 'How's your singing, Edina? Will you be giving us a song tonight?'

'I'm an okay singer. Normally, I would be first up, but for obvious reasons, I've lost my confidence a bit tonight. Maybe next time.'

Edina joined her work colleagues at the table. The music was loud, and the conversation between them was basic. Looking around the table, she could see Struan was happy to sit admiring Marnie. Next to Struan was Suzie, who held on to her drink as though it was about to be stolen from her. Since they arrived, only one round of drinks had been bought, and yet Suzie's eyes told a different story. Edina glanced at Freddy, who had already noticed this situation; he shrugged his shoulders at her, indicating that he had no idea why Suzie seemed inebriated.

Edina could recall one colleague in Edinburgh who was always drunker than everyone else. He appeared to be drinking the same amount, but his behaviour was that of someone who had been drinking all day. She remembered that when everyone moved on to the next pub, he would tell them that he'd catch up with them shortly. Who knows how many drinks he downed in the extra half hour he snatched alone.

Edina's attention focused on Freddy. He was Mull born and raised, and by the looks of things, he was known to everyone. His focus appeared to be on the pretty females sitting on the table near the rear of the room.

They were probably the alpha, mean girls at school. I'm a tough cookie, but they still managed to intimidate me when I walked in tonight. I wonder which one he likes.

She looked at Freddy to see who his eyes were fixed on, but it was too difficult to tell.

I will put my money on the skinny tomboy with the short hair. She is the prettiest, perhaps even the sexy one of the group. The rest look like airheads.

A quick movement caught her eye from across the table. It was Freddy rescuing Suzie's drink as it slipped from her limp hand.

Seeing Struan so fixated on Marnie made Edina realise that if she *had* made a play for him, she would have been left looking like a fool… for the second time that night. This man had eyes for only one woman. This was obvious for all to see.

Oh well, the good ones do generally get taken first.

Even she could see that Marnie was pretty special.

Edina's position at the table was facing the bar. The fishermen were to her right. Out of reluctant curiosity, she stole a surreptitious glance at the table of trawlermen. As she did so, she caught the eye of the *humpback* driver. His gaze was already on her. When their eyes met, his face formed a scowl before he turned away. It pained her to admit this to herself, but he was really quite gorgeous.

Horrible, but unquestionably gorgeous. There, I've said it, and I hate myself for thinking it.

It was Edina's turn to buy a round of drinks.

'Who's ready for another drink?' she asked, pointing at the almost empty glasses on the table. 'What are you all having?'

'Yes, please, rum and coke,' Struan said. 'Do you want me to give you a hand?'

Edina lifted the silver tray from the spare seat at the table. 'No, I will manage fine with this.'

Freddy pointed his thumb upwards. 'It's Tennent's lager.'

'Got it,' she told him.

Suzie was swaying backwards and forwards on her seat, not noticeably so, but Edina spotted it. Buying drinks for people who were already drunk had never bothered her in the past, but looking at Suzie's lost expression somehow took a swipe at her conscience. She looked to the boys at the table for guidance.

Struan screwed up his face, holding his hands out to the side.

He mouthed, 'I don't know.'

Once again, Freddy shrugged his reply.

'Suzie, what would you like to drink?'

'Same again,' she slurred, with an exaggerated wave with her arm in the air.

There was a two-human deep queue waiting to be served. Edina joined the ranks at the back. The Edina of a bygone time would have wiled her way to the front with the excuse of a made-up emergency. Her fingers drummed one, two, three, four beats on the tray while she waited, then ever so casually, she stole a squint at the fishermen.

He's looking again. I can't believe it. He is actually looking at me again. He can't keep his eyes off me. Unbelievable!

At that moment, she made the bold decision to smile over at her admirer. Keeping it sweet and coy, she tilted her head and displayed her best smile in his direction.

The handsome fisherman stared back. He then burst out laughing at her attempt to appeal to him. He shook his head before continuing his conversation with his friend next to him.

You've done it again, Edina. You've made a first-class arse of yourself for the second time. That guy must think I am an absolute nut job.

'What can I get you, Edina?' Marnie asked.

Grateful for the distraction, Edina gave forth her drinks order, adding, 'Could you make Suzie's vodka a small one? I don't know how it's happened, but she's smashed already.'

'It's the same story every week,' Marnie explained. 'I've said to Struan about it because I shouldn't really be serving her at all. He doesn't understand why it happens either. I'll just put a small splash of vodka in, then top it up with the coke.'

A book containing a list of the available Karaoke songs was passed from table to table. One of the alpha mean girls brought the book to Freddy after she and her friends had selected their choices. She laid it down in the middle of the table, managing to give Edina a look of disdain at the same time.

How impressive! The mean girl is a multitasker. She can make a karaoke book delivery while giving the evil eye to the pretty new girl.

The girl's hand then rested around Freddy's shoulders, leaning in to whisper something in his ear. There was an awkward moment that followed while she stood waiting for a response.

Freddy sat motionless, looking everywhere but at her. A shake of his head sent her scuttling off to her friends who were waiting eagerly for news.

Struan reached for the list of songs. 'Okay, who's getting up? Come on, Freddy, you can hold a tune.'

'No, not tonight,' he said. 'I'm not in the mood.'

Turning to Susie, Struan could see that she was really quite out of sorts, although she still managed to cling tightly to her tilted glass.

'Something tells me that Susie won't be treating us to a song tonight,' Struan commented.

'Whatever gave you that idea?' Freddy agreed.

Edina threw a disapproving look at Freddy. 'Okay, that's enough. We've all been there,' she told him.

It was difficult for Edina to work out why Susie was in such a state.

She got on the bus with us straight after her shift. Perhaps she hasn't eaten anything today. She is very petite, so it probably doesn't take much to push her over the edge. On the other hand, she has actually only had one drink. Whoops, there goes her glass!

Edina leaned over to rescue the tumbler, which sat at a precarious angle in Suzie's hand.

Suzie's large handbag lay open at her feet, and something within the bag caught Edina's eye as she took the drink from her gripless hands.

Okay that explains it. Edina the investigative journalist figures it out again. We would all be sitting in that state if we brought a large bottle of Smirnoff out for the night.

'Hey, Edina, from Edinburgh!' Struan coaxed. 'What about it? Let's hear if you can sing or not.'

Before she could answer no, one of the songs in the book practically leapt off the page at her.

Ah ha! The perfect song. If these clowns at the back table think I'm looking for a cowboy with this dress on, then I might as well play along.

Scribbling her name across from her chosen song, she then handed the book back to Struan to pass on to the next table.

'Good on you, Edina. You're a good sport,' Struan told her with a pat on the back. 'You had better be good, or we'll be embarrassed.'

The karaoke got underway, with the singers performing on the small stage area near the bar. The majority of the entertainment was painful and impossible to zone out from. Edina listened in disbelief to most of the singers who had taken to the stage with confidence.

What are they hearing in their own ears? If only they knew what they really sounded like to the audience.

There were all the classic karaoke songs such as I Will Survive, It's Raining Men, and every Adele song available.

Why are people so predictable?

The background chatter of the disinterested crowd became as loud as the singers. Freddy was mimicking a girl in the spotlight who dramatically shut her eyes, making learned arm gestures as she belted out, For One Night Only.

Marnie came over to the table to whisper in Edina's ear, 'You're up next.'

She walked past Struan, ruffling his hair. He grabbed her arm, pulling her towards him. He whispered something in Marnie's ear, which made her laugh, but she jokingly slapped him, pretending to be shocked.

Edina's name was called, igniting for a few seconds the flutter of nerves in the pit of her stomach. She knew she was a good singer, but she was in a room full of strangers who hadn't taken kindly towards her.

The song she had selected was, Cowboy Take Me Away by The Dixie Chicks. She loved that song. With both hands trembling, she gripped the microphone, waiting for the words to appear on the screen in front of her.

When she heard the music coming through the speakers, she began singing the verse, which was slow. The crowd listened, but merely from curiosity at the newcomer. Suddenly, the powerful chorus broke forth, showing everyone in the room that Edina was more than worthy of a place on the makeshift stage in The Shell Seekers. Effortlessly, she had sung this song many times before to far bigger audiences than this, but tonight, she was proving a point. Using all the emotions of the previous few months, she sang with everything she had. Many of the onlookers were moved to tears, mainly due to her talent, but the surprise element was also a factor.

The talking had ceased, and everyone was now focused on the performer. Those seated at the back rose to their feet to get a better view. From where she stood at the microphone, she could see that the audience was with her all the way. Nothing pleased her more than gaining the room's full attention, including the table of hecklers. Never before had there been a performer of this quality at the karaoke night; deep down, Edina knew it.

As she stood under the spotlight, she felt elated. She was no longer embarrassed to be wearing her red saloon girl dress. She was proud.

For the final time, she broke into the emotional chorus, asking her cowboy to take her away, but this time, she focused her attention on the table of fishermen, beckoning with her finger as she sang.

Impressed by her sass, they replied with a cheer.

When the final note ended, there was a moment's hush before the crowd went wild. Even the fishermen at the back were on their feet. Some people were shouting, *encore* and *more, more*. Edina gave a tiny bow before returning to her seat. Struan and Freddy were speechless. They couldn't believe what had just happened. It was one of those nights that would be talked about on the island for years to come, a night to remember. The shouts of *again* and *more* continued to echo around the bar, but Edina smiled coquettishly at her audience.

There, how'd you like them green apples!

Chapter 10

Edina awoke the following morning happy with the knowledge that her shift at the hotel did not start until 3pm. Her head felt woolly, a thirst raged in her throat.

'Water, water,' she croaked with exaggeration as she ran downstairs to fill a tall glass from the tap.

The sight of her journal caught her eye, it dawned on her that she hadn't written in it the previous night. She lifted the book from where it lay on the threadbare carpet and saw that, yet again, it had been defaced. Strangely, this phenomenon no longer had the dramatic effect on her that it had in the early days. In a sense, it was beginning to feel normal.

It was 8.30am.

Edina was torn between housework and heading back up to the comfort of her bed. It took less than three seconds for her to decide to turn around and climb the stairs to her bedroom. Her limbs and bones were exhausted from the physicality of her job. Her previous career had been much less demanding on her body but far more pressurised mentally and emotionally. Considering everything she had been through back on the mainland, the idea of completing a shift, then returning home with nothing to think about was preferable for her.

On the floor at the side of the bed, she slipped her feet out of her slippers and climbed back under the duvet. Dreams of the previous night at The Shell Seekers began to play out in her mind as she fell deeper and deeper into sleep.

A deafening whirring sound intruded on her peaceful slumber. Bolting to the upright position, she looked around her, feeling disorientated.

What the hell is that noise?

Throwing back the quilt, she bounded towards the window.

Oh, Stan!

He was pushing the lawnmower across the grass.

Did it have to be today?

It was no use. The Saturday lie-in was off. The only option remaining for her was to get up and greet the day. After showering, she headed downstairs for breakfast. Her cupboards and fridge were fairly full from the shopping she had managed to get through the week in between shifts.

With a cup of tea in hand, she looked out the window to see Stan wiping his brow. She opened the front door and waved frantically at him to get his attention.

At first, he simply dipped his cap in response, believing she was merely offering him a good morning greeting. He then noticed she continued waving her arms in the air at him, so he switched off the heavy petrol lawnmower.

'Were you looking to speak to me, lass?'

'Yes, Stan, I just wanted to thank you so much for taking us in and picking us up last night. That was very good of you.'

'Don't mention it,' he told her. 'I don't do both runs every week, but I thought because it was your first time out with your workmates, I'd make a special effort. Hey, I hear you can belt out a tune.'

Well, there's one thing for sure, I'll never get a job as a journalist here. There is no call for newspapers when the island jungle drums can carry the news way faster.

'Yes, I do enjoy belting out a song whenever I get the opportunity. Do you fancy a couple of bacon rolls and a cup of tea?' she offered, hoping to get a chance to speak to him about her strange nightly problem.

'That would be great. I was up with the lark this morning.'

She summoned him into the house and told him to sit while she cooked breakfast.

From the kitchen area, she shouted, 'Do you take tomato sauce with your roll, Stan?'

'Oh no, never tomato sauce with bacon rolls,' he said seriously. 'It has to be brown sauce with bacon rolls. Tomato sauce is for fish and chips, brown sauce is for bacon rolls. It's a rule of thumb. In the books!'

'Well, could you make an exception just for today because I don't have any brown sauce?'

'No,' he said with conviction. 'I will refrain from having any sauce if you don't have brown.'

'I am so sorry. I'll do better next time.'

Edina carried the tray through to the lounge, where she set it down on the coffee table. After pouring two mugs of tea from the teapot, she decided against asking him if he wanted milk and sugar. It was best to avoid another sauce-style debate, instead, she would allow him to help himself from the milk jug and sugar bowl.

When she saw that Stan had finished eating, she asked him about the history of the area.

Stan's face broke into a semi-toothless smile. This was his area of expertise.

'Well, where do I start?' he began. 'Mull has been inhabited since the end of the last ice age, which was around 6000 BC.' His face took on a faraway look as though he was straightening out the main events in his mind. 'You see, the Bronze Age inhabitants built brochs, cairns, stone circles, pottery and standing stones which all provided compelling evidence to the island's past.'

Oh no. What have I done? I've gone and unleashed the beast.

'The early Christian period on the island began around the 6th century, with AD563 being particularly relevant as it was thought that Christianity was brought to this part of Scotland by St Columba when he arrived on the Island of Iona to set up a monastery.'

Arrrghhh! I can't take anymore.

She began to see her precious morning off slipping away as fast as her will to live.

'By the 14th Century, Mull became part of the Lordship of the Isles—'

'Stan, I am so impressed with your knowledge,' she interrupted. 'Could I fast forward you to say, the past one hundred years or so?'

Stan stared at her with a look of bewilderment. The past one hundred years was a long way off from his timeline.

'Any reason in particular?'

'Sort of, although it might sound a bit random. Would you know if there are any stories about a small boy who was connected to Pennyghael House Estate in some way? A tragedy perhaps?'

'Why do you ask?'

He was clearly intrigued.

Edina fetched her handbag from the sideboard.

'My phone's in here somewhere,' she told him, rooting around the contents. 'Ah ha, now let me show you the oddest thing.'

Balancing on the arm of the wingchair where Stan sat, she flicked through each photo, enlarging the subject matter as she showed him.

'Aye, lass, that is one of the strangest things I've ever seen. I agree with you that it looks like a young lad. His clothes are highly peculiar. Where would you even be able to buy a hat like that for a youngster? I have no explanation for this.'

'Wait, Stan, there's more. The photos were only the start.'

'The first few nights, I could hear something downstairs, a ripping noise. I was terrified out of my wits, so I just hid under the duvet until morning. It still happens every night, but now I simply go to sleep. It doesn't scare me anymore. If it had wanted to harm me, it could have done it before this.'

Stan sat forward on his seat, spellbound by Edina's ghostly tale.

'Did you ever find out what the ripping sound was?'

'Yes, in fact, I'll show you what the ripping noise was.'

Edina showed Stan the defaced journal, with pages scribbled on and torn.

'And you say it happens every night?'

'Every night,' she confirmed.

'Do you think it's the boy from the photos?'

Edina shrugged. 'I don't know. I am presuming it's him because surely there can't be more than one ghost that wants to contact me.'

'Yes, that's a good point. Are you writing things about the boy in the journal?'

'No, I haven't mentioned anything about him. I just write about the really mundane things that I do every day.'

Stan rubbed his chin, nodding.

'In my opinion, thereby lieth the problem, Edina from Edinburgh.'

'Explain, please, you've lost me.'

'The boy has shown himself to you, right?'

'Right.'

'This means that he thinks you can help him, although I don't know why he would choose someone from the mainland and not a Mulloch. He is possibly able to make some kind of connection with you… Don't ask me to explain that. I just made it up. So if he is reaching out to you, then he wants you to notice him, talk about him, write about him. Until now, you've pretty much ignored him. I presume you haven't told anyone else about this strange occurrence?'

'No, I haven't told a soul and yes, I even ignore him when he is downstairs in my house. I know I'm not a Mulloch, but maybe that is why he has chosen to reach out to me. Oh, and there is the possibility that he somehow knows that I am an investigative journalist. Although, how ghosts could ever do a background search on mortals is beyond me.'

'Edina, it is not for us to question why.'

'Good point Stan. So what do you suggest?'

There was a lengthy pause from Stan.

'I am going to find out anything I can about the estate, starting with my own mother, who has lived in this area all of her life. She's ninety-six in June.'

'Wow, that's a good age. Island life must suit her. So, what do you think that I could be doing?'

'Starting today, I want you to write all the information you have so far about the boy appearing in the photos. Then, catalogue the events of the night-time visitations. Let's see if that angers or pleases him. I have a feeling it will be the latter. This kid wants to be noticed.'

'Good idea. I'm so glad I told you about it. Thanks for not laughing at me.'

'You can't laugh at what is there in black and white in front of your face. Don't worry. We'll get to the bottom of this. Now I have to leave. The grass out there needs cutting. Thanks for the breakfast.'

Chapter 11

Stan's advice was foremost in Edina's thoughts as she drove along the potholed road, skilfully avoiding every crater. The road, with all of its pitfalls, had become second nature to her. It was as though road and girl had reached a working compromise, each respecting the other's flaws.

The chat with Stan had been highly beneficial to her. It encouraged her to look at the situation from a different angle and with different eyes. Test the theory he had suggested. She would do just that tonight when she returned home.

When she entered the double glass doors of the hotel, she was greeted with a smile from Struan, who was standing at the reception desk.

'Hey, what about you last night?' he said, laughing. 'You really smashed it. Everyone is talking about it.'

'Oh, stop it,' she joked. 'That wasn't even my best singing!'

She walked away in the direction of the dining room, which needed setting up for the evening ahead.

Struan shouted after her. 'Hey! Edina, come here for a minute.'

'What?' she asked, returning to the reception area.

'I nearly forgot,' he said, producing a note from behind the desk. 'This was handed in for you.'

A curious look passed across her face as she took the piece of paper.

Who would send me a note? I don't know anyone on Mull.

Walking back towards the dining room, she opened it.

I enjoyed your singing last night. You are a shit driver but a great singer!
Tom.

He had added his mobile number at the foot of the page.

It was impossible to prevent a smile from spreading from her mouth to her eyes. She knew exactly who had written this note. It was obvious now that he had forgiven her for nearly killing him that first day at the humpback bridge. Question was, did she want to call him? He had been so nasty to her last night when she had walked into The Shell Seekers.

Who does he think he is, embarrassing me like that in front of everyone? Then he finds out I'm a half-decent singer and can't throw his phone number at me quickly enough. Oh no, I don't think so. He can go and find some other girl who is willing to put up with all of his unpleasantness.

The note was stuffed into the side pocket of her skirt.

I don't have time to think about phoning men who aren't even nice to me. I have a lot of work to catch up with.

The restaurant and bar were not particularly busy, but by midnight, the few people who were left showed no sign of leaving. A table of residents, who were golfers, had just ordered another bottle of Taittinger Champagne. Edina was tired, and it was now after closing time, but she knew that Struan and his mum needed all the business they could get. So, she willingly obliged with a smile and brought the bottle in an ice bucket over to the table, where she poured each a glass.

I think I'll prepare some bowls of nuts and twiglets for them. Hopefully, the saltiness will help them drink the bottle faster so they can then get the hell up to their beds.

When she took the salty treats over to the golfers, she noticed the young couple holding hands at the table near the window. They arrived at seven for dinner and were still there. Earlier in the evening, they had explained to Edina that it was their first wedding anniversary.

She saw the couple watching as the table of golfers shared the champagne. The hour was late, but Edina decided to approach the love birds.

'We have less expensive bottles of champagne if you are looking to have a proper celebration.'

They looked at each other, smiling.

Egging them on a little further, she said, 'Go on, a one-year anniversary is something special. Make it a night to remember. I can prepare you some little snacks with it.'

The young man exchanged a look with his pretty young wife, then turned to Edina.

'You're right, let's go mad. But could you make it one of your cheaper bottles?'

'One cheap bottle of good quality champagne coming up. Maybe next year you can buy the Taittinger.'

The couple suddenly became excited about their impulse buy.

Downstairs in the kitchen, Freddy was on dishwashing duties. His house was walking distance to the hotel, so he could be brought in at a moment's notice. The money came in handy for him as he was leaving the island in September to take up a place at college in Glasgow.

Ever since he was a young boy, he worked alongside his father in their family-owned garage. It was the only garage on the island, so everyone used it. In the early days, Freddy's father coped with the workload, but the rising population on the island, as well as the need for every family member to own a car, meant that he now had a growing backlog of cars to service.

Freddy's father was well aware that his son knew as much about cars as he did, perhaps more, but he wanted him to get the qualification on the mainland. He believed it was healthy for a young person to have a broader life experience.

Freddy reluctantly accepted the place at college as he had no desire to be anywhere but the Island of Mull. Small as it was, it was the only life he wanted.

When the restaurant finally emptied of merry customers, Freddy appeared in the bar to help Edina finish up.

Pulling out one of the bar stools, he climbed up saying, 'A pint of your finest lager, please, wench!'

'Call me wench again, and you'll experience the fine lager poured over you,' Edina joked back.

Freddy watched as she ran the sale through the till. 'You're not honestly going to charge me for a drink, are you?'

'Yes, Freddy, I am. If this were your bar, would you allow me to give away free drinks?'

'No, I suppose not.'

'Business is slow here, and if we don't help boost the profits, then we'll all be out of a job.'

'I know. I heard Struan and his mum talking the other day. They didn't know I was there. Struan said that if business didn't pick up in the next few months, they would be shutting the doors before next summer.'

Edina felt strangely saddened by the news of this conversation. Although it couldn't be said that she loved her life on the island, she would admit that its peaceful rhythm was having a positive influence her.

'Hey, you are a really good singer,' Freddy said, changing the subject.

'So people keep telling me. You were a bit quiet last night. Was there anything wrong?'

'No, I'm fine really, just a bit flat about stuff.'

'Do you want to talk about it?' she asked him.

'There's a girl I really like, she was at The Shell Seekers last night. I can't speak to her because I start tripping over my words until I don't make any sense, then I run off. I'm leaving for college soon, and if I don't tell her how I feel, it will be too late.'

'Have you any idea if she likes you too?'

'No. She would never be interested in me,' he said, pushing his finger into the froth of his lager then supping it off.

'Next Friday, when we all go out, you show me which girl it is, and I could have a quiet word with her.'

Edina had a pretty solid suspicion that it was the quirky one of the alpha females.

Those girls hated me from the moment I walked through the door. If I went over to have a quiet word with one of them, they'd lynch me. Still, a week is a long way off, and Freddy looks a bit happier now.

'By the way, Freddy, have you ever seen anything strange in this hotel?'

No harm in putting out feelers.

'Strange how?' he asked.

'Unusual, creepy, odd,' she clarified.

'Not really, but the bedroom beside the tower gives me the shitters. I've been in there twice, and I've had the chills with an odd feeling that someone was watching me. I had to change a lightbulb once. I know I put the light off at the switch, but when I put the new bulb in, it flickered on and off, on and off. The next thing I knew, it nearly electrocuted me. I fell off the ladder. I got a hell of a fright. I've never been in there since.'

Now that's interesting.

'Did you tell anyone at the time?'

'No way, who's going to believe me?'

'I do,' she assured him.

'It was one of those experiences I would rather erase from my memory.'

If only you knew how many of those I have in my life.

Edina offered Freddy a lift home, but he told her she would laugh if she saw how close he lived.

'I'd be no sooner in the car, but it would be time to get back out,' he joked.

'Okay, thanks for your help tonight. I'll see you on Friday, if not before,' she told him.

They went their separate ways on the front steps of the hotel.

As she opened her car door, she heard Freddy shouting.

'Don't forget that you're going to speak to that girl at The Shell Seekers for me!'

'I won't, that's a done deal.'

Chapter 12

On the drive back to the cottage, Edina became aware of the aching pains in her neck and shoulders. Her body was unfamiliar with the physical efforts she bestowed on it. Sitting down on the short car journey had allowed her feet to swell considerably.

I have no idea how I'll get my shoes off tonight. I may have to go to bed with them on.

She felt them straining against the leather. On the potholed road, although she was tired, she glided smoothly over it, like skates on ice. When she saw the window in the lounge illuminated, she applauded her decision to leave the lamp on. Returning home to a dark, empty space was something she did not relish.

She parked in the space beside the trees, switching off the car engine. An unexpected memory entered her head. It was brought on by the thought of entering a dark house. Her mind was taken back to that night in Edinburgh, when she had walked home with the editor, whose name was too painful to say. They had left the celebrations in the pub to walk toward their homes.

'Would you mind walking with me up to the main door? I get a bit scared sometimes.'

He obliged.

In truth, nothing scared her, certainly not walking home alone in the city.

Men like to feel like the brave protector. Show your vulnerable side, and your wish will be their command.

They walked together as far as her apartment building. Until now, she had formed the opinion that he was shy, but that night he had shown a humorous, outgoing side to his character that was normally kept hidden. It dawned on her as she watched him throw his head back slightly while laughing, that although he had been her boss for seven years, she didn't really know him. Her thought at that moment, standing there outside her house, was he was so attractive, so different from other men.

'Would you like to come up?' she said, completely on impulse.

He looked down at his feet without replying.

Here goes. This usually seals it.

'Oh my goodness, what am I saying. I'm so sorry. I shouldn't have asked you that. You must think I'm terrible. What does that look like? Thanks for walking me home.'

He reached for her hand, allowing himself to be led up to her apartment.

Turning the key in the door, she took him into the dark, empty house. No words were exchanged as she stood close to him in the hallway, brushing her hand across the top of his leg. Unsure of what he was thinking, she didn't care. He was there in her apartment, open to seduction. Taking his face in her hands, she kissed him gently on the lips. His interest in her was obvious, but she could tell he was fighting with his conscience. A sexual tension built up in the air around them. Still no words were spoken.

In a moment of weakness, unseen in the dark, he grabbed her with both hands, pushing her to the wall. He pressed hard against her, enabling her to feel how aroused he was. Kissing her roughly, he touched her between her legs. *She* became the lamb to the slaughter. The editor was completely in charge. She was helpless. Unexpectedly, he then turned her to face the wall.

All she could hear, apart from their laboured breathing, was the sound of him fumbling with the zip on his trousers. The next thing she knew, her dress was pulled up, with an expectation that he was about to enter her.

It didn't happen.

Pulling her dress back down, he then zipped up his trousers, apologised, and left.

In the darkness of the hallway, in her empty apartment, she stood wondering what had just happened. *I can't believe it,* she remembered thinking.

I am actually in love.

Never before had she experienced passion of that intensity. The experience stayed in her thoughts day and night, as did the editor. Even back then, she knew that the wise thing would be to leave well alone, but that would never happen. He was all she needed, all she wanted, all she desired. There was no one else that came close. She had to have him, and that was final.

Thinking back to that time was not good for her, but she allowed the memory to play out for some reason.

Edina, you have to shut the door on that chapter. It's over, and it can't be changed. What's done is done. Keep looking forward.

She had been sitting reflecting in the car outside her cottage for almost half an hour. The time could be described as late or very early when she finally entered the front door. All she wanted to do was fall into her bed and sleep.

This was her first experience of fatigue, real fatigue, the kind that removes every ounce of your energy. Her swollen feet needed careful tending as they had become one with her shoes. Sliding down the wall at the front door, she sat and gently dislodged the leather from skin. *These two things on the end of my legs don't even resemble feet.* She stared at the puffed flesh. *Now, let's see if I can actually walk on them.* Hobbling with a limp, she made her way to the staircase. A thought occurred to her before she climbed the stairs. It stopped her in her tracks. *The journal! I forgot about the wretched journal. I promised Stan I'd write about the boy to test his theory. I can't be bothered. Should I wait until tomorrow? Yes, I'll start it tomorrow.* She placed her swollen foot on the first stair. *No, I promised. I need to do it tonight to see if it stops the ghostly activity. I'll keep it brief.*

There was barely enough energy in her arms to pull the tartan blanket from the back of the chair to drape around her shoulders. Once wrapped up comfortably, she began thinking about how she would start the journal entry. The words came flowing from her pen, almost as though she was being aided in her quest.

The first time I set eyes on Pennyghael House, I was overcome by its splendour. I had an overwhelming urge to photograph the magnificent dwelling from every angle...

Without missing a single detail, she described the boy that had appeared to her in the photos. She then moved on to the unsettling activity occurring each night as she lay in her bed. It was important at this stage to point out that the boy and the destruction may not be connected. It could be a disturbing coincidence. On the second page, she asked hypothetical questions and gave possible explanations. The final paragraph described the range of emotions she had experienced during this time, beginning with fear and ending in complacency. Two pages were filled with ease.

The process of creating a piece of work again felt good. It had been cathartic to write about the boy, discussing him in such a way seemed to make him more real. Only when she ran out of material to write about did she stop. The journal was closed with the pen resting on the spine. She left it on the sideboard to be inspected in the morning.

Now she could climb the stairs with a clear conscience to claim her prize of a well-deserved sleep.

Chapter 13

The night sky was beginning to show signs of the arrival of morning. Edina pulled the duvet up around her neck and gazed out the window at the remaining pinholes of stars. Before sleep consumed her, she sent out a request to the endless universe.

Mum, if you are peeking down on me, I need to tell you that I love you and I'm sorry for everything. I will make you proud of me.

In Edina's dream, she found a note which read:

Meet me at the humpback bridge.

I can't meet anyone at the bridge. I have to investigate the tower room at the hotel so that I can write about it in my journal. Maybe instead of meeting him at the bridge, I could meet him in the tower.

The dream turmoil ended when Edina's alarm woke her at nine. Feeling incredibly groggy, she sat up in bed, realising that her dilemma was not real.

The note… Why did I dream about the note from this Tom character? I thought I'd shut the door on that idea. Do I want to send him a text? Well, he had gone to the trouble of taking a handwritten message to the hotel. How did he know where I worked? I thought I'd be anonymous when I came to this remote island. It's been quite the reverse. Everyone knows everything about me. I feel completely onymous… if there is such a word.

She pushed her feet into her sheepskin slippers.

Yes, I think I will send him a message to see what he has to say for himself. I certainly won't be meeting him on the humpback bridge or the tower. The tower room is something I will investigate alone.

Her shift at the hotel started at eleven. This gave her plenty of time to wash her hair and make breakfast. The sun had dramatically appeared by shining through all the front-facing windows. Edina entered the lounge and saw it looked almost nice as the golden rays fanned across the back of the sofa, landing on the back wall where the sideboard rested. She stood with her eyes shut, enjoying the warmth on her face. A thought entered her mind.

The journal!

Frantically, she looked around the floor where it was usually left, but there was no sign of it anywhere. Her eyes then turned to the sideboard where she had left it. It sat untouched with the pen still tucked tightly against the spine.

I don't believe it. Stan was so right about the boy. He just wanted to be noticed.

Inside the cover, she saw that the sheets she had written on were just as they had been the night before.

This boy really wants my attention. Now, I just have to find out why.

On the drive up to the hotel, Edina spotted Stan trimming the edge of the lawn with long-handled shears. She brought the car to an abrupt halt in the middle of the road, hollering out of the window.

'Stan, Stan, I've got news!'

Throwing his shears to one side, Stan hastened over to the car.

'I wrote only about the boy in my journal last night, and guess what?'

'Your notebook was intact?' he guessed.

'Yip! I think we are really onto something. Have you spoken to your mum yet?' she asked.

'I'm going to see her today at teatime. I'll let you know what she says. Meanwhile, keep writing down everything you find out. We'll get to the bottom of this, lass.'

Edina bounded into the hotel, waving at Struan as he stood talking on the phone.

He returned her greeting with a two-fingered salute.

This made Edina laugh as she remembered the ridiculous curtsey she had given him on her first week in employment.

This is beginning to feel like a game of 'How many ways can you say hello without speaking?' I'll try to think of something clever tomorrow.

Down in the kitchen, Edina saw Suzie folding the sheets and towels as she took them out of the industrial tumble dryer.

'Hi Suzie, I wonder if you can help me?'

'I'll certainly try.'

'As you know, I'm living in the cottage on the estate, and it is pretty basic inside, to say the least. Would you know of anywhere that would sell second-hand pictures and bric-a-brac items?'

'Yes, I do,' Susie answered quite excitedly. 'There's a big warehouse that sells all second-hand goods for charity. I'll take you there on Saturday morning if you like?'

'That would be great. It's a date!'

Edina skipped off in the direction of the cupboard where the hoover resided.

I never dreamt that I'd feel excited about going to a big charity shop. I actually can't wait.

'Hey Edina,' Struan shouted when she passed through the foyer. 'Did you ever do anything about that note from Tom the fisherman?'

'I'm still pondering that one. I'll keep you informed.'

In the broom cupboard, she reached into the pocket of her skirt for the note. She took her phone from her apron and typed out a message.

Hello Tom, Your note was quite a surprise because you told me I was a maniac. Does this make you a psycho for wanting to be in touch with me? Edina

She pressed send.

Within seconds, a message vibrated back.

I promise I am not a psycho. Ask anyone who doesn't know me. Tx

The message made her laugh. *I don't think I'll reply for a while. It's best to keep him hanging on a bit.*

Chapter 14

Struan's mobile phone rang while he was setting up the dining room for lunch.

'Slow down, Marnie, I don't know what you're saying. Oh no, not another one. Read it to me.'

Marnie read the latest letter posted by hand through her letter box.

**MARNIE,
I THINK YOU KNOW BY NOW THAT I AM WATCHING YOU.
I KNOW EVERYTHING ABOUT YOU
EVEN THE SECRETS OF YOUR PAST.
TIME IS RUNNING OUT**

'Was it written in the same way, with the letters cut from a newspaper?' Struan asked. 'Did you see anyone delivering it to your door?'

'No,' she sobbed.

'Just calm down. Lock the doors and don't go out. I will go to the police station, then I'll be straight over to check all the locks.'

Struan could hear Marnie's stifled cries on the other end of the line. He knew that Marnie's fear came not from the letters she had received but from the potential identity of the sender.

Leaving Edina in charge of the hotel, he headed to the police station in Tobermory. He knew about Marnie's ex-boyfriend, Ashton Brook, who believed she had ruined his life. His career as a professional footballer was now over, and Struan suspected that he was seeking revenge. In truth, he had ruined his own career. He had carried out the serious assault, Marnie simply reported him.

Today's letter had been the fifth to be posted through the door of The Shell Seekers, all written in the same style. Struan had wondered why Ashton hadn't approached her before now. Was he being cautious or did he just enjoy instilling fear in his victim before moving in for the kill? Either way, alarm bells were blaring in his ears.

How can I keep my sweet girl safe? If anything ever happened to her, my life would be over.

His foot pressed down harder on the accelerator pedal.

Chapter 15

Stan walked the full length of the lawn, then back, pushing the lawnmower. The bag at the front of the machine needed emptying every ten minutes or so. At one point, he had made a request to Struan for a mower that he could sit on and drive around, but Struan had told him that they couldn't even think about it until next year. The grounds were spacious, made up mainly of lawn and woodland. The area at the front of the hotel had to be prioritised, as Stan was the only groundsman on the estate.

Before Stan left for the day, he had neatened the borders of the lawn with the long shears, pulled weeds from all four flower beds, and scraped moss from the hotel's front steps. He had worked for over half an hour longer than the time he was paid for, but there was nothing unusual about that. It was important to him to have the grounds looking just right before he finished for the evening.

His mother's house was only a few minutes from the hotel by car. When he pulled into her street, he could see that she was already standing at the front door, eagerly anticipating his arrival.

'Hello, son,' she called to him as he stepped out of the car.

'Hi, Mum, you look well.'

He wrapped his arms around her frail form, kissing her on the cheek.

'Come on in, you've probably had a tough day. I've made you your favourite for dinner. You put your feet up, and I'll set the table.'

Stan walked into the familiar lounge of his family home. The dining table dominated the already cluttered room. The weather was mild, but there was a blazing fire in the grate, nonetheless. Stan automatically walked to the side of the sofa nearest to the fireplace.

'How have your swollen ankles been, Mum?' he shouted in the direction of the kitchen.

'Oh, not too bad, son. I try to stay off my feet as much as I can.'

'I feel bad that you're running around after me.'

'I love running after you, son. I made you a chocolate cake this afternoon.'

Stan helped his mum to set the table, then the two sat down together to eat. It never ceased to amaze him that his mother, who was now in her nineties, was still a wonderful cook.

'So your ankles are feeling a bit better?' Stan asked her.

'Yes, they are, but now I've got an itchy scalp. I'm scratch, scratch, scratching all day long, even at night sometimes.'

Stan made a sympathetic face. 'We can't have that,' he told her. 'I'll go to the chemist in Tobermory and ask for advice about that.'

'That's good of you, son.'

'Now, mother, I want to ask you about any information you may remember about a boy who must have lived long ago. I think he was possibly connected to Pennyghael House. I know you worked as a maid there when you were a teenager. Do you have any memory of a young lad living there at that time?'

'What's this all about?' she asked him.

'Nothing really, it was an inquiry from someone at the hotel.' He did not want to frighten his elderly mum with stories of ghostly happenings.

'I worked for Lord and Lady MacGillivrey, but they had three daughters, no sons. Now, what were their names?' she asked herself. 'Oh yes, Alicia, Rosemary, and Francesca. They were such lovely children, as I remember. No, wait, Francesca was a handful. She could be defiant. A little cheeky at times. Alicia was the arty one. Some of her paintings were so beautiful. Then—'

Stan interrupted her to keep her from going off on a tangent.

'Any memories of little boys at the Pennyghael House?'

'No, son, it was all girls that I remember from my time there.'

'It doesn't matter. So what about this chocolate cake that you made? Am I getting some, or am I not?'

'Now, wait a minute. This may not be connected, and we are talking almost eighty years ago now but I have a memory of Alicia making a drawing of a boy. She said she sometimes saw him when she looked out of her window. I think it was her imagination because there were no children nearby.'

This might be something. 'Can you remember how the boy was dressed in the drawings?'

'Yes, I can, because she always drew him the same. He wore a little black suit, and she drew a black hat on him.'

Bingo!

Stan listened to his mother's recollections.

The boy must have lived way before that time. That young girl was seeing the boy as a ghost too...

Chapter 16

Only three bedrooms in the hotel needed changing, so it didn't take Edina long to finish her work upstairs. All the dirty sheets and towels were gathered to take down to the kitchen for washing. Edina pushed the laundry trolley along the hallway.

I wonder why Struan had to see Marnie in such a hurry? It was nice that he put me in charge, although it was only a choice between Suzie and me. Still, good that he chose me. I can't believe that only two staff members are working in this beautiful hotel at the height of the summer season. Where are all the holidaymakers? If this were a hotel in Edinburgh, it would be busier than this in the quietest time of the year. I can't understand it.

At the end of the hall, she saw the door to the tower room. It was a bedroom, no different from the other guest rooms, but it never needed changing because no one was ever checked in to it. Thinking back to her first day on the job, she had no memory of Struan showing her inside the room when he gave her the guided tour.

A text message vibrated through her phone, which she kept in her apron pocket.

When she saw it was from Tom, she secretly pleased.

Are you going to The Shell Seekers on Friday?

Of course, she was going. A night in was a night wasted, as she always used to say. And she had certainly wasted more than enough nights since she got here.

She texted back: *Possibly.*

A message was returned instantly: *Great, I'll see you then.*

She replied: *Perhaps.*

I am actually looking forward to seeing that fisherman on Friday. Maybe he was just nasty the first time I met him because I nearly killed him. A near-death experience can really change the mood of a person.
She brought the trolley to a halt outside the tower room.
When I've finished my shift, I'll go in and have a look around. I don't think I'll find anything but it would be good to get a sense of the place.
At the top of the curved, rosewood staircase, Edina paused for a moment. It was difficult to believe that the hotel had, until fairly recently, been a ruin. The photographs taken at the start of the project showed the staircase with gaping holes and foliage growing around the banister. Struan and his mum had taken on such a mammoth task to preserve a vital part of Pennyghael's history and Edina commended them for this. How much easier it would have been to demolish the crumbling walls and start again with a modern build. Halfway down the stairs she stopped again to marvel at the framed photos of the old Pennyghael House in its heyday. The first photo showed the building with servants lined up outside the front door. A horse and carriage waited expectantly in the background. She

wondered what remarkable stories were embedded in the house's history and what secrets lay within its walls.

They must have spent every penny they had and more. What can I do to help this venture be a success? I can't exactly call all my friends and ex-colleagues to come and book a holiday because everyone back home hates me. I need to come up with a plan. I want to help Struan, but I also want to help myself. If something doesn't change soon, I'll be out of a job. I never thought I'd think this, but I actually like it here.

Edina set the washing machine to a hot temperature. The cycle would lead straight into a tumble-dry setting. This gave her time to arrange the dining room for evening guests. There were two residents and two bookings for dinner, so it would be a quiet night unless customers phoned within the next few hours.

She stood at the end of the bar, folding the napkins into her speciality swans.

Should I take a quick look at the tower room now? I only need to stick my head in the door to know if there's anything untoward about it.

Swan number four lay unfinished on the table as Edina ran upstairs to see the room for herself.

I must be objective here. No preconceived ideas that the room is eerie. I shall enter with a completely open mind.

Turning the door handle of the tower room, she attempted to open it but was met with a force on the other side pushing against her. With the help of her shoulder, she put all of her strength against the door. The pressure from the other side stopped suddenly, causing her to fall into the room. Quickly getting to her feet, she looked at the space around her.

Okay, there is no rocking chair moving of its own accord, no wind-up toys beating on drums, no porcelain dolls with staring eyes.

Apart from the curved wall where the tower was situated, the room looked identical to every other bedroom in the hotel. However, the air within the room delivered a drastic drop in temperature.

She pulled her cardigan tightly around her.

Maybe it's cold because it's never used. No, it doesn't feel right in here. I can't put my finger on it. The atmosphere is just wrong.

She decided that she had seen enough.

Time to leave.

Chapter 17

The police officer on duty at the station was an elderly gentleman who had possibly bypassed his retirement age. Although he was kind, he was of little help to Struan. The letters contained nothing of a threatening nature; therefore, no crime had been committed. The look of frustration on Struan's face was apparent to the officer, but there was really nothing he could do but offer advice.

'I can see that this is a very upsetting matter for you and your girlfriend, especially now that you've told me the ex-boyfriend's history, but the content of the letters, albeit unnerving, are not breaking any laws. The only advice that I can offer you is to be vigilant.'

Struan shrugged his shoulders. There was nothing left to say.

The police officer came out from behind the counter and stood next to Struan. 'Have you ever thought of installing a security system with cameras outside the property?'

Struan perked up at this suggestion. It was an obvious idea but it hadn't occurred to him.

'Actually, that is a really good idea. Thank you.'

He made to leave.

The elderly gentleman rested his hand on Struan's arm.

'I can give you the business card of a company that we have used in the past.'

'That would be helpful, Sir.'

'In my opinion,' the officer concluded, 'the person doing this means no harm to your girl. Either that or he is cleverly wording the letters. The sender knows that if he leaves out any abusive or menacing language, then there is not a damn thing anyone can do about it. He could be enjoying the game of cat and mouse.'

'Yes, I think you're right. I believe he wants to scare her, but eventually, he will want to take it to another level, surely?'

'Get the cameras installed, and we'll see what they uncover.'

Chapter 18

Marnie stood nervously watching from the window of her lounge, in the flat above the Shell Seekers bar. Her taut shoulders dropped in relief at the welcome sight of Struan driving into the car park.

By the time he exited his car, she was running towards him with her arms outstretched.

'I'm so sorry to drag you away from the hotel. Oh, Struan, I have been going out of my mind. I am really frightened that Ashton is behind this. I know that this time he won't just put me in the hospital. He'll kill me.'

She sobbed onto Struan's shoulder.

'Look, Marnie, I will never let that happen to you. Either we will move you into the hotel, or I will come and stay here with you.'

'That would be all right through the week, but you know how inconvenient it would be when we both work until late. Anyway, this is my home, I love it here at the beach. I can't let him ruin my life anymore.' She exhaled a sigh of despair. 'Did the police say that they would try to find him?'

'No, not yet. We need something more concrete to prove that it's him. The officer at the station has given me the number of a company that installs security cameras. I will phone them tomorrow. If we get a camera at the back of the house and one at the front, we'll catch him on film. I can then go back to the cops with the footage.'

The Shell Seekers was located at the end of a single-track road; one way in, one way out. Originally, Marnie had loved the isolation of the pub and her living quarters. No one from her previous life knew of her move to the Island of Mull, except her friends, Lockhart and Bee. Not even her parents knew where she lived now, not that they would care. Until recently, she had never felt so safe in her entire life, but now everything was spoiled. She had become so fearful, constantly imagining that she saw movement in the trees across from the pub.

Turning to Struan, she asked, 'How do you think Ashton managed to find me?'

'I don't know. The two friends that you told, are they trustworthy?'

'They are the most trustworthy people I know, apart from you, of course. I have never had such loyal friends as Lockhart and Bee. After I was released from hospital, Lockhart took me into her home and cared for me until I got back on my feet again. Remember, Bee was the one who brought me here on her holiday with her husband. They changed my life.'

'Yes, I know, but I thought I'd ask. I really don't know how he tracked you down, but we are going to catch him. It's only a matter of time. Now, you go and put the kettle on. I'm going to take a wander across to the woods.'

There was a steep embankment to climb before entering the wooded area across from the bar. With the absence of tread on his formal shoes, this was no easy feat for Struan. After climbing three steps up, he slid two back down. Eventually, he grasped a tree root that protruded from the soil. The sinewy root took his weight as he hauled himself to the top of the small hill.

His socks began to feel wet from the mossy, waterlogged ground underfoot. Dressy shoes were not made with the intention of coping with the trials of the outdoors. He squelched his way far enough to be hidden from view, but with The Shell Seekers still in plain sight. The density of the forest pines prevented the light from entering, making it easy to be concealed in the darkness. Looking around him, he could see it was a perfect vantage point for a stalker. To his left-hand side, he noticed that the shrubbery had been flattened. Crouching down to take a closer look, he saw a sheet of plastic tarpaulin. Strewn around the sheeting lay several crisp wrappers and two empty cans of lager. This confirmed that there had indeed been someone in the shadows, watching, waiting, preparing to strike. Anger raged within him at the thought of sweet Marnie, a defenceless duckling to this dangerous, vengeful predator.

A cup of tea was on the table waiting for Struan when he returned from the woods. To prevent frightening Marnie further, he told her there had been no sign of any intruders but to keep the doors locked and the curtains closed as a precaution.

'I will come after work tonight to stay with you. If Ashton knows where you live and work, then he will also know that you and I are a couple. It may ward him off if I'm here as often as possible. I will park my car near the front door where it can be seen. Hopefully, we'll get the cameras in place next week.' Struan reached for Marnie's hand, giving it a squeeze. 'This will come to an end, I promise.'

Marnie kissed the back of his hand. 'I know you'll fix it. I love you, Struan.'
'I love you too.'

Chapter 19

Struan decided that Edina would be in charge whenever he left the hotel. Knowing that the place was in good hands, he took the opportunity to go over and see Marnie in the afternoons for an hour or two. The nights that he stayed over at The Shell Seekers, Edina offered to do the early morning start for him. He accepted this offer with the knowledge that she was more than capable of running the show.

Each day, in the morning or afternoon, before he left Marnie, Struan checked the viewpoint in the trees to see if there had been any change to the way he had left it. The day he discovered the wrappers and cans, he had strategically placed them on the tarpaulin so that he would know if they had been moved. After his daily inspections, he noted that the area remained untouched.

Although it had been a stressful time worrying about Marnie, in a strange way, Struan had enjoyed comforting her and finding extra time in his day to be with her. The idea of proposing marriage to her had been in his mind for several months. He had always been sure of his love for her, but the past week had sealed the deal for him. Being with Marnie every day, looking after her, sleeping beside her, and waking up next to her beautiful, serene face was now all he wanted in the world. The success or failure of the hotel had filled him with angst from the day it opened, but the events of the past week made him realise that the only thing that truly mattered was being with Marnie and keeping her safe. Now that he had

Edina to rely on, it was perhaps time to make some changes in his life.

When Struan arrived at the hotel, Edina was at the reception desk, talking on the phone.

While still conversing professionally with a customer on the line, she winked at Struan, pointing her two fingers like a gun at him.

Screwing up his face, he shook his head at her. For some inexplicable reason, she had invented a greeting game that he had never agreed to be part of. How long was she going to keep this nonsense up? Of course, he would never have told her this but he found it mildly endearing, even a little amusing.

When the phone call ended, Edina shouted to Struan, who was standing in the doorway of the bar, 'Any news on Marnie? How is she holding up?'

'Okay, considering. I am worried about her. Don't mention this to her, but I saw evidence in the trees across from the pub that someone had been hiding and watching her. We are almost positive that it's her ex-boyfriend, who is a very dangerous individual.'

'Struan, that's awful. When we go to The Shell Seekers later, should I offer to stay on Sunday night with her? I'm off the next day.'

'Yes, I think she'd really appreciate that.'

As they stood discussing the Marnie situation, Stan entered the main door of the hotel.

'Hey Stan,' Edina shouted. 'I haven't seen you all week. Are you our chauffeur for tonight?'

'Yes, yes, as always. Who else is daft enough to do it?'

'Stan, you're the best. We all really do appreciate it,' she told him, knowing that he enjoyed a bit of a fuss.

When Struan left the reception, Stan moved in closer to Edina. He looked left, right, then behind him to ensure that no one was around to hear what he had to say. His voice dropped to a conspiratorial whisper.

'I've got a bit of information for your journal.' He paused for effect. 'I went to see my mother through the week and I subtly questioned her about the boy. I had to do it ever so gently because I wouldn't want her knowing anything about a destructive ghost roaming around your house, scaring the hee-bee-gee-bees out of you. I didn't get anything concrete but she did say something interesting, very interesting indeed.'

'Oh Stan, that's brilliant. What did she tell you?'

Using his index finger, he tapped on the side of his nose. 'I'll tell you later. We have to keep all of this research on the QT.'

Edina saw that Stan was loving every moment of this secret mission. 'Okay, we'll talk as soon as the coast is clear and it is safe to do so.' She allowed herself an inward chuckle, unbeknownst to Stan.

Suzie walked downstairs carrying an armful of laundry. She was singing the chorus of a song then humming the verse as she had no idea of the words.

'My goodness,' Stan said, as she walked past the reception area. 'Someone doesn't have a care in the world.'

Suzie stopped to stare in disbelief. 'If only you knew Stan, if only you knew.'

Edina was intrigued by her response.

If only he knew what? Something is going on in this young girl's life. Does she drink to forget it?

Suzie turned to Edina. 'Are you still on for visiting the big charity shop tomorrow morning?'

'Are you kidding?' Edina joked. 'It will be the highlight of my week.'

Suzie gave directions to her house, then stressed specifically, 'Don't come to the door. Just send a quick text that you are outside. I will be ready.'

'Great, thanks for doing this for me. Shall we say ten o'clock?'

'Ten is perfect. Remember, don't come to the door.'

Chapter 20

I'm incredibly nervous about going to The Shell Seekers tonight. Edina watched from the hotel window for Stan to arrive in his bus. *It's not just because I've been a hermit since I arrived on Mull. It's this guy, Tom. I am really excited to see him. I know he's been mean to me, called me names, and laughed at me, but I can't stop thinking about him.*

For convenience, she had brought her change of clothes with her to work. This meant that she wouldn't have to waste valuable time driving home and back. The very moment her shift ended, she ran to one of the unused bedrooms to get changed. Being the first one ready meant that she found herself getting a little irritated with her colleagues, who she noticed were still milling around the hotel, finishing minor tasks of no importance.

Freddy hadn't been working that day but drove to the hotel, intending to leave his car there until the morning. Lately, he was finding that he had more and more spare time on his hands since the hotel guest numbers were becoming fewer. His dishwashing job didn't pay much, but it enabled him to save up for going to college after the summer. He helped his father in the garage most days, but that was an expectation, an apprenticeship really, rather than a paid job.

Dressed smartly in jeans and a black shirt, Freddie entered the hotel, an overpowering smell of aftershave followed closely behind him. He smiled when he saw Edina standing staring out of the window in the bar.

'Hey Edina, are you standing there waiting for Prince Charming to arrive and whisk you away from all of this?'

'I suppose you could say that, if you can call Stan, Prince Charming. I'm just watching for the bus.'

'Where is everyone?' he asked.

'Still faffing around. It really irritates me. I'm always prompt to arrive anywhere. I despise lateness,' Edina growled, unable to mask her displeasure.

'Calm down. It's no big deal, Stan's not even here yet. By the way, did you get a chance to check out the tower room?'

Edina softened, 'Yes, you were so right about that. I experienced the oddest sensation as soon as I went in. It's very hard to explain. No wonder they don't put any guests in there.'

'Actually, when the hotel first opened, they tried filling that room, but within a few hours, the guests would ask to be relocated. You can check with Struan, but I think it happened at least four times. They don't even try to fob it off onto anyone now.'

'No wonder. So, about this girl you like,' she said, changing the subject. 'Do you think she'll be in the Shell Seekers tonight?'

'Probably.'

'What are you going to do about it?'

'Same as always, nothing,' he told her. His face displayed an expression of defeat as he shrugged his shoulders.

'Nothing, my backside! We will get you all fixed up before you go to college. All you have to do is point her out to me. I'll soon know if she is interested.'

'Edina, I'm not like you. I'm not confident and outgoing. Sometimes, it's just easier to watch from afar. I like to keep my cards close to my chest.'

'Well, it's time you dealt yourself a new hand because the one you're playing with is for losers.'

They were interrupted by the sound of the crunching of gravel under wheels. Stan drove into the carpark with three short toots on the horn followed by a long fourth.

'We'll continue this conversation later, Freddy. I'm not letting you off the hook that easy.'

Edina ran through to the dining room where Suzie and Struan were finishing off setting up the tables for dinner guests.

Struan's mum volunteered to work at the hotel every Friday to allow the staff a night out together. Along with the chef, she ran things fairly smoothly. The downside was that the dishes were left until the morning, the tables were uncleared and the bar remained unstocked. Still, Struan weighed up that it was a small price to pay for a night out with a few drinks.

'Hey guys, the pleasure bus has arrived to transport us to wonderland,' Edina announced with great arm-waving theatrics.

'You know Edina, you can be quite a crazy girl at times,' Struan told her, shaking his head.

'I'm not ready yet,' Suzie screeched. 'Just give me five minutes.' She ran off in the direction of the bathroom.

The remaining three made their way out to the bus. They all knew that Stan didn't like to be kept waiting.

'Where's your fancy frock tonight?' he asked Edina as she boarded.

It was an innocent comment, but it made Edina blush. The memory of the previous week's embarrassment returned abruptly to her thoughts. Being laughed at was not something she wanted to remember.

'I'm toning things down a little, Stan. I don't want the reputation of being a show off.'

'Too late!' Struan shouted from his seat on the bus.

Stan threw a scowl in Struan's direction. 'Aw that's a shame, I thought you looked smashing. You showed these scruffs a thing or two.'

One last toot of the horn brought Suzie running out of the hotel. They had all been warned some time ago that if they weren't out after the final toot reminder, Stan would drive off without them. This warning had never been tested, so no one was quite sure whether he was tough enough to carry it through.

With her oversized handbag slung over her shoulder, Suzie climbed aboard, and the electronic door shut behind her.

Edina looked across the aisle of the bus to where Freddy was sitting. Sliding over to be closer to him, she said, 'Listen, Freddy, the best advice I can give you, if you really want to get to know this girl better, is to start by making eye contact with her. That will get her attention, then perhaps you could send her over a drink. If Marnie is too busy to take it over, I'll do it. Problem is though, if it's the girl I think it is, well, I'm not convinced that she likes me, so I may hinder your cause. I think you should just relax about the whole thing. Chances are, she's crazy about you too.'

Discussing matters of the heart was not something that Freddy felt comfortable with. The deepest conversations he had at home with his parents were, 'Do you want chips or potatoes with your fish, tonight?' or 'Pass me that spanner, son. No, not that one, the small one below it.' In Freddy's household, you didn't discuss girlfriends, emotions or heartbreaks. Career paths and marriage choices were the only subjects headings on the discussion table. This wasn't a laid down law, it was simply an unrevised guideline that had been adhered to from generation to generation.

'Look Edina, I know what you're saying but I think she has a boyfriend and I don't want to rattle any cages around here. She is never with him at the weekends but I know that they are a thing, if you know what I mean.'

'Freddy, that doesn't mean anything. Sometimes, people get stuck in a relationship that's gone stale. They coast along until someone better comes their way. You could be that someone better. It's not like she's married or engaged or anything. All's fair in love and war, as they say.'

Edina couldn't quite believe the advice she was handing out to this young man. Hadn't she ruined her own life by going after something that wasn't hers?

She stared out of the window, lost in her thoughts. *All is not fair in love and war. No one deserves to die because two countries have a disagreement and no one's life should be destroyed because a selfish girl decides she wants something that isn't available.*

'You know, Freddy,' she said, turning to face him. 'Maybe if this girl is in a relationship, things are best left alone until she's free.'

'What the hell, Edina? You have just given me two completely different pieces of counselling. You've really confused me now. Do I give her eye contact or stay away from her?'

'Wait until she's single. There will be plenty of pretty girls in The Shell Seekers who are available.'

Chapter 21

'Everybody out!' Stan shouted, as he turned the bus around in the car park of the pub. 'If I come back, I come back, if I don't, I don't.'

As usual, Struan ran ahead to see Marnie.

Edina waited for Freddy and Suzie. There was a feeling of security in being part of a group. A nervous energy had taken over her emotions. It was partially due to her unfortunate experience the previous week, but the thought of seeing the fisherman was a little overwhelming. Apart from hurled insults and a few texts, no conversation had actually taken place between them.

Pushing open the door leading to the bar, she found herself pausing to take a few deep breaths before entering. This was a side of herself that she had never seen before. In the past, she breezed into an establishment alone, waving with both hands in every direction. It was highly probable that many people viewed her as an overconfident pain in the ass.

The bar was busy, and the music was loud. Customers queued for drinks, and others bunched around talking, catching up on the news of the previous week.

Edina found herself scanning the crowd for Tom. She spotted him. He was there at the back of the room, already looking at her. *Oh my goodness, he looks gorgeous, incredibly gorgeous.*

Tom, the fisherman, gave Edina a wave.

She returned his greeting with a smile.

Struan watched Marnie smiling as she served the customers. Considering the sleepless nights she had endured and the stress brought on by her stalker, he thought she looked radiant. Between customers, she looked over and blew him a kiss. He knew that as soon as things quietened down, she would come straight to him, wrapping her arms around his neck. The wait only heightened his excitement to speak to her, hold her for a moment and smell the essence of her. Marnie was his world, nothing else mattered.

The quiz nights at the pub were always popular, attracting the same people week after week. It had never dawned on Struan until now that Marnie began pouring the drinks for customers before they even told her what they wanted. Everyone who approached the bar was given special treatment and their drink of choice had been learned off by heart. In the early days, Struan offered to help her when things became frantic, but she declined his offer, telling him she would manage.

From the table Marnie had reserved for them, Freddy looked longingly at the only girl he had ever loved. He had been devoted to her from the first moment he saw her. Although she was always pleasant, she showed no signs of being interested in him. He waited eagerly for her to laugh. Only when she laughed did the dimple on her left cheek become visible. Not so long ago, he observed something quite unique about her. Whenever she finished talking, her nose crinkled slightly. He would have bet everything he owned in the world that no one else had picked up this barely noticeable idiosyncrasy of hers, not even her so-called boyfriend. Yes, he knew a boyfriend was on the scene, but he had never really seen them together. He made a solemn promise to himself that if she ever reciprocated his feelings, he would make sure they were inseparable. Until that day, he would be there, waiting for her to notice him.

Edina was first up to buy the drinks. While she stood waiting at the back of the queue, she became aware of someone standing close to her, perhaps too close. Subtly, she glanced around and saw the blue of his shirt from the corner of her eye. Aware that the fisherman was wearing a shirt of identical colour, she looked up at the face of the man standing beside her. It was indeed Tom. Adrenaline sprinted, at full throttle, through her. *Oh no, I'm nervous, I'm nervous, I'm nervous. I don't want to make a fool of myself. What will I say? Oh, quick, what will I say?*

She needn't have fretted. He opened the conversation between them.

'How have you been since we last bumped into one another?' he asked, giving her a nudge.

'Well, I've stayed well away from humpback bridges,' she answered, without turning to look at him. *He smells unbelievable.*

'Are you just here for the summer?' he asked.

'I don't know yet. My contract at the hotel is until September. After that, I have no idea,' she answered honestly. *I love that highland twang in his voice.*

'Did you know that your name is from the mediaeval times? It means, from Edinburgh. My parents also gave me an ancient Scots mediaeval name, but I use my middle name, Tom.'

'Yes, I knew the meaning of Edina.'

'Was it hotel work you did on the mainland?' he asked her.

'No, I was an investigative journalist for The Scottish Independent newspaper.'

She stood at the height of his chest. Too shy to look him in the eye, she focused on his perfectly formed muscles and how they strained against his shirt's fabric.

'Why did you leave?'

Because of the editor, whose name is too painful to say. Oh, and the fact that I caused something terrible to happen. Not forgetting that everyone I know hates me.

'I just needed a change.'

'Well, island life is a change, all right.'

Having completely run out of questions, Tom turned to leave.

He's leaving. I can't let him go. Quick, think, what should I ask him?

Grabbing onto his arm, she asked, 'So, you're a fisherman, eh? Is it dangerous?'

'Yes, my whole family are fishermen. My father has his own boat. I just kind of drifted into the family business. It wasn't a lifelong dream, and I don't want to do it forever. Usually, there is no danger involved, but it can be a bit harrowing sometimes, particularly in bad weather.'

She loved the way he answered the questions so fully, as though he was being interviewed. She continued with a good thing.

'Have you always lived on Mull?'

'No, I have worked on the oil rigs in the North Sea and lived in the Middle East for nearly three years,' he told her. 'Oh, wait a minute, I worked in a bar in Ibiza when I was twenty, and the following year, I did some bar work on the Greek Islands.'

He related these facts about his history as though suddenly remembering them.

It was Edina's turned to be served at the bar.

'I'll talk to you later,' Tom said, as he turned to leave. 'I hope you lose the quiz.'

'Right back at you,' she joked, watching him as he walked away.

Marnie leaned over towards Edina on the other side of the bar. 'Do you like him any better this week?' she asked.

Edina laughed, 'Oh yes, a whole lot better.'

'Is it the usual for your colleagues?' she inquired, already pouring the pint for Struan.

'Yes, please. By the way, I wondered if you wanted any company on Sunday night? I could come over and join you if you like.'

Marnie was so obviously pleased. 'Edina, that is so kind of you. I would love that.'

'It's a date.'

The music ended when the quiz master walked onto the stage area of the bar. Everyone cheered. Using his hands, he waved downwards for silence.

Edina thought that he bore a resemblance to her late grandfather, and surprisingly, this gave her a pang of sadness. Quickly brushing her feelings aside, she watched as the quiz master took the microphone from the stand to read out the names of all the teams participating. Edina realised, when she heard her colleagues cheering, that they were The Bad Pennies.

She looked over at Struan, 'What does that mean?' she mouthed over, raising her hands, palm up.

'The bad pennies of Pennyghael because we always turn up. That's the name we've always used.'

Edina nodded. 'Okay, I get it.' She then listened out for the name of Tom's team.

'And over at the table in the far corner, we have, Fisherman's Friends,' the quizmaster announced.

A resounding cheer came from Tom's team.

Edina looked over at him, only to discover that he was staring at her.

She smiled. *I think this is the start of something really good. Try not to ruin it, Edina.*

Between the two of them, Edina and Struan answered almost every question. Their specialised subjects complemented one another perfectly. There were some educated guesses among their answers, but, nonetheless, they were quietly confident that they had won the prize of a bottle of champagne.

Struan had promised her that she could keep the winnings as this was the first time they had ever come close to completing the questions.

When Struan headed over to the quizmaster with the team's answer sheet, Edina moved around the table to sit next to Suzie. Once more, Edina saw that Suzie was in a dreadful state with alcohol. She propped her up straight in her seat, fearing that she would soon fall over. From the limp grip of her hand, Edina removed her glass, which bore only a dribble.

What makes you want to enter oblivion? Are you drinking to forget or escape, or has alcohol just got you in its clutches? I wonder if she thinks that we don't notice what's going on.

Across the table, Edina saw that Freddy was, for want of a better word, looking wretched.

'Hey Freddy, the quiz was fun, wasn't it?' she asked him.

'Not really. I never know any of the answers. How come you and Struan know so much stuff?'

'We've been alive for longer for a start.'

What else could she say?

She saw that Struan was at the bar laughing with Marnie.

I want that. I want someone nice who will adore me.

The company at her table was anything but scintillating. This left her sitting looking at the ceiling. Quite unexpectedly, she sensed someone standing close, perhaps too close, behind her.

It was Tom. A thrill travelled through her when she looked up at her suitor's smile.

'Do you want to go out some night this week?' he asked her.

'Okay. I finish early on Tuesday. Why don't you come over, and I'll make you dinner?'

'Sounds good. Can you cook?'

'Don't be so cheeky. Of course, I can cook.'

'Are you living in that cottage on the grounds of Pennyghael House?' he asked.

'Have you been spying on me?'

'No, but everyone was discussing you last week after you sang. You've been the talk of Mull, you know. I just listen in on the interesting bits, like where you live.'

'Well, how about seven o'clock on Tuesday? Don't bring anything and don't be late.'

Over the microphone, the quizmaster announced that the results of the quiz were in.

'I had better go back to my table to hear the news that we've won... again,' he said, feigning boredom over this outcome.

'Don't be too sure about that. I think you may discover that you are not ranked at the top this week.'

He laughed at her ludicrous suggestion.

'By the way, you said your first name is mediaeval like mine. What is your real name?' She was curious to know.

'Somerled,' he told her. 'See you on Tuesday. I'll bring the champagne that I win tonight.'

He left to join his friends at the table near the back.

The quizmaster announced that the team in third place was, The Thornbirds.

Everyone clapped.

'Second place, with a very high score, goes to the Bad Pennies.' There was more clapping, a few cheers, and a whistle.

Edina and Struan stared in disbelief. 'We've been robbed,' she whispered to Struan.

'Let's demand a recount,' Struan told her in jest.

'And in first place with a perfect score and the winners of the bottle of champagne, let's hear it for, The Fishermen's Friends.'

The room cheered wildly.

Tom smiled smugly over at Edina.

Chapter 22

Edina asked Freddy for some assistance as they left the bar at closing time. Suzie was a dead weight, making it impossible for Edina to support her alone. Taking a side each, they attempted to walk her out to the car park. To Edina's delight, Stan was parked in one of the spaces at the side of the building.

I don't know what I would have done with Suzie if Stan hadn't come back for us tonight.

Knowing that Stan would drop her at her house was a relief.

The toes of Suzie's shoes dragged across the gravel while Edina and Freddy desperately attempted to keep her upright.

'Is she always as bad as this?' Edina asked.

Freddy strained under the weight of her. 'No, things have become worse in the past couple of months. She used to just stagger out the door. I don't know for sure, but I think she's unhappy at home.'

Getting Suzie on the bus was no mean feat, but when she finally flopped into one of the seats, Edina raised her hand to high-five Freddy.

Stan watched the whole scene from his rear-view mirror, and when he saw that Edina and Freddy had taken their seats, he drove off. He was not the type to interfere, but there was something not right about a young girl making herself incapacitated, and becoming the responsibility of others.

The previous week, he had taken her to the front door of her house. In her inebriated state, she had shouted, 'I don't want to go in there. I don't want to go in there ever again.'

Stan wondered if he should have asked her about it when he next saw her at the hotel, but the moment did not arise, and Suzie behaved like it had never happened.

The bus meandered along the winding road leading onto the turning for Edina's house. The physical work of the previous week had left her exhausted, so it was a treat to be dropped off first.

Turning to Freddy, who was beside her, she asked, 'I saw you over at the table of girls at one point. Did anything notable happen?'

'How do you mean notable?'

'Did you get a chance to speak to the girl you like?'

Freddy shrugged. 'Yes, I spoke to her a couple of times, but things are still the same. She is very nice to me, but she doesn't really know that I exist.'

The passengers were flung forward as the front wheel of the bus nosedived into a pothole.

'Stan! You have to treat this road the way you treat your women, with love and respect,' Edina advised him.

'I'll try to remember that,' he told her, hitting a crater on the right, then another one on the left.

Stopping the bus at the opened gate, he suggested that she climb out now as getting turned would be impossible.

'Thanks for the lift, Stan, it is really appreciated. See you through the week, Freddy.'

The bus drove off, leaving Edina standing in the darkness alone. The welcome glow of the lamp she left on could be seen through the trees.

'Go towards the light,' she said aloud, in a mysterious voice. This made her laugh. She had a sneaking suspicion that she may be a little tipsy.

On entering her spartan little home, she was reminded that Suzie was taking her to the charity shop for house furnishings. *I'll be surprised if she's up for it. I'll go to her house for ten and toot the horn, as requested, but if no one answers, I'll come right back home to bed.*

She flopped down into the big wing chair next to the fireplace.

'Somerled, Somerled,' she said over and over to herself.

Somerled, what a fantastic name. Somerled, who would even have known that was a name. Somerled, Somerled. She repeated his name over and over in her head.

It was difficult for her to fathom that this fisherman had the power to turn her into a babbling fool. Perhaps if he had known the girl she used to be, he would have run for his life. But that girl was gone, he would never encounter her. Yes, it was fair to say that this fisherman, Somerled, ticked all the boxes of her dream man and had even created a few new categories.

When she had relived every moment of the evening with Somerled, she decided it was time to take the little stairway to Heaven and turn in for the night. Slipping her cardigan on over her pyjamas, she scrambled under the duvet. She looked out the window from where she lay and saw that the army of stars was in full force. One of the sparkling pinholes shone brighter than the others. She chose it as her own.

Mum, I'm sorry I didn't appreciate you and spend time with you. I was wrapped up in my own life, and I wasn't there to care for you when you became ill. Please forgive me. I've met someone really special, mum. His name is Somerled, which is a mediaeval name, just like mine. I'm so tired now, but I will talk to you tomorrow…

Sleep enfolded her within minutes.

Chapter 23

A sound from somewhere in the house awakened Edina from her dream-filled sleep. It wasn't a loud noise, but even the tiniest creak was intrusive in the vacuous silence. Sitting upright, she tried to pinpoint the location of the sound. It had the rhythm of movement across floorboards. Someone was in the house. The only thing worse than that would be that *some thing* was in the house. The noise appeared to be coming from the landing at the top of the stairs. There was a creak, then a pause. Creak, then pause. Fear began to tighten its grip around Edina. Whoever or whatever it was had made its way upstairs. The noise moved closer to her bedroom. Edina's heart rate accelerated to an almost unbearable level. It had now entered her room. Unrecognisable sounds came from it. It then stopped, silence, then a light thud could be heard, as though someone had dropped to the ground. Peering over her quilt, she forced herself to look but saw nothing. She was frightened to stay in bed, yet too immobilized by fear to get up. The phrase fight, flight, or freeze entered her mind, and she realised she had fallen into the last category.

After the thud on the floor, everything around her turned ominously quiet. Nervous anticipation filled her mind. W*here is it? What is it? Am I going to survive this night? Why me?*

The sound that shattered the silence was truly chilling. The fact that it was not human meant that it was her otherworldly visitor. To her absolute horror, she then became aware of something dragging itself across her bedroom floor in the direction of her bed.

A thought entered Edina's head as she hid under the duvet, gripping the edges tightly around her.

Petrified, meaning turned to stone. I feel like I am turning to stone. I am becoming rigid.

To worsen the horror of the situation, Edina felt the foot of her quilt being pulled away from her bed. It was the only meagre protection that she had, so she fought hard to keep it. A tug-of-war began with her faceless opponent. It took all the fight she had left within her to hold on to her defence, her shelter, her security blanket.

When eventually her well of strength was dry, she let go of the quilt. Lying uncovered in the foetal position, she sobbed. *Please help me, God. Release me from this abominable, unearthly situation.*

A final, short burst of energy filled her heaving lungs as she sat up and shouted, 'Leave me alone, *now*!'

A divine calmness filled the room. Edina could feel the fear leaving her body. It was miraculous and tangible. Her muscles loosened, her breathing slowed.

It was over.

Retrieving her duvet from the floor, she wrapped it tightly around herself. *Thank you for protecting me.*

Chapter 24

Bright morning sunshine filled Edina's bedroom when she opened her eyes for the first time since her horror film experience. What relief she felt to know that the night had ended, taking with it the unwelcome visitor that had terrorised her. She had grown incredibly fond of her spartan little home, but she would leave if she faced another night like that again. Moving into the town was not an idea she relished. If everyone knew her business in this isolated location, then how much more intrusive would it be in a close-knit village.

When she rose from her bed, she decided to change the duvet cover. The very idea of a faceless entity touching it gave her the creeps. It was just after eight o'clock, giving her time to shower and have breakfast before she went to look for Suzie's house.

The last thing Edina wanted to do was charity shop trawling, especially when she was working later that afternoon. If given the choice, she would have slept for at least another two hours.

I have to remember that Suzie is also giving up her free time to help me. How she'll manage to be up and ready after the state she was in last night, I'll never know. If no one comes to the door, I'm heading straight back to bed.

Downstairs in the kitchen, the whistling kettle began to boil. There was arguably a case to be answered for a two-spoonful cup of coffee. Not just two spoons of granules but two spoons of sugar. Edina could not think of a more effective way to kick-start her morning.

A frivolous thought flitted into her mind while she carried the oversized, chipped mug into the sitting room. *Somerled, Somerled, Somerled.*

She sat down slowly in the wing chair, being careful not to spill a drop. She had a bad habit of overfilling her cups.

The view was mainly of the Scots pines across the way from where the wing chair sat. Edina stared out at the greenery, sipping gently on the steaming coffee.

What happened to me last night? What kind of supernatural being has the strength to pull a duvet from my bed?

The events of the night ran through her mind. In the broad light of day, it hardly seemed possible that it had really happened. No one would ever believe her, except perhaps Stan. This thought led to her thinking of Stan's advice about writing in her journal.

The journal! I didn't write in the journal last night. My head was full of thoughts of Somerled.

Setting her coffee mug down on the table, she headed over to the sideboard to see her journal. It lay open. Edina's hands covered her mouth in shock. The pages had been torn and scored. This was not like the previous damage. This was frenzied, angry almost.

A ghost with a temper! Why has this boy made a connection with me? Can't he leave me alone so that I can dream of Somerled in peace?

Chilling as it was, she knew that she could not avoid this situation. Last night, the boy had so obviously tried to make himself known to her so that she would help him. But what exactly did he want her to do?

'I won't ignore you again,' she said aloud. 'I will help you in any way I can.'

When Edina had finished tidying the kitchen, she headed upstairs to lay out her uniform for a quick change before starting her shift. Because the weather outside was pleasant, there would be no need for her to take a jacket on her excursion. She grabbed her car keys and ventured off on her quest of giving her drab little house a makeover.

On the straight road, after the turning for Pennyghael House Hotel, Edina thought about Somerled coming to her house on Tuesday night. This would be her first visitor, using the visitor's parking space in front of her house.

I wish I hadn't invited him for dinner. I can't cook. Why did I say I could cook? I was even offended when he asked me if I could cook. I was indignant about it. I can be really stupid at times. I'll just have to rustle up something and then make an excuse for it. Alternatively, I could buy ready meals and tell him that I can't cook. Starting the relationship off with honesty. No more lies and half-truths. That girl is long gone.

If the directions were correct, Suzie's house was the first turning on the left, just after the BP garage. Edina drove along this narrow road, which was in almost as bad condition as the one that led to her own home. The wheels of her car thudded into a couple of potholes before she reached the house that she presumed must be Suzie's. Turning off her engine, she stared at the dilapidated hovel before her.

No one can possibly live here.

She stared at the torn net curtains covering the filthy windows. Edina remembered Freddy saying that he thought Suzie was unhappy at home. When she looked at the house, she could begin to understand why.

Stepping over the car tyres and items of junk that lay around the front garden, she made her way to the front door.

This place looks uninhabitable. It's like something straight out of a horror movie.

She banged twice on the front door.

Oops. Suzie's instructions were that I was to stay in the car and toot the horn for her. She told me not to come to the door. She must have been embarrassed about the state of her house.

When the front door opened, Edina all at once realised exactly what Suzie was embarrassed about and it wasn't just the property.

A man, possibly older looking than his actual years, stood smiling at her. His grey, wiry hair lay on his shoulders. Neither his hair nor his clothes had recently been washed, which was obvious for a variety of reasons. Stepping out from the doorway, he moved closer to her.

'Can I help you with anything?' he asked, with an odious smirk on his face.

Edina saw his eyes drop from her face down to her breasts. Instinctively, she covered the small V of flesh at her neckline. Everything within her told her that this man was a deviant and she should run as far away as she could.

'Hi, I've come to pick up Suzie,' she told him.

His eyes roamed over her body, with a grin that Edina suspected was brought on by his ungentlemanly thoughts.

'Why don't you come in and wait,' he offered.

'No, it's okay, I'm...'

Fortunately, there was no need to finish the sentence as Suzie appeared in the hallway, looking anguished.

Edina walked swiftly towards her car, feeling the man's eyes boring into her back. The moment Suzie closed the passenger door, Edina hit the accelerator and drove off. Such was her need to distance herself from the house and its occupant, she hit every crater on the road.

'Who was that?' Edina finally asked, after a short silence.

'That's my dad,' she said, in a way that should have had 'believe it or not' tagged on to the end.

'Does your mum live with you too?' Edina probed.

'Nope, just me and him,' she told her.

Edina was filled with such compassion for this girl. Maybe she was way off the mark, but she started to join a few dots around Susie's life, and it wasn't creating a very pretty picture.

On the way to the charity warehouse, they passed a quaint church by the roadside. Edina commented on how pretty it looked, almost like a child's drawing of a church.

'That's the oldest church on Mull. It stood there when there was only farmland and a few crofts around. They never lock the door, so you can go in anytime, sit all day if you want. I walk along most days, just to get away,' she told Edina.

Edina put her foot on the brake, then reversed all the way back to the church.

'Let's go in,' she announced.

It was cool inside, with an ancient, musty smell hanging in the air. The flagstones were worn away in furrows where people had come to worship for generations.

Susie sat in one of the pews, staring up at the cross.

In the far corner of the church, there stood a tiered stand which held unlit tealights. Edina reached into her bag for a pound coin, which she dropped into the honesty box. The first candle she lit was for her mum.

Closing her eyes, she prayed quietly. 'Please forgive me.'

Choosing another candle situated on the back row, she lit it for the editor's wife. 'Please forgive.'

Seeing that Suzie had taken a seat in the front pew, she walked over to join her.

Bowing her head, she prayed a silent prayer. *Please protect me from the spirit that is allying itself to me. Show me how I can help it so that we can both be free to move on. Forgive me for the terrible things I have done and help me to make the right decisions from now on. Amen.*

Leaving the peaceful atmosphere of the charming little church, they continued on their quest for second-hand goods. They drove along the coast road until they reached a sign for the village of Dervaig.

Edina asked Suzie for the official pronunciation of the town's name.

'Dervig,' Suzie told her. 'The village dates back to the Viking times. Dervaig means good inlet. I remember that from my school days.'

'You're a proper font of knowledge, Suzie. Oh look,' Edina said, pointing at the small white van at the side of the road. 'What are they selling?' she asked, seeing the queue lining up along the pavement.

'They're not selling anything. It's the mobile library.'

'A mobile library? I didn't know things like that still existed.' Edina laughed at the idea of it.

'We still have a mobile bank, grocery van, and a fish van.'

Edina had a thought when she saw people carrying their books. 'Can anyone borrow a book from the library, or is it just for the residents of Mull?'

'Do you want to take some books out?' she asked.

'Yes, I've got no internet and no television. I can only find a radio station that plays old music hall classics. Having books to read would be great. I'm actually looking for one on the history of Pennyghael. Do you think they would lend to me?'

'Of course, you're a resident of Mull now, are you not?' Suzie laughed.

Edina pulled into the side of the road, parking behind the library van. She took up her place at the end of the queue of borrowers and returnees.

It took a little longer than she had anticipated, but she waited patiently until she was the only one left standing. There were two stairs to climb before she found herself in the odd, little travelling book emporium.

I wonder if this white van will hunt you down if you don't return your book on time?

Edina pondered this while she looked at the timid librarian, who had spinster written all over her.

No, they probably just write it off as a loss. She doesn't want any trouble in her library. There will be no combing the streets of Mull looking for book thieves.

The librarian informed her rather officiously that if she wanted to join the Mull Library, she would need two forms of identification.

Fortunately for Edina, she had her driver's licence and a copy of her lease agreement for her cottage on the estate.

From a black folder on the top shelf, the librarian then unclipped an information form for Edina to fill in before she chose a book.

The time was moving on, and Edina knew she had used up a fair portion of her allocation. The information, which included previous addresses, seemed so unnecessary. This left her wondering if she should come back another day when she had more time. That, of course, would mean that the long wait in the queue had been for nothing. She scribbled down the answers to the questions, fabricating the details she was unsure of.

Would they really hire someone to do a background check on a library information sheet? I don't think so.

On the completion of the form, the librarian clipped it back into the black folder before returning it to the shelf.

'Welcome to Mull Library,' she announced, becoming suddenly warm and friendly as though things had changed now that she was a member. 'Was there any book in particular you were looking for? All the books are in sections…'

'Yes, I am interested in reading about the history of Pennyghael.'

'I can offer you a geographical book on Mull which will include information about Pennyghael, or I have a first-hand account of life in Pennyghael by a woman called Catriona McLeod. Do either of these books sound like what you are interested in?'

'Possibly. When was the Catriona McLeod book written?'

The librarian used her finger to help her scan along the shelf of books set out in alphabetical order.

Eventually, she said, 'Ah-ha,' as she expertly flicked the book out from its position on the shelf. 'Let me see,' she said, searching the first page for a publication date. 'There it is. The book was first published in 1969.'

'That's no use, I'm afraid,' Edina told her. 'I need something dating back further.'

'Oh, but this one is particularly interesting because it is beautifully written in Catriona's own words.'

'I'm sure it is great but it won't have the information that I am looking for. Thanks anyway.' Edina felt cheated out of the half-hour she had invested in the little library. She turned to leave.

'Before you leave, I should tell you that Catriona McLeod lived in 1847. Her book lay in a box in the attic for many years until the family member who inherited the house found it and sent it off to a publisher. The story was on the Scottish news at the time. It was a big talking point here in Mull for many years.'

'I'll take it.'

Edina apologised to Suzie for keeping her waiting in the car for so long in. The clock on the dashboard told her that she would only have a short time at the charity shop. Both she and Suzie were due to start their shift at

3pm. She found herself putting her foot down heavily on the accelerator.

I'll slow down if I come to a humpback bridge.

Suzie directed her to a large, windowless warehouse with nothing around it but a single car parking space. When they entered the building, the standard odour of second-hand goods caught the back of Edina's throat. The fusty dampness caused her to cough quite uncontrollably.

'It's a bit whiffy in here,' Suzie informed her.

'Phew! I had noticed.'

They wandered around the furniture and bric-a-brac section, where Edina found two paintings she loved. They were large works of art by an artist called Val Scott. Both paintings were similar, but one was predominantly red, the other yellow. Leaving them at the check-out, she continued to look around for items that would turn her house into a home. Edina smiled gratefully when she saw Suzie pushing a shopping trolley towards her. It was just what she needed, and she filled it with cushions, mugs, wine glasses, and a pretty mirror for hanging in the bathroom. The time was charging on, and although Edina could have stayed browsing all day, she knew they had to make their way back home.

Suzie opened the boot of the car, ready for Edina to pack in her purchases. It had been a fruitful day, full of surprises. Meeting Suzie's father had given Edina an insight into why she appeared so unhappy. Stopping at the Jacobean church had been a wonderful highlight, especially the lighting of the forgiveness candles for those Edina had hurt. It was an unexpected bonus that she managed to get her hands on the Catriona McLeod book, although she was dubious as to whether it would unlock any beneficial secrets. Still, she would begin reading as soon as she could, and then perhaps her destructive little ghost would see that she was trying.

The road was winding and hilly, which meant Edina had to concentrate on her driving. Keeping her eyes fixed firmly on the road ahead, she asked Suzie, 'Have you ever thought of getting a flat or house of your own?'

'I would give anything for a place of my own away from that man, but I don't have any money for a deposit. He takes nearly all of my wages from me. I despise living there, and I despise him,' she said.

Edina could hardly believe how honest and open she was being about her situation. Had it not been for her heavy drinking and, of course, the fact that Somerled had just come into her life, she would have offered Susie a room at her house. What Suzie needed was a long-term solution. A fresh start.

'If things are that bad, then we need to get you out,' Edina told her. 'Does he hurt you?'

Suzie put her face in her hands and said nothing.

Her reaction told Edina all she needed to know. Yes, he was hurting her, probably in ways that would get him locked up.

It was with an unbearably heavy heart that Edina dropped Suzie off at her house.

'We will discuss this further. We will work out a solution. You're not on your own. You have friends here, including me.'

'Thanks, Edina. I've had a really good time this morning.'

Edina watched the poor girl walk with shoulders drooped, towards her house. Who knew what horrors took place within those walls. The door of the house opened before she reached it. It looked like her father had been eagerly awaiting her return.

Chapter 25

Dressed smartly in her uniform, with her long hair tied back, Edina entered the main door of the hotel. The shifts were long and physically exhausting, but she no longer dreaded them. If she were being completely honest, she would confess that she not only enjoyed hotel work but that she was actually good at it. The future of Pennyghael House concerned her, not only for Struan's sake but for the impact it would have on her own life. The idea of starting all over again in another job, in another town, filled her with dread. Mull was already beginning to feel like home, and she viewed these people as her friends. And as for Somerled...

Struan appeared from the dining room door.

Edina raised her thumbs to imaginary lapels. She then bent her knees down as she said, 'Ello, ello, ello.'

A look of bewilderment spread across Struan's face as he said, 'Edina, you can be really strange at times. Do you know that?'

'I'm just playing the greeting game with you,' she told him, feeling slightly offended by his insult.

'What greeting game?'

'Have you not noticed that we always think up new ways to greet one another? Curtsies, salutes, bows, and things like that.'

Struan was mystified. 'No, I haven't noticed. Do you know that it's only a game if we both know about it and we're both playing it? That's generally the rule. Anyway, we were robbed of the top spot last night at the quiz, don't you think?'

'Yeah, I was sure that it was ours. Still, if we had to be beaten, then I'm glad it was the fishermen. They seem like a nice bunch of guys.'

'Well, you've changed your tune. They were the ones that were laughing at your dress last week. Did you not almost crash into one of them on a humpback bridge?'

'Oh, forget that. We've made up since then. He's coming over on Tuesday night for dinner. I can't cook, so I don't know what to give him. Any ideas?' she asked.

'I could get the chef to make something for you to heat up in the microwave. You could pick it up in the afternoon. Does that sound good?' he offered.

'Oh yes, that sounds brilliant, but the quaint but basic house I rent from you has no microwave. Could it be something that could go in the oven?' she asked.

'Leave it with me.'

'Two more favours I'd like to ask you,' she said, taking advantage of his amenable mood.

'Oh, here we go. What now?' he asked, pretending to be exasperated.

'When you get the cameras installed at Marnie's flat, could you have one set up for me?'

'Where?' he asked. 'No one ever goes anywhere near the cottage. By the third pothole, they turn back.'

'You're going to find this very strange, so please don't ask for an explanation. I want it set up in my lounge.'

'Wait a minute!' he said, taken aback. 'Is this some kind of kinky thing going on because you are having your fisherman friend round?'

'No, don't be ridiculous! There is some strange stuff going on, and that's all I'm saying on the subject,' she replied.

'Right, what's the next favour?' He was now a little intrigued.

'I've had a chat with Suzie. She's desperately unhappy at home, and I have a bad feeling about that father of hers. I was wondering if you had more cottages with a low rent or a spare room here at the hotel?'

'I can't help you with that one. We don't have any properties left available, and I need to keep all the rooms free at the hotel, just in case. Oh, there is the tower room, but no one ever wants to stay long in there.'

'Oh, don't worry,' she said. 'I'll think of something else.'

'Two out of three is not bad,' he said, just as the phone rang.

'Good afternoon, Pennyghael House Hotel, Struan speaking, how can I help you?'

Edina mouthed, 'Thanks.'

Down in the kitchen, Suzie folded the clean sheets straight from the tumble dryer.

'How is your house looking with all the new things you bought?' Suzie asked, as she began folding the fresh towels.

'I didn't have time to hang the pictures, but the cushions look great on that old sofa. I was really pleased with everything that I bought.'

Unsure whether to speak of Suzie's situation, she decided that there was no time to be wasted. They had to act fast on this, or something dreadful may happen. This young girl's life was being systematically ruined and she was the only one that could help her.

'I hope you don't mind, Suzie, but I asked Struan if he had any more cottages or spare rooms in the hotel. He doesn't have anything at the moment, but he will look out for something suitable.'

'Don't worry about it, Edina. I know there is nothing that can be done. I just have to get on with it the best way I can.'

'You've taken the first step, telling me about it. I will do anything I can to fix this for you.'

'Thanks,' Suzie whispered, as she continued to fold the washing.

It had been a week since Edina steam cleaned the floors in the main reception area, and she now noticed that they were looking lustreless. It was not a job she relished, as the machine used for carrying out this task was a cumbersome piece of equipment. First, the floor had to be swept because the wilting flower display had shed petals across the table, which were subsequently blown over the floor each time the front door opened. Edina made a mental note to replace the arrangement in the vase. The reception hall was the customer's first glimpse of the hotel, the frontline, if you like. Therefore, it had to be just right. Withered flowers would create a negative impression as far as Edina was concerned.

With all of her strength, she dragged the steamer back and forth across the wood. A chemical had been added to the water to give the floor a rich shine.

Struan walked across the polished floor on his tiptoes behind her, mouthing *sorry*.

'Hey, Struan,' she shouted after him. 'Did you order flowers for the vase?' She pointed at the sepia-edged leaves.

'Damn! I forgot.'

'Tut, tut, tut. Don't worry, I'll fix it.'

By the time she had finished, the floors were gleaming. Mr Sheen helped polish up the walnut table in the centre of the room until you could almost see your face. After returning the steam cleaner to its rightful home under the stairs, Edina left in the direction of the kitchen on a mission to find scissors hardy enough to cut plant stalks.

Directly across from the hotel grew a densely wooded area with many trees and bushes. Armed with a sharp pair of kitchen scissors, Edina walked across the mossy woodland floor. She filled her lungs with the aroma of peat soaked in rainwater. The smells of the country were still being discovered by Edina, who had been a lifelong city girl.

The scissors were not a match for the woody stems, but she managed to snap through them, nonetheless. The assortment of foliage she soon held in her arms was made up of cerise rhododendrons, the snowy white flowers of the elderberry plant, and sprigs of rowanberries. The vase she would be filling was deep, so she made sure the stalks were long.

In the stillness of the wood, a twig snapped behind her, causing her to turn around startled. Within the section of the trees, which was denser, she could see the outline of a figure. Instantly, she knew by the hat who the figure was. She did not feel alarmed or afraid. Laying her cut plants to one side, she walked slowly towards the boy. His face was not visible as his hat cast a shadow over it.

'I think you need my help,' she shouted. 'Just tell me what you want me to do.'

The boy remained silent.

'Please, help me to help you.'

Raising his hands up to his face, he began to cry. His sobs seemed to echo through the woodland.

The sight of the distressed boy upset Edina terribly.

This child is in so much pain that he has managed to make himself visible to me in order to get help. What on earth must have happened to him?

Slowly, she began to walk towards him to offer comfort. He turned and ran until he could no longer be seen.

Edina stood for a moment, processing what she had just seen. Then, gathering up her plants, she made her way back to the hotel.

Struan stared at her as she came through the front door.

'Are you all right?' he asked. 'You look like you've just seen a ghost.'

'You have no idea how close to the truth that is. I will tell you about it someday, just not today.'

'Is this anything to do with the camera you want set up *inside* your house?'

'Yes, it's got everything to do with it.'

With trembling hands, she used the scissors to snip off the ends of the plants.

'Are you sure you don't want to talk about it?'

'Another day.'

After filling the large etched glass vase with clean water, she arranged the plants into what could only be referred to as a spectacular display.

For the remainder of the evening, Edina functioned on autopilot. Her mind was filled with thoughts of the boy. What if she couldn't help him? Would he simply haunt her forever? She was unsure how many more of these supernatural events she could take.

I can't believe I have said I don't believe in ghosts in the past. Who would ever have thought that a ghost would become part of my day-to-day life now?

On the way home, after her shift, she replayed the events of the woods in her mind. Regardless of how tired she was, she had to write everything in the journal. She would describe the visitation the previous night and the sighting of the sorrowful boy in the woods.

He wouldn't like it if she ignored him again.

Chapter 26

Thankfully, Edina awoke refreshed after a ghost-free night. The two pages of writing she had completed the previous night had obviously been enough to pacify the boy, as the journal was left perfectly intact. It was such a relief to sleep all night with no interruptions and no damage to her property.

For Edina, Sundays were slow, tedious days for the simple reason everything closed down for the sabbath. Today would be different because she had arranged to go over to Marnie's flat to keep her company. Female company was something that she lacked in her previous life, either she was wary of women or they were wary of her, she wasn't sure which.

Marnie wasn't expecting her at any particular time, which was good because she had lots to do around the house. Hanging the Val Scott paintings was first on the agenda, and it was no easy task. Each painting needed two nails at the same level, two feet apart. For this, Edina had to stand on the sideboard. She then had to balance on the arm of the wing chair to complete the job. The oranges, reds, and yellows were so vibrant, and Edina knew the room would be transformed once they were displayed on the walls.

Thoughts of Somerled coming to the house on Tuesday gave her a schoolgirl churning in the depths of her stomach. It would be a chance to have him all to herself, perhaps until morning. The dawn of this relationship was different from anything she had ever experienced. It simply couldn't be compared to what she had with the editor, whose name was too painful to say. Somerled was not forbidden fruit, nor was he her boss. The seeds of this romance began with mutual attraction between two strangers who knew nothing about one another. The less Somerled knew of her past, the better. With any luck, the Edina he would hopefully fall for would be the new, improved, reinvented girl who had walked barefoot through refining fires.

She plumped up her colourful cushions, admired her artwork, and lifted the wine and cakes she had bought to take to Marnie's house. The leather holdall, which contained her pyjamas, change of clothes and toothbrush, was hurled into the car's back seat. This would be her first girlie sleepover, not just on the Island of Mull, but ever in her life. Thinking back to her previous self, she could see she hadn't invested any real time in friendships. Her life consisted of keeping up with the men at the newspaper, chasing the story, and playing hard in the evenings. It wasn't until everyone found out what she had done that she realised she had no friends. No one to love her no matter what she did. Her mum would have been there for her, but Edina was too busy to make contact with her until the day it was too late. Now, there would be no more calls from her mum.

If only I had been there for my mum, then I wouldn't have to talk to the stars at night to tell her about my life. I know she would have stood by me with no judgement attached. I'm so sorry, mum.

Marnie was delighted to see Edina at the door. Since the letters had started, she hadn't experienced a full night's sleep. Every sound she heard in the night had left her feeling anxious. Latterly, on the nights that Struan couldn't stay, she slept with the radio on in order to mask any unfamiliar noises.

'Thank you so much for offering to stay with me, Edina.'

'I was looking forward to coming over. I'm not exactly plagued with visitors at the cottage.'

Edina was given a tour of the tasteful little apartment, which came with Marnie's job as bar manager. The surroundings were stylish and comfortable, giving Edina a few ideas for her own home. The spare room had been prepared for her with white bedding and a fluffy, emerald green towel lay folded on the chair.

Edina left her holdall on the floor beside the bed before being led through to the lounge, which was, in her opinion, 'very Marnie' in an unexplainable way.

'Please, have a seat, and I'll make you a coffee,' Marnie suggested, gesturing towards the armchair at the window.

'That would be good. You have the place looking great, Marnie.'

'Oh, thanks, I just look out for things that I like and I buy them. It was pretty basic when I first moved in.'

Edina laughed. 'You don't need to tell me about basic. I have just hung two paintings and put a few scatter cushions on my sofa, and the place is unrecognisable.'

Marnie smiled. 'You'll start seeing it as home before you know it.' She headed into the kitchen to put the kettle on.

Framed photographs were lined along the mantlepiece. Edina stood up to get a better look. All the pictures were of Marnie and Struan; together, happy. *That's what I want.*

There were no photos of Marnie's family, Edina noticed.

Nothing strange about that. Not only did I not display any photos of my mum, I did not possess any. How could I have forgotten all about her? She must have been so hurt that I didn't call her or visit her. The loneliness must have been awful... Stop it, Edina. You can't change what is done. Hopefully, she will see I am different now, not that selfish girl I once was.

Marnie brought through a tray containing cups of coffee and the cakes Edina had brought. 'I will make us some dinner later. This will tide us over until then.'

While the girls sat together in the lounge, Edina asked, 'Have there been any more letters?'

'No, it seems to have gone a bit quiet. Maybe he knows that Struan will be getting security cameras installed.'

'Struan says that you suspect your ex-boyfriend is the perpetrator?'

Marnie sipped her coffee. 'Yes, I do. It's not difficult to believe he would do something like this.'

'Do you mind telling me what happened between you two?' Edina inquired.

'It's a long story.'

'We've got all night.'

Marnie sat back, coffee in hand, and attempted to explain the past.

'I was in a relationship with Ashton Brook, the footballer, for several years. We were even engaged to be married. The problem was his jealousy, even though he was the one who was the cheat. I was only ever loyal and faithful to him.'

Edina nodded her head. 'That's the way these kind of guys work. They are unfaithful, so they suspect you must be too.'

'Exactly. Anyway, a very good friend of mine called Lockhart worked in a bridal shop, and she organised a competition through the local newspaper, which had me wearing several of her wedding dresses. The readers could go online and vote for the one they thought I would be the nicest in for my wedding day. It was really successful, and some of the bigger newspapers even got involved.'

Edina sat upright in the chair, 'Oh my goodness, are you Marnie from Marnie's in a Quandary?'

'Yip, that's me.'

'I can't believe it. The newspaper I worked for didn't get involved, but before I left, we had plans to steal your idea.'

'That's so funny,' Marnie said, hardly comprehending that someone from Edinburgh would have heard of her. 'Anyway, cutting a long story short, Ashton found the phone number of the newspaper's photographer in my bag. Lockhart had given it to me because there was an offer of more photographic work if I was interested.'

Edina's face showed that she had pre-empted what was coming next. 'If you don't want to talk about it, Marnie, it's okay.' She could see Marnie reliving the experience in her mind.

'There isn't much to tell. I only remember the first blow to my face. It knocked me out. All the other injuries happened when I was unconscious.'

'That is so terrible. I can't believe he did that to you.'

'I was in hospital for a while, and then I stayed at Lockhart's house until I felt stronger. My other friend Bee took me on holiday here to Mull during this time, and that's when I met Struan. Meantime, Ashton was arrested and served a short prison sentence. His football club dropped him, and people shouted at him in the street. It was the first time I ever pressed charges against him for hitting me. So you can see why he hates me. I just don't know how he found out that I was here on the island.'

'He can't hide out in such a small place forever. The police will find him.'

'I hope so. Anyway, enough about me. Tell me about yourself. Why did you come to Mull? It sounds like you had a great job back in the city.'

There was a moment of silence before Edina said, 'I'll tell you about it, but I think you had better open the bottle of wine for this one.'

Chapter 27

Edina reached for the glass of Prosecco as Marnie handed it to her. She never intended to share her story with anyone in her new life. After all, the past was the past, what's done was done and all that... But somehow, sitting with Marnie, she felt the need to open up. There was even a chance that speaking the events aloud would cleanse her or at least unburden her of some of the guilt she carried.

'So, Edina, why did you end up in Mull?' Marnie asked, almost afraid of what she was about to hear.

'Before I begin, I need you to know that I am not that person anymore. I don't expect you to be understanding but trust me, you can't judge me any more harshly than I've judged myself.'

Marnie leaned forward on her chair, reaching for Edina's hand.

'Don't be sympathetic towards me until you hear what I've done.' She pulled her hand away from Marnie's.

She explained that the newspaper editor, whose name was too painful to say, was a happily married man with a family. She wanted to make it clear that this man was a victim, her victim.

'Marnie, I set my cap at him and pursued him relentlessly. We had shared a few moments in my flat in the dark, but he stopped and said he didn't want to take it any further. He didn't want to hurt his family. I should have left well enough alone, but after tasting a bite of the delicious cherry, so to speak, I desperately wanted more. I had fallen for him, but I also relished the challenge.'

Marnie listened intently.

'I seduced him in the room where the photocopiers were kept, stroked him under the table at the staff's morning meeting, I even followed him into the gents. I was like the Terminator, I absolutely would not stop, but he resisted me every time.' She squirmed as she thought back to how ruthlessly destructive she had been. All she cared about was her feelings and desires.

Marnie refilled the glasses.

'About a week later, I was sitting in my flat watching a film, and there was a knock at the door. It was the editor, whose name I still find too painful to say. I had been on the verge of giving up my quest to have him, but he came looking for me. He walked into my home. Not one word was exchanged. We had the most wild and frenzied sex, several times. It was an unleashing of pure passion. The thing was, Marnie, we had both been fantasising about it, so when it finally happened, there were fireworks.'

'Wow, that sounds like a great time,' Marnie said. 'You can't blame yourself. You were single, he wasn't. He came to your door, no one forced him.'

'Thanks for your words of encouragement, Marnie, but it got worse. We embarked on the affair of the century. You have no idea the wild and outrageous things we got up to. We even went away on trips to beautiful hotels. By this time, I was crazy in love with him. If we weren't together, I had no interest in going out. Nightlife held no appeal for me. It was magical, and it lasted almost two years. No one knew. No one even suspected. We were so careful.'

'So, what went wrong? Did his wife find out?' Marnie probed, lifting the wine bottle to top them both up.

Edina could feel the sting of tears in the corner of her eyes.

She continued. 'One day, he sent me a text saying he needed to talk to me. He arranged to come to my flat at half past six that evening. It wasn't like his usual texts, it was solemn, like we were strangers. I was so nervous. I paced the floor back and forth like a lion in a cage. I was in torment.'

The memory of that day encouraged the tears to spill. Marnie stood to offer comfort, but Edina shook her head and waved her off. After a deep breath, she continued with her story.

'I answered the door to him, but he wouldn't come in. He said that he never wanted to see me again. He then told me that he would ask for a transfer to another newspaper and was changing his phone number. His last words to me before he left that day were, '*Stay away for good, I mean it.*''

Edina put her face into her hands. She had never repeated this story out loud before. All the gut-wrenching pain came flooding back.

Regardless of whether Edina wanted her to or not, Marnie gently laid her hand on her shoulder. 'Oh, you poor thing, that must have been torture,' she comforted.

'I am not a poor thing, Marnie. I'm a monster. After he left that night, I cried and cried. When the sun came up, I had cried myself dry. That was when I got angry. I got incredibly angry at him for using me and dumping me. I see the truth now, he didn't use me, we enjoyed each other. He didn't dump me, he finished an affair with me, it's allowed. You don't have to stay with someone forever just because they would be hurt if you left.'

Marnie tilted her head to the side slightly. 'Oh no, I've got the feeling that you wanted your revenge on him.'

'It was morning, a work morning. I got dressed up and did my hair. I looked just like the assassin that I was. I didn't go to work that day. I walked straight round to the editor's house. I knew he would be in the office. I pressed my painted lips together, pushed up my cleavage, and then knocked three times on the door. I heard footsteps coming. I nearly chickened out at that point. A pretty, smiley-faced woman came to the door and said, 'Yes?'

'I braced myself because I knew deep down this wasn't right, but I wanted her to hurt as much as I was hurting. I introduced myself and told her that I thought she should know that her husband and I had been having a wild affair for the past two years. I told her about the incredible sex and the secret overnight stays. I even told her that he said he didn't get this kind of sex at home. The truth was that he never said that. He only ever told me that he loved his wife. She stood staring at me for a few moments, and then she quietly shut the door. I walked away and more or less rubbed my hands together as if to say, job done.'

'That was brutal, Edina,' Marnie said quietly, screwing up her face.

'The following day, I went to work, and one of my fellow journalists, who I considered a friend, shut the door in my face. Everyone stared at me, then ignored me. I went over to my good friend, Clare, and asked her what was going on. She looked at me like she despised me before telling me to fuck off. Everyone hated me, and they didn't hold back in telling me so.'

'How did they know?' Marnie asked.

'It turns out the editor's wife had just been diagnosed with motor neuron disease. The editor was devastated by this news, obviously. After all, she was everything to him. I was just sex. He ended our affair to focus on taking care of her.'

Edina paused to take a sip of wine.

Marnie looked aghast, 'So, that's when you applied for the job at Pennyghael House?'

'Wait, that's not all, Marnie, it actually got worse, a lot worse. When the editor got home that night, he found his wife dead in the bathroom. She had taken her own life. The children were in the house. There was a note left. It said that she had met me and I had told her everything. She didn't want to be a burden on him with her deteriorating illness, so she basically gave us her blessing. That's when I looked for a job far away from Edinburgh.'

Marnie silently shook her head. 'I don't really know what to say right now. It's a really bad story.'

Edina nodded in agreement before replying. 'I know, it is a *really* bad story. There is nothing you can say.'

Having drained the last dregs of the wine, Marnie rose to her feet, 'I think I'll put some dinner on for us. All that bearing our souls stuff has given me an appetite. If you want a shower, help yourself. I've left a towel in your room.'

'Thanks, Marnie. I hope I haven't put you off me.'
Marnie smiled. 'We all have skeletons of some sort in our cupboard. It's not about what you do wrong. It's about what you do to make amends.'
Edina welcomed her words.

Chapter 28

The flat was filled with the aroma of onions frying when Edina came out of the shower. It wasn't until her nostrils caught the scent that she felt incredibly hungry.

'Are you happy to have your dinner on your knee in the lounge, or would you like to sit at the little table here in the kitchen?' Marnie hollered to Edina.

'My knee in the lounge is great, thanks! Do you need any help?'

'No,' Marnie shouted. 'Go and sit down. I've opened another bottle. Help yourself.'

As Edina sat down, the buzz of a text came through her phone, giving her a start. She clicked on it and read the words:

Two more sleeps until I get to enjoy the magnificent dinner you are making for me. I cannot wait. See you Tuesday. T x

Edina laughed aloud.
He must be thinking about me as much as I'm thinking about him.
She sent a text straight back:

I'm sitting here trawling through recipe books to find a dish suitable for a man of your stature. E x

She waited for a response. And it came.

Good to hear that you are giving this some serious thought. I'm off to bed, I have a 4am start in the morning. Goodnight, sweet girl. T x

Feeling touched by his description of her, she sent a reply:

Goodnight Somerled. Be safe at sea. E x

Marnie walked through to the lounge with a dinner plate in each hand. Cutlery had been stuffed into the pocket of her cardigan.
Edina reached for one of the plates, marvelling aloud at the delights it held. She reached into Marnie's pocket for a knife and fork. They sat together eating in silence, enjoying the many flavours of the restaurant quality meal that Marnie managed to have rustled up in no time at all.
No wonder Struan loves her so much. She's a superwoman.
Sharing her deepest secrets with Marnie had been cathartic for Edina. Having an evening away from her house, in the company of such a great girl, had been the best medicine she could have asked for.
When she could no longer keep her eyes open, she said, 'Marnie, I hate to be the first to ruin the party, but I have to go to bed. I have had a great night, it was just what I needed. Thanks for everything.'
'Oh, you are so welcome,' Marnie told her. 'We will do this again soon. It's been great to have your company. I want to say one last thing about what happened in Edinburgh. It was awful, I can't deny that.'

Edina hung her head in shame.

'But you were young, carefree, and could never have predicted the outcome in your wildest dreams. Some people, like Ashton, for example, go through life hurting people, a bit like a logger, leaving destruction behind them wherever they go. You are not that person, Edina. You made a terrible mistake, but you've learned from it and changed your heart. It's time to forgive yourself and let it go.'

Edina wrapped her arms around Marnie, whispering, 'Thank you,' in her ear.

Edina was up first in the morning. She felt great after a restful sleep with no interruptions. There was no fear of strange dragging noises and scribbling sounds to keep her awake in the night. However, the thought entered her mind that she hadn't written in her journal. The boy wouldn't be pleased. There was a strong possibility that she would be facing some vandalism to her property when she got back. The idea of it disturbed her.

I must be the only person in the world with a ghost who takes tantrums.

To avoid waking Marnie, she dressed, grabbed her things, then tiptoed out quietly. She took the stairs gently, one at a time. As she reached the back door, she saw a hand-delivered letter lying on the floor.

Oh no. I know exactly what this is. I can't leave Marnie to discover this alone. I need to stay with her. I'll explain it to Struan. He'll understand.

Her stomach churned as she lifted the envelope. She stared at the lettering on the front, which read MARNIE in capitals. Instinctively, she then held it to her nose to detect any familiar odour from it. Her nose picked up a trace of aftershave, but it was so faint that she could not identify it.

Marnie looked so peaceful as she slept, blissfully ignorant of what was awaiting her. Waking her with such awful news was somehow cruel. As she sat on the edge of Marnie's bed, she saw that she was beginning to stir.

'Marnie, are you awake?' she said gently, using it as a prompt, not a question.

Marnie rubbed her eyes, then pushed her hair from her face.

'I found this letter downstairs at the front door. I wanted to stay just in case it's from him.'

Marnie sat up in bed, looking at Edina, then the letter. Her sleep had been deep, so it took a moment to register what was happening. Suddenly, the reality hit. 'Oh no, please, no more.'

Opening the envelope, Marnie recognised that it had been written in the same style, with the letters cut from newspaper headlines, then stuck on to make the words.

IT IS GOOD TO SEE THAT YOU HAVE FRIENDS.
WE ALL NEED SOMEONE TO SHARE OUR SECRETS WITH.
RIGHT NOW, I AM NOTHING TO YOU BUT ONE DAY I WILL COME OUT FROM THE SHADOWS.

Marnie read the words aloud as Edina listened. Edina took the letter, rereading it silently. She held it up to the light for clues, then smelt it again. The aftershave scent was stronger on the actual letter than it had been on the envelope. Edina was good with smells, and this one was familiar to her; she had no idea why.

'What kind of aftershave did Ashton wear?' she asked Marnie.

'I can't remember the name, but it was by Hermes, I think.'

Edina had never come across any aftershaves by Hermes before, so why was this smell familiar? It was a bit of a dead end as a clue, but it was worth thinking about. When she was a journalist, she followed every line of inquiry, no matter how small or seemingly meaningless.

'There are two things that we know for sure from this letter, Marnie. He knew I was with you last night, so he was watching. He also doesn't intend to stay hidden for long, so time is running out to catch him. We need those cameras installed soon. The part I can't work out is how did he know we were talking about secrets? Was that just a lucky guess?'

Or was he in the flat?

She didn't voice this to Marnie.

Chapter 29

As soon as Struan arrived at The Shell Seekers, Edina got ready to set off to the hotel.

'Thanks, Edina,' Struan said. 'Can you hold the fort until I get back? It might be in the afternoon, but the police are coming over to speak to Marnie. I want to show them the place where I think Ashton hides out when he's watching.'

'Take as long as you need, guys. Do I have Suzie and Freddy today at the hotel?'

'Yes, you have the full complement of our extensive staff at your disposal,' he joked.

'One more thing,' Edina asked. 'Any news on the CCTV cameras? I think you need to hurry them along.'

'I called again before I left. They said it would hopefully be tomorrow.'

Edina drove to Pennyghael House. Her mind churned over the events of the morning. Thinking about it logically, if Ashton Brook were here on Mull, then he would have to find somewhere to stay. The only way to the island was by the ferry, leaving from Oban. There must be CCTV cameras on board the boat. Was he intelligent enough to devise a plan where he would mess with Marnie's head by secretly stalking her? From what Marnie had told her about him, he was more likely to get the ferry over, beat her to a pulp, and then leave. If he had paid someone to come over and find her, then things were going to become a lot more complicated.

Freddy was at the reception desk when Edina walked through the hotel doors.

'What's going on?' Freddy asked, confused by his sudden promotion from dishwasher to receptionist.

'Oh, nothing really. Marnie's not feeling that good today, so Struan didn't want to leave her on her own,' Edina explained.

The fewer people that knew the details of this situation, the better. The last thing she wanted was for it to become the gossip story of the island.

'When do you start your course?' she asked, changing the subject.

'In about six weeks. The start date is the 25th of August. My dad is paying for a flat for me, which is just around the corner from the college,' he told her. 'That means I can lie in my bed until ten minutes before my class starts. I hope to get a flatmate to share with me so that my dad gets help with the monthly payments. I know that he can't really afford it.'

'You'll have to work hard and do him proud. If he is sacrificing for you, then you'll have to make it worth it. It's good that you are not just taking it for granted. When I was your age, I just took, took and took, and I didn't think of the compromises my mum was making for me.'

Yet again, regrets regarding her mum fleeted through her mind. *She did without so much to give to me. A winter coat had been one of those sacrifices.* It physically hurt her to think about it.

A text came through Edina's phone. It was from Somerled.

One more sleep. T x

She smiled at this welcome distraction. She texted back.

Started preparing the meal already. I want it to be just right! E x

You're cutting it a bit fine. Are you sure it will be ready for tomorrow? T x

Trust me. I am a MasterChef. E x

Struan arrived back at the hotel late in the afternoon. He had spoken with the police, and, as yet, they had no leads in finding out who was sending the letters. The police did point out, once again, that there had been no crime committed. The letters were sinister looking, because of the unusual format, but the content was not threatening nor slanderous in any way. However, they conceded that because they were anonymous and implied that the sender was watching from afar, they could be construed as distressing to Marnie. They agreed to check Ashton Brook's name against the list of people who had booked their car for the Mull ferry in the past four months. Additionally, Struan asked them if they could do a search on the type of vehicle that Ashton drove. If he knew what to look for on the road, it would put him one step ahead.

The police explained to both Struan and Marnie that the CCTV cameras outside The Shell Seekers would give the most hopeful lead in solving this case. The sooner they were installed, the better.

Chapter 30

On the drive home, Edina scolded herself for hitting two potholes. She and the road had an understanding now, so dipping into not one, but two craters, was just not on. She blamed it on her focus being somewhere other than what was ahead.

It had been a long shift at the hotel, and the thought of immersing herself in a hot bath was her deepest desire at that particular moment in time. Unfortunately, the bath would need to be put on hold as she was met with a most distressing sight when she walked through the front door. At first glance, it appeared that a burglar had trashed the house in search of valuables.

Of course, she knew that this was not the work of an intruder, not a live one anyway. In hindsight, she should have taken the journal to Marnie's or written in it before she left. *Do I never learn?*

'I'm sorry,' she shouted to the empty room. 'I haven't forgotten about you. I was visiting my friend.' *What am I doing apologising to an invisible child in my own home?*

Sitting down on the coffee table, she looked all around her at the devastation caused by one troubled little spirit. The Val Scott paintings hung at an angle. The radio had been thrown across the room with force, leaving a dent in the opposite wall. Edina shook her head, asking herself the same old question. *Why me?*

On the floor, at her feet, lay her journal, that cursed journal that she wished she had never started. She was astonished by the state the pages had been left in.

Amidst the scribbles and scores, she noticed something. Yes, it was unmistakable. The word 'help' could be clearly seen. Staring down at the page, she saw the desperate urgency in those sad little letters. *Okay. This changes everything.*

The mammoth task of fixing up the house could wait until tomorrow. The boy needed help tonight. On the sideboard lay the book from the mobile library, 'Memories of Pennyghael' by Catriona McLeod. Pulling the tartan throw around her shoulders, she tucked her legs under her and began reading.

Her intention was to read as much of the book as she could that night, skimming past the irrelevant chapters. After reading the first chapter, she questioned whether anyone had ever read it before, apart from family. It wasn't exactly a high-octane, thrills and spills page-turner. That said, it was beautifully written in a simplistic language, all of its own.

Catriona described her experiences from childhood where she played Hopscotch, Mumblypeg, and Farmer's in his Dell. She described her dolly, Shona, made from an old shoe brush. This made Edina laugh out loud. The tales of Catriona's youth were lovingly told. They incorporated the tragedy of death with anecdotes filled with humour. Edina was transported back to a time that she had only ever seen in films or read in history books. Although she was exhausted, physically and mentally, she was unable to put the charming novel down.

The birds were chirping, and the sun's rays were appearing over the treetops by the time Edina reached chapter twelve. This was a chapter that covered

Catriona's years in service at the grand Pennyghael House. Edina believed that if there was anything relevant to her situation, it would be within this section of the book. She read on.

There was a detailed description of the staff and their positions within the house. This was followed by a breakdown of the daily chores carried out by each employee. Edina skimmed the pages until she saw the sub-heading, The Fire at Pennyghael.

Catriona painted a vivid picture of the house on fire, which had started in the roof. She explained that all the villagers arrived with buckets, bowls, and receptacles of every description to fill with water from the stream.

As Edina read the words on the page, her mind filled with images of the terrifying scene. Gripped by Catriona's interpretation of events, she read of the black plumes of smoke filling the sky, accompanied by the deafening crackle of the wooden eaves burning. The story then focused on a young maid named Lottie and her son Jeremy, who was described as being born out of wedlock. Edina sat upright, reading with great interest that the boy was six years old. The story unfolded that Jeremy worked incredibly hard that night, filling pots with water, then running close to the fire to help to douse it. The frantic trips back and forth, along with the inhalation of black smoke, caused the boy to collapse. The master of the house had stepped in at this point, instructing one of the stable boys to ride to Tobermory to fetch Dr Innis.

Edina raised her eyes from the page, voicing aloud, 'Jeremy, is that who you are? Are you Jeremy that helped with the fire at Pennyghael?'

Catriona explained further that Lottie and her son were given the cottage on the grounds of the estate. Several staff at the house were not pleased about this and couldn't understand why she would be awarded such a privilege.

Catriona had written, 'It raised a few eyebrows.'

Edina stopped reading again to say, 'Did you live here, in my house, Jeremy?'

I couldn't have been more wrong about this novel. It's turning out to be very high octane indeed. I can't be sure, but I think Catriona has supplied me with a few important pieces of the puzzle.

Further news of the mother and son was documented in the following chapter. Catriona talked about a memorable day when her sister, who also worked at Pennyghael House, came running home to tell the family of a momentous argument that had taken place in the parlour. The door had been shut, but some of the staff were huddled outside, listening. The Master of the House was alone in the room with Lottie. His voice was raised. At first, they were filled with concern for the young woman, but they needn't have, as they soon heard Lottie retorting back at her boss in a mocking manner. The final words shouted from the room were from the Master saying, 'How dare you try to blackmail me.'

Edina was spellbound by this chapter. Her mind began to sew in some loose threads that had hung around the story.

It was now official daylight hours, but still, Edina kept reading.

Catriona wrote that Lottie had not turned up at work the following day. She did not appear the day after that nor the day after that. Some of the staff, including Catriona's sister, had gone to the cottage on the estate to check on Lottie and her little boy, but they had simply vanished. The cottage had been emptied. All that remained was a spiral of smoke, pirouetting heavenward from a bonfire in the back garden.

'Where did you go?' Edina asked aloud. 'What happened to you and your mother?'

According to Catriona, the staff had taken strength in numbers and approached his Lordship for information on the whereabouts of Lottie and Jeremy.

Infuriated by their audacity, he told them curtly, 'They left on a boat bound for Ireland. I do not wish for it to be spoken of under my roof, ever again.'

Catriona's sister had been particularly aggrieved by the departure of her good friend Lottie and the lack of a farewell.

The final chapter of the book had moved away from the subject of Lottie and Jeremy. Catriona told of a fair that took place on Port n Ba Beach. There had been stalls and entertainments, including Punch and Judy. It then described how she and her sister had been led along the white sands on little Shetland ponies. Edina decided to stop reading. She had found out all that she needed to know from Catriona McLeod. Tired as she was, she had no regrets about pulling an all-nighter.

Edina climbed the narrow stairs as though scaling Everest. It was not sleep that awaited her at the top, but a change of uniform for work. Her shift was due to start in under an hour. When she reached the top stair, she stopped.

'Oh, Jeremy, you didn't get on a boat for Ireland, did you? So, where are you?'

Chapter 31

Edina arrived at the hotel just as her phone vibrated with a text. She clicked on it.

No more sleeps. Today is the day. I can't wait. See you at 7. T x

Oh that's right, it's tonight! I'm getting Somerled all to myself tonight, I can't wait... oh shit! My house is ransacked and I have no food. Oh well, these things are no barrier to love.

Already watching at the window for you. Don't be late E x

Struan approached her as soon as she entered the main hall. 'Edina, can I have the key to your house? The engineers are setting up the CCTV cameras today for you and Marnie.'

Edina was pleasantly surprised by this because Struan hadn't actually confirmed to her that she was getting a camera. Somehow, it didn't seem so urgent that she spied on her little visitor. As long as she played by his rules, he left well alone. Things were now beginning to make sense regarding who the boy was. In her heart, she believed it all came down to finding out the truth about mother and son and the fate that befell them. Still, it wouldn't do any harm to have a camera, just to catch a glimpse of what she was dealing with.

'You don't need my key. I've never locked the front door. Tell the workmen to go on in and make themselves at home. Eh, Struan, could you also tell them to ignore the mess? I had a sort of, shall we say, mishap.'

'A mishap? What the hell is a mishap?' Struan asked.

'Never mind, you wouldn't understand. By the way, is the offer still on for the chef making me something for my date tonight?' she asked, now feeling completely desperate.

'I've asked him to prepare you a lasagne and some garlic bread. He will cook the lasagne, then all you need to do is heat it up in the oven at the same time you cook the bread. Do you think you can handle that?'

'Well, I was hoping for something a bit more exotic,' she told him. 'I'm only joking, that's great, Struan, thanks.'

'Hey, have you heard anything from Suzie? She hasn't turned up this morning, which is very unusual for her.'

Knowing Suzie's situation, Edina felt immediately concerned. 'No, but I'll drive to her house during my break, just to check everything is all right.'

Freddy was in the kitchen when Edina got there. He explained that Struan had given him a call to come in because Susie hadn't turned up for her shift. Edina was pleased to see him, and she gave a quick rundown on the jobs that Suzie would normally cover in the morning.

'Suzie is a bit of a dynamo when she gets started, so don't worry if you don't finish everything she normally does. I will race through the work upstairs, and then I'll come down and help you.'

'Thanks, Edina, that would be great,' Freddy told her. He then began emptying the dishwasher.

Edina could hear him whistling an unrecognisable tune.

He'll manage fine doing Suzie's work. Good old Freddy, always there in a crisis. Freddy at the ready!

It was now time for Edina to perform her least favourite task, which involved wrestling the industrial hoover out of the cupboard. Once out in the open, she had to carry it upstairs before she could start hoovering every square inch of the thick, wool-twist carpets.

Having completed the hallway upstairs and two of the bedrooms, Edina glanced at her phone to check the time.

10.30, I'll take my tea break now. I'll check on Suzie, then come straight back.

She found Freddy scrubbing out the ladies powder room downstairs. It made her smile to see him on his hands and knees cleaning the floor around the toilet. Somewhere in the kitchen cupboards, he had found himself a pair of bright yellow marigold gloves.

I'm really going to miss that boy when he leaves. She watched him singing as he worked. *He doesn't have much to say, but things are not the same when he's not around.*

Freddy looked up from the floor. 'Hey Edina, I didn't hear you coming in.'

'I just came to tell you that I'm driving along to Suzie's house to check on her. I'll be back in about ten minutes.'

'No problemo, amigo.'

Edina smiled at Freddy's response. She could tell by the look on his face that he thought it was clever.

He gave her a brief wave with his marigold covered hand before continuing cleaning the toilet bowl, lifting the seat, and scouring all around. His singing changed back to whistling.

Edina drove with a tense knot embedded in her stomach. As far as she was concerned, a dark, foreboding cloud was hanging over this situation. Suzie wouldn't let Struan down without good reason or without phoning to let him know. Edina hadn't known her long but was sure that this was not Suzie's style. She was reliable. Edina had a bad feeling about going to the house in normal circumstances. This was a whole new level of dread.

Pulling up into the junk-filled driveway, she looked from her car window for signs of life. Oh, what she would have given for Suzie to walk out the front door. But the house appeared deserted. Uncollected mail was clamped halfway in the letterbox; Edina knew this was a bad sign. Taking a deep breath, she stepped out of the car. Rubber tyres lay strewn over the grass, causing Edina to take a zig-zag route to the door.

She hammered the front door with her fist. No reply.

She repeated the three loud knocks. There appeared to be no one home.

For a few moments, Edina pondered what to do next before deciding that she couldn't simply drive away. She walked over to the front window, unwittingly screwing her face up at the filthy net curtains hanging askew. The gap between the hem and the windowsill was enough to see through into the living area. With her fingers, she rubbed the grime from the glass in a circular motion, making herself a small peephole.

She peered in.

From what she could see, Suzie's father was sitting in the armchair with his back to the window. Suzie was perched on the floor in front of him; her hands covering her face.

Edina tapped on the glass. Susie looked up from her hands. Her face portrayed a look of bewilderment. Edina then saw her rising to her feet to make her way through to the hallway. Much to Edina's relief, Suzie's father remained in his chair in the lounge.

The front door opened a fraction.

'Hi Edina,' Suzie said.

Her eyes were wide and carried a faraway look.

'Suzie, we're all worried about you. You didn't show up for your shift today. Are you all right?'

'Yes, I'm sorry. I'm not feeling too well. Could you explain this to Struan for me? I'm really sorry. Thank you for coming to see me.'

Her voice was weak and breathy.

'I don't know what's going on here, Suzie, but I will get you out of there. I give you my word. Can you hang on a little longer?'

Suzie nodded, mouthing, 'Thanks.'

No sound came out.

Edina drove back to the hotel, her mind searching for a solution to Suzie's predicament. The only option she hadn't considered was to phone the social work department. On Suzie's behalf, she could explain that she was living in an unhealthy environment. Maybe they could rehouse her anywhere, as long it was far away from that man.

There was something about Suzie's behaviour that was especially odd, to say the least. The father sitting in the chair, Suzie at his feet with her head in her hands.

What is going on in that house? I don't think I should have left her there. I must phone the housing department as soon as I get home.

Chapter 32

Back at the hotel, Freddy had almost finished his cleaning chores. He stood with Struan at the reception, awaiting the news about Suzie. Edina was greeted by both men as she entered the main door.

'Well?' Struan asked, throwing his hands up.

'Is she okay?' Freddy added, genuinely worried.

'I don't know. There is something going on in that house, and it is not right. There was something strange in the way that Suzie was acting.'

Struan adopted a puzzled expression. 'Strange in what way?'

'I can't put my finger on it. Just odd. I have a nose for these things and things don't smell right.'

Freddy thought about this for a moment. 'Was she smashed?'

'No, she hadn't been drinking. I'm going to make a few calls to the housing department. I don't think that a young girl should be living with that man. He is no good for her.'

'He is her dad, though,' Freddy argued. 'Family ties in Mull are tight, Edina.'

'I get that, but don't forget, not all dads are good fathers like yours, you know.'

'I agree, Edina,' Struan told her. 'We need to get her out of there. Look, you've got a big date night tonight, and you need to make a call for Suzie before the offices shut. We are not busy here, so why don't you finish upstairs, then go home. The lasagne is in the big fridge in the kitchen. Take garlic bread from the freezer if you want.'

'Struan, you are a great boss. Thanks so much. I'll pass on the garlic bread. It could ruin the night, if you know what I mean.'

Edina ran off to finish hoovering the bedrooms upstairs.

Freddy ran after her, shouting, 'Edina!'

She stopped halfway up the staircase.

'You know how you've got a date tonight, well so have I,' he told her, smiling.

'Freddy, that's great. Who is it?'

'You know that girl with the blonde curly hair who goes to The Shell Seekers?'

Edina racked her brains before saying, 'Yes, I think so.'

'Well, it's not her. It's her cousin, Rose, from the mainland. She is staying with her for a few weeks.'

'That is so exciting. Where will you take her?'

'I thought we could go into Tobermory to the seafood restaurant. It's called Clam Rock. It has the best mussels in the world.'

'Freddy, that's a big statement to make, especially when you've never been off the island.'

'You know what I mean.'

Edina laughed. 'Have a great time. I'll hear all about it when I next see you.'

'Aww, thanks.'

Freddy headed back downstairs to join Struan.

When Edina arrived home, the CCTV engineers were just finishing off. The man in charge explained that Struan had arranged for Wi-Fi to be installed so she could see everything going on from her phone or laptop. The film would be stored for forty-eight hours, but she could save a film if she needed to for any reason. Once everything was set in place, he showed her how to use it.

'Your house is in some state. No wonder you wanted the cameras. Do the cops have any idea who would do this?' the engineer commented.

'No, but I'm sure they'll get him.' She had neither the desire nor the inclination to explain what was going on in her life. 'Thanks for doing that for me,' she told him, ushering him to the front door.

When the engineers had left, she took the opportunity to phone the social work department. It was a luxury to have her phone in use again. It made her feel safer and more connected to the outside world.

The phone number she required was easy to find now that she had the internet. The automated voice on the end of the line gave her several options, which were coordinated to a number on her keypad. When she was finally connected to the housing department, she explained to the woman who answered the call, that she had serious concerns about her friend and work colleague, Suzie Bannerman. She explained that she had reason to believe that abuse may be taking place in the home. She was met with silence on the other end of the line, so she continued by asking if there was any accommodation available on Mull for situations like this.

After what felt like an overly lengthy pause, the woman asked Edina, 'Does your friend have her name down on the council house waiting list?'

'No, I don't believe she does.'

'There is a process to follow when seeking a house from the council. Your friend should start by phoning this department herself. Then she can request an application.'

'I do understand all this, but I feel that her situation is quite desperate,' Edina said, unwilling to give up without a fight.

'Did your friend confide in you that she was being abused in her home?'

'Not exactly,' Edina answered.

'Have you seen any abuse taking place in this girl's home?'

'No.' Edina knew that this was not going well.

'So, can I ask what you have based your assumptions on?'

'Just a bad feeling, really.'

'You must understand, Madam, that we have many desperate people on the housing list, and there are very few available properties on the island.'

'I understand that.'

'The best thing I can suggest for you to do is to bring your friend in to talk to us. We can then guide her onto the first rung of the ladder in finding her own home.'

'Thank you for your help,' Edina said, pressing the 'end call' button by applying a little too much force.

The next thing on her agenda was to write in her journal. It would not be convenient for any celestial happenings to occur tonight. Plus, she owed it to the boy, or more precisely, she owed it to *Jeremy*, to record everything that she had found out. Catriona McLeod's book gave her insight into the events leading up to the disappearance of mother and son. If Lottie and Jeremy didn't leave on the boat to Ireland, what happened to them, and where were they buried? This was what she needed to find out. Stan was the only one she had confided in about this matter, and now she needed to talk to him.

Chapter 33

Somerled was due to arrive in just over an hour. The havoc caused by Jeremy, the friendly ghost, had been all straightened out, and the room looked habitable again. Having Wi-Fi meant Edina wasn't relying on the old wireless for background music. The playlist for the evening was selected carefully to create an atmosphere-enhancing mood. It was too early to light the candles she had previously picked up at the supermarket, but she laid the kitchen matches down on the table ready. *It's not cold tonight, but I think I'll light a fire just for effect.* Having had plenty of practice, she knew it would take her no more than fifteen minutes to have a decent fire burning away in the oversized fireplace.

Once changed, she inspected her outfit in front of the mirror. Tiredness revealed itself around her eyes in the form of dark shadows. *I must apply a bit of make-up to these circles under my eyes.* Standing side on, she could see that she had lost weight since her arrival in Mull. *I am so much slimmer. It must be because my new job is more physical, and there is a lack of business lunches accompanied by alcohol. Alcohol! My weekly units have gone from dangerously high to dangerously low.* Looking herself up and down, she decided that she looked good, considering how sleep-deprived she was.

A loud knock from the front door resounded around the house.

'Oh shit, oh shit, oh shit,' she said, feeling more nervous than she had ever been in her life before.

Somerled stood on the doorstep smiling, looking incredibly gorgeous. The sight of him caused a rush to her head as well as an involuntary sharp intake of breath. A peal of laughter escaped Somerled's lips when he saw her standing at the door wearing her red saloon girl dress.

'Your cowboy has arrived!' he announced. 'Here, I bought you this.'

He brought a bottle of champagne out from behind his back.

'You big liar,' she corrected him. 'You won it at the quiz the other night.'

Laughing again, he said, 'Oh yes, so I did.'

Gesturing for him to come in, she stood aside to let him pass. He planted a kiss on her cheek as he passed her. Edina liked that.

'Hey, this is cosy. You've made it really nice. Did anyone ever tell you that this cottage has the reputation of being haunted? I mean, it's just local talk, nothing to worry about. The people of Mull really go in for that kind of thing.'

'Well, thanks for telling me. That is just what I wanted to hear when I live alone in a remote location in dark woods.'

'Oh, sorry, I didn't mean to frighten you.'

'It doesn't scare me. In fact I've befriended one of them. I'm glad of the company,' she joked.

'You look absolutely beautiful,' he announced, completely unexpectedly.

Her cheeks reddened with embarrassment, 'I don't,' she said, giggling.

'You do.'

'I don't.'

'You do,' he said firmly.

'Okay, I do.'

She laughed as she walked away to the kitchen to put the oven on. *What temperature did Struan tell me to put the oven to? Was it 180 or 200? I can't remember. I'll take a gamble at 180. Did he tell me to heat the oven before I put the lasagne in, or did he say it could go straight in? I'll take a gamble and put it straight in.*

When she reappeared in the lounge, Somerled was admiring the Val Scott paintings.

'I'm just going to get something out of the way before we move on to more interesting things,' she announced.

Somerled turned around to look at her, unsure of what was coming next.

'I can't cook,' she told him quickly. 'I do have dinner, though, but the chef at work made it. Okay, I've said it. Let's not speak of it again.'

'Ah ha! I suspected as much. It's fine by me. I'd rather have something made by a chef than something I'd have to force down that was made by a girl who can't cook. If you see what I mean.'

'My thoughts exactly. Now, let's change the subject. Tell me what your name means,' she asked, sitting him down and opening the champagne.

Somerled cleared his throat for effect. 'It means summer traveller. It was the name of a 12th-century Scottish warlord who created a kingdom on the Scottish islands. My father had read a book about the warlord and decided that his first son would be called Somerled. My mum said it suited me because I travelled every summer when I was younger. I took a job in a bar on a Greek island one summer and then on a Spanish island the following summer. I always seem to get the itch for travel when the summer comes.'

'What about this year?' she asked him.

'Yes, I did get a twinge, but someone caught my eye, and it has anchored me for now.' He gave her a little half wink. 'Maybe I'll become Autumnled,' he added, smiling.

I really hope not. I need you to stay forever.

The wine was beginning to go to her head, which reminded her that she hadn't eaten all day. Her lunchtime had been taken up with checking on Suzie.

'I'll go and put the dinner out,' she told him. The smell of cooking was drifting through from the kitchen.

'It's about bloody time,' he said. 'I'll be gnawing on my fists soon if I don't get something to eat.'

The slab of lasagne somehow looked a little wanting as it sat alone on the dinner plate.

I should've taken the garlic bread or at least made a salad to go with it. I didn't really think this through. I've got nothing for dessert, either. Why did I invite him for dinner? I could easily have said come for drinks. Why do I always make things so difficult for myself?

'I'm sorry it doesn't look like much. I should have made a salad,' she explained, feeling embarrassed by the meagre offering.

'Stop apologising. It's great. Anyway, I came to see you, not the chef's cooking.' Again he laughed.

After they had eaten, Somerled smiled. 'I have left just enough room for dessert.'

'Oh, that's a shame because I don't actually have anything for dessert,' she told him, avoiding the sorry word. 'I'll tell you what I can give you… a digestive biscuit. Interested?'

'It's incredibly tempting, but I think I'll resist. I'm watching my figure.'

She glanced at his muscular frame, which filled every inch of his shirt. Without a doubt, she knew that there wouldn't be one ounce of fat on that perfect body.

As they chatted, he rose from the wing chair, making his way around the coffee table to sit beside her on the sofa. Removing his shoes, he joined her by resting his feet beside hers on the coffee table.

The smell of his aftershave was torturously delicious to Edina's nasal passages. *This is the most perfect man I have ever encountered, and he is here with me in my house. How lucky can a girl get?*

They sat together, watching the flames dancing in the fireplace. Somerled had slid his arm around her shoulders and was now playing with her hair.

'Hey,' he said. 'This is nice, isn't it?'

'The nicest,' she told him.

'Why did you leave Edinburgh?'

Unsure how to answer the question, she decided on, 'I got myself in a whole lot of trouble.'

Somerled sat up to look at her. 'Do you mean with the police?'

'No, of course not. Relationship trouble.'

He nodded. 'I get it. I presume that you don't want to talk about it.'

'Let's just say that I messed things up so badly that I had to leave and make a fresh start. I came here to learn to like myself again. I had planned to keep a low profile, you know, try not to upset people. The first person I met was you on the humpback bridge.'

He laughed at the memory. 'I thought you were an absolute nutcase when I met you on the bridge.'

'And now?' she asked.

'Jury's out.'

'Hopefully, I will prove to you that I am completely normal,' she told him. 'When I arrived here at first, I thought, what the hell have I done. But now, I like it here, and I have to say, life is never dull. I'm glad I came.'

'I'm glad you came too. Mull is a more exciting place with you in it.' He drew her close to him. Her head rested on his shoulder. The warmth of the fire could be felt in her cheeks. The music playing in the background was soothing.

Edina woke up sharply in the darkness. She was alone. Not even an ember remained in the fireplace. The tartan blanket from the back of the sofa covered her up to her chin. *What on earth is going on? What happened to the wonderful night we were having? Did Somerled just up and leave?*

Throwing the blanket from her body, she felt the chill of the room. She shivered. To her astonishment, the clock showed 3.45 am. As she stumbled her way to the staircase, she glanced at the dirty dishes in the sink, which had a centrepiece of the lasagne dish with its baked-on remnants. *Don't look, it will only upset you.*

Still wearing her make-up and saloon girl dress, she rattled her way under the duvet on her bed. Before she slept, a thought came to her mind, making her peer her head out from under the quilt. Good, the stars were out. This meant that she could tell her mum how wonderful Somerled was.

Chapter 34

In the morning, Edina opened her eyes with great difficulty. Memories of the previous night with Somerled invaded her thoughts immediately. The ending of the night was a dead zone. Did she say goodnight to him? She struggled to remember as she rubbed furiously at her mascara clogged eyes. No, she couldn't remember their parting, it wasn't vague, it just wasn't there. Rising from the lying position, she sat on the edge of her bed, looking down at her crumpled dress and black hold-up stockings around her ankles. She kicked the stockings off her feet, one by one before stumbling her way into the bathroom. The sight that faced her in the mirror was not a pleasant one. Black panda eyes, matted hair on one side and a mouth that resembled the Joker. *Oh dear, if Somerled could see me now. I look just like a zombie.* The state of her was almost funny. She straightened her legs, put her arms out in front of her, and made an undead moaning noise all the way to the bathroom.

Her shift didn't start for another hour, so she headed downstairs for breakfast and an indulgent think over the events of the previous night. Apart from the ending, it had been a perfect evening. Somerled was someone special, she believed, perhaps even put on the earth just for her. *On second thoughts, he's too good for me. What did I ever do in this life that earned me the gift of Somerled? Somerled. I love that name. Somerled, Somerled, Somerled. Wait a minute, the camera!*

On her mobile phone, she found the footage of the previous evening. Her heart double thumped as she saw

Somerled standing there in her house. Pressing the fast-forward button, she found the part where he stood up from the wing chair and came to sit beside her. The view was side-on, but she could see him laying his arm along the back of the sofa. It was adorable watching him twirling away at the ends of her hair. The orange glow from the fire was the only light, but she could see them both clearly. Then her head slumped onto Somerled's shoulder. Moving the film forward, she saw that he stayed beside her for nearly an hour. When she saw movement on the film, she began playing it again. She watched as he carefully positioned her head onto a cushion before covering her with the blanket. The next part was her favourite. He tucked the blanket tightly around her and then kissed her forehead. It was a most touching and tender scene. No one had treated her so considerately.

Before setting off for work, she rewound the film again to watch Somerled tucking her in. The smile soon dropped from her face when she looked into the background of the lounge. With her fingers she enlarged the film to get a better look. Yes, there he was, large as life… or death. Jeremy could clearly be seen standing in the shadows near the kitchen. *Was he standing there all night?* Glancing around the room, she wondered if he was there now. This problem needed to be solved sooner rather than later. Until then, she would have no privacy.

A text vibrated her phone. She clicked off the camera and onto the text.

Sorry I left you sleeping, but I didn't want to disturb you. I slipped away because I was due out on the boat at 6am this morning. I had a great time last night. How about we do it all over again tonight? T x

She texted him back immediately.

I had a great time too. I love that you are so keen, but let's make it tomorrow night. We'll ditch the dinner and just have drinks. E x

You're on. Same time, same place? Tx

Unless you've got a better idea.' E x

'How was your night?' Struan asked as she walked into the reception of the hotel.

'Oh, Struan, it was great. I really, really like him,' she said, avoiding the details of the abrupt end to the evening. 'Is Suzie in?' she asked, looking around.

Struan adopted a very stern-looking face. 'No, she didn't appear this morning and has given no explanation as to why she hasn't turned up. I'm furious. In fact, she is making things easy for me because if business doesn't pick up soon, I will have to choose a member of staff to let go. I can't believe she would let me down like this. She's probably just hungover. I don't know what I would do without Freddy. He's so reliable.' The rant finished just as the phone rang. 'Pennyghael House Hotel, Struan speaking. How can I help you?'

Edina walked away with a mix of emotions. On one hand, her stomach fluttered with the excitement of new love. On the other, she was uneasy about Suzie, as well as feeling deeply troubled for the future of the hotel.

Before she entered the kitchen, she could hear Freddy whistling away. *Thank goodness this place is not all doom and gloom.* The loud rumbling of the dishwasher meant that she could sneak up behind him without being heard.

'Hi Freddy,' she said, making him jump. 'I had a great time last night. How was your night?'

'Not good,' he said, shaking his head and screwing up his face. 'She was a very irritating person. She thought she was funny and literally honked with laughter at her own jokes, all night. Everything about her annoyed me. Oh, and she spat when she talked, and I didn't like how her mascara formed a sticky goo in the corner of her eyes.'

Edina laughed aloud. 'Don't hold back, Freddy, just tell me what you really think.'

'I have never been so glad to get home. I left early with the excuse that my dad needed me to work on a car with him. It was ten o'clock! She believed me, though, phew.'

'So when are you seeing her again?'

'Ha ha, very funny. The problem is that I told her that I would text her. If I don't text, then I'll become public enemy number one from her nasty group of henchwomen. They'll give me a dog's life. I really don't fancy walking into The Shell Seekers on Friday night to get heckled the way you did. No offence.'

'None taken. Just tell her that you are not ready for a relationship now, but it was great meeting her.'

Freddy stared at Edina. 'Hey, that's so good. I'm going to use that. Where do you learn all that clever stuff?'

'Just comes naturally, I guess.' She laughed.

Edina decided that it was necessary to follow the same routine as the previous day. So, after racing through her morning chores, she headed off in the car to check on Suzie. *I'm going to have to be firm with her this time. If she loses her job, she will have nothing. I will offer to take her to the housing department to fill in the application.*

Just like the previous day, she banged on the door several times. Again, no one answered. She peeked through the space under the grubby net curtains. Again, Suzie was sitting with her head in her hands. Her father was in the chair across from her. Edina knocked on the glass, startling Suzie, who then bolted towards the hallway.

Suzie stood at the door, looking at Edina. She was silent.

In Edina's opinion, Suzie looked unkempt, unclean, and unnaturally pale. Her hair was folded behind her ears, but Edina could see it hadn't been acquainted with shampoo in days.

'What is going on in there, Suzie? Let me in. I want to speak to your father.'

Tensions were now soaring within Edina, her blood pressure was up, her mind was filling with worst case scenarios. The state of this young girl was distressing, and the situation needed attending to, now. She had no intention of leaving it for one more day, one more hour, one more second. Pushing the door all the way open, she barged her way into the house. No resistance came from Suzie. Edina walked straight into the living room to face Suzie's father head on. This time there was no holding back.

Edina could not quite process what she was seeing before her. In the chair sat Suzie's father. His pallor was grey, and remnants of dried foam had crystallised around his mouth. He stared ahead, fixed on something. She didn't know what. The whites of his eyes had turned blood red. It became obvious to her that he had died some time ago. It was not a scene that would be easily erased from her memory. The putrid stench was not something that would leave her nostrils anytime soon.

Edina called the ambulance service before getting in contact with Struan. She then held Suzie in her arms. It was now obvious to her that Suzie's abnormal behaviour was borne out of shock from the event she had witnessed.

'I hated him.' Suzie sobbed on Edina's shoulder. 'I wished him dead every day. I sat in the little church along the road and prayed that God would take him. I wanted him to vanish off the face of the earth. I willed it to happen every minute of every day. Now it has. I'm not sorry that he's gone, but I know that it must have been me that did it. Surely, if you wish for something for long enough, it happens.'

Edina held her tightly. 'Of course, it wasn't you. It must have been his time. Our names are all up there on the big heavenly calendar. A day to be born, a day to die. It's the cycle of life. Don't feel guilty. None of this is your fault. You are free now to start afresh. We are all here for you.'

The ambulance drove up in front of the house. One of the paramedics headed straight in the open front door. The other, a young woman, came to speak to Suzie.

'Are you okay to tell me what happened?' she asked softly.

Suzie nodded.

Edina released her from her grip but placed a supportive arm around her narrow waist.

Suzie composed herself as she thought over the order of events leading up to her father's death. 'He was watching the television when I brought his dinner through to him. He took it and I walked away. He then shouted, *'Where the hell is the tomato sauce?'* I went to the kitchen to fetch it for him, and when I came back into the living room, I heard what sounded like an animal noise. I rushed over and saw that he was having a stroke or a seizure or something. It was horrible. He writhed and squirmed. Foam began appearing from his mouth, and I was terrified. His arms and legs jerked a few times, then it was over. He went still, but his eyes stayed open.'

'Thank you,' the paramedic said. 'I know this is not easy for you.' She then turned to Edina. 'Is there anywhere you can take her for a couple of days so she is not alone?'

Edina nodded. With an arm around Suzie to steady her, she led her to the car before the sheet covered body was brought out of the house on a stretcher.

There was a thought-filled silence in the car as Edina drove Suzie to the hotel, which had been Struan's suggestion. He had explained to Edina that there were currently plenty of spare bedrooms for her to sleep in until she recovered from the trauma.

In a rear-facing, single room in Pennyghael House, Edina ran Suzie a bath. She then gave her privacy by disappearing off to the kitchen to prepare something for her to eat. By Edina's calculations, Suzie's father could have been dead for anything up to three days. During that time, she guessed that Suzie hadn't slept or eaten.

When Suzie was tucked up in bed, Edina drew the heavy curtains shut.

'Do you want to talk about it or do you just want to sleep,' she asked.

There was silence. Suzie was already asleep.

Coming down the main staircase, Edina saw Struan and Freddy standing at the reception desk, deep in conversation. She joined them.

'Are you all right, Edina?' Struan asked. He admired the competent way she had handled a highly distressing situation.

'Yes, I'm fine. It's Suzie I'm worried about. She seems to think that she killed him because she has wished him dead for years. I would hate to see her carrying a burden of guilt over this for the rest of her life. It is actually a blessing for her that this has happened. I think the abuse she has suffered at her father's hands has been the root of her alcohol problem.'

Struan nodded in agreement. 'Maybe we'll see a different Suzie emerging over the next few weeks and months. All we can do is support her.'

'Okay, I'll start by going down to the kitchen to finish the washing. I'm actually quite enjoying doing Suzie's job,' Freddy said as he walked away, whistling.

Edina and Struan stood for a moment at the reception.

'Edina, thanks for dealing with this for Suzie and for all the support you've given Marnie. I'm glad you came to

Mull. No matter what happens with the hotel, I will try to find something for you here on the island.'
'Thanks Struan. You have no idea how much that means to me.' *I am so happy that I am liked. The old me didn't have a true friend in the world. I want so much to help Struan save the hotel. I'll think of a way to get the visitors through the door.*

Chapter 35

Driving home over the potholed road, an ironic thought entered Edina's head. *Now I can add staring into the red eyes of a corpse to my experiences in Mull. I have a friend who is being stalked by a violent ex-boyfriend and a ghost who appears to reside in my house at all times. Why did I think that island life would be boring? I never experienced anything like this in the city.*

Curled up in the wing chair, in her spotted pyjamas, Edina picked up her journal and began writing her daily entry. She described the little figure standing in the background of the CCTV camera film.

'Jeremy, I just want you to know that I am writing about you in my journal. There is a lot going on in my life at the moment, but I will never forget about you,' she promised aloud. This was done for both Jeremy and her own sake. She couldn't cope with her house been trashed again.

When she had finished writing, she began reading over everything she had written since the beginning. It read like a novel, which made her feel proud of her ability to write well. *I must have been about eight when my teacher read my work to the class and told me that I was a good writer. I was so proud. If memory serves me correctly, I was commended for my writing every year until I left.* Her thoughts drifted back to her school days when she founded the school magazine. A smile spread across her lips as she remembered the seriousness with which she took the whole venture. *What were some of the articles I included in my magazine?* She tried to recall. *Oh yes, I took a hot topic each month and asked the teachers to give their opinions on it.* She laughed, thinking about how she interviewed the head teacher with her post. *Everything you wanted to know about Mr Simpson but were too scared to ask.*

I think I asked him about his favourite film, book and song. Then, I tried to make it a little edgier by asking him if he ever got in trouble at school. He answered, 'No comment'. I also think I asked him what he was scared of and if there was any other job he wanted to do other than being the head of a school. He said he wanted to be a pilot but had a fear of flying. Ha, that was a good answer.

She suddenly remembered.

Billy Robertson. I hired him to help m; well when I say hired, I didn't actually pay him, just bossed him around. He took photographs and wrote about all the sports fixtures. I was never interested in that kind of stuff. Did I ever mention Billy Robertson in the magazine for all of his hard work? No, I don't think I ever did. Maybe I'll track him down on social media and thank him someday.

A memory from those times returned to her unexpectedly. She hadn't thought about June Smith in years, yet now she was turning up in her recollections. Perhaps she had deliberately pushed all thoughts of June out of her head for good. But, the mind had a funny way of churning up unwanted memories when you least expected it, as she well knew. She recalled what happened when June had approached her asking if she could come on board with the magazine. *I told her absolutely not. I was so unwilling to share the glory with anyone else, and yet, looking back, the project would have benefitted from an extra pair of hands and opinions. I remember walking away from her. She had shouted after me that she had a really good idea and that she had written out a plan for it.*

Edina's memory transported her back to the playground, where she turned around with interest on hearing June shout this. New ideas were becoming scarce, so she was curious to hear what she had to say.

I remember loving June's proposal for an anonymous agony aunt. What was it again? Pupils posted their problems in a box in the main hall of the school. The agony aunt chose ten to answer each month. Replies were written up in the middle pages of the magazine. From what the kids told me back then, most of them liked this problem page more than any other item. It was such a success. I even wrote the problems myself if I didn't get enough interesting ones.

Edina became uncomfortable thinking back to this time. The unleashed memories acted as a mirror, reflecting the ugliness of her character. Was she going to be forever reminded of her selfish acts towards people throughout her life? Perhaps, she needed to face the past before she could completely morph into a better version of herself.

I told June that I liked her idea and that I would be in touch. I never was. I became 'Cathy Cares' and took the credit for her idea. Why didn't I let her get involved? I was so tired of writing all the articles and answering all the problems myself. I think that was why my exam results suffered. June must have felt so betrayed. Maybe one day I will track her down and apologise.

Shortly after the betrayal of June, she remembered, a new head teacher was appointed. His name was Mr Coyle-

Brackenridge, and he did not approve of letting children write their own material. The magazine continued, but it was under the leadership of the school's English department.

The crystal clear recollection of events surprised Edina. Was everyone visited by ghosts of their selfish past or just her, she wondered. How about Suzie's father? Did his crimes flash in front of him before he died?

Lying her journal on the table, she then took her phone out to search through her photos of Jeremy on that first day she arrived. The photo of the dark shadow standing at the tower's window was a mystery to her. There didn't appear to be a door to the tower anywhere. No way in, no way out, so why would there be a small window? Her mind began mapping out the location of the tower. Its circular walls protruded into the corner of the dining room, but no door was there. The bedroom upstairs that no one wanted to sleep in also hosted the tower, but again, there was no door. The tower did not lead into the attic because it narrowed into a turret, which stood adjacent to the house's roof. There must have been a door for the tower at some point in history. Otherwise, there would be no purpose for the window.

This might be something, or it may be nothing, but I think that I will try to find out about this. I will try to speak to Stan.

A text came through Edina's phone.

What time will I come calling tomorrow? Can I bring anything? I know I'm not the most interesting guy in the world, but could you make an effort to stay awake this time? You've really knocked my confidence! T x

Why don't we go out? I've heard that there is a nice seafood place in Tobermory called Clam Rock. That will help me resist the temptation to sleep. E x

Great idea, I'll pick you up at eight. Don't wear anything embarrassing! T x

Just for your cheek, I will! I'll look forward to it. E x

As sleep began to pull her in, she heard a noise coming from downstairs. She was too exhausted to be afraid. Noises occurred so often in the house she was becoming quite comfortable with them. Old houses take a while to settle at night, as did ghosts.

Chapter 36

When Edina awoke the following morning one thought was firmly planted in her mind, Somerled. Tonight they were going out together in Tobermory. With a population of a few thousand, it really felt like she was entering real civilisation for the first time since she arrived. Lying on her back on her pillow, she slipped her hands behind her head. Somerled, Somerled, even his name excited her. Images of his wide smile, his ruffled hair and the way he made a joke without smiling, filled her thoughts. *What am I feeling here? Is this why people say love is a drug? I feel ecstatic, high, abnormally happy. I can't believe this fantastic man seems to feel the same about me. Don't spoil it, Edina, please don't spoil it, you tend to ruin everything.*

Reaching for her dressing gown from the peg on the back of the bedroom door, she slipped it on as she headed downstairs in a quest for tea. She poured the boiling water from the whistling kettle into the china teapot. Whether the key factor was the island water, the teapot or the whistling kettle, she had no idea, all she knew was the combination made the tea taste better. Mull had turned her into a self-confessed tea Jenny and she wasn't ashamed to admit it. Perhaps life in Edinburgh was too full on to take time over such trivial things. Edina found that she was now walking more in step with life around her, especially now that she was slowly letting go of the memories that tied her to the mainland. No longer was she making unfavourable comparisons between life now and then. Most days, the bright lights of Edinburgh did not enter her thoughts.

The journal caught her eye when she entered the lounge carrying her tea. It had changed its location from where she left it. *Oh, oh, something's afoot.* She expected the worst as she looked around the room. No, nothing was touched except the journal, which now sat neatly on the chair. It had not been torn or scribbled on, but on closer inspection, she saw that on the first blank page, there was a picture that had not been drawn by her. The infantile picture depicted a long tube with a square in the centre. *Mysterious!* She stared at it for answers.

'What are you telling me here, Jeremy?' she said aloud, turning the page around to inspect the tube from a different angle.

I wonder if last night's events are on the CCTV film?

She took her phone from her dressing gown pocket. The footage showed Edina sitting on her chair, writing her journal. Pausing the footage for a moment, she checked for anything untoward in the background. Yes, there he was, over by the sideboard. Playing the film again, she saw herself talking into the room. Of course, she knew that this was her asking Jeremy questions. The following section was of her sitting staring into space. This lasted a lengthier time than she remembered.

I must have been thinking about the school magazine at this point and how I steamrollered over June Smith. After that, I looked at the photos of Jeremy and the tower. That's it! It's the tower. Jeremy has drawn the tower. The tower is a long tube with a square window. Oh, my goodness, I reckon that Jeremy and his mother might be bricked in behind the tower walls.

The film played on, showing her laying the journal on the sideboard before heading to bed.

Nothing happened for several minutes. Jeremy then entered the frame from the shadows. Dressed in black and wearing a tall hat, he walked over to the sideboard. Stretching up on tiptoes, he reached for the journal, taking it to the coffee table.

I actually don't believe what I am seeing here.

She was effectively watching a dead child doing an earthly task. In astonishment, she watched the boy carefully drawing on the page. He then took the book and placed it on her chair.

Edina sat back, processing what she had just witnessed with her own eyes and the connotations of the drawing. Over the decades, she wondered how many people Jeremy had tried to alert to his plight? The fact that she was in the same cottage that he had resided in with his mother and the added bonus of her being an investigative journalist, made her a prime candidate to solve the mystery. She may never have listened and understood had her life not been so isolated. *How many opportunities or cries for help do we miss by being caught up in the chaos of life,* she wondered.

The dilemma facing her now was, what could she do about the revelation she had uncovered.

Chapter 37

It was no good. Edina couldn't settle. She had to head to work early. This newfound discovery needed to be shared with Stan. He would soon tell her if she were getting carried away with an outlandish idea.

The driveway up to the hotel snaked and turned. Its manicured lawns followed. Edina searched out of every window in the car for Stan as she drove. By not keeping her eyes on the road, she veered onto the grass several times, leaving tyre gouges as a reminder.

Where is he?

Slowly, she drove to the top of the hill until she reached the hotel. *Great! There he is.* All she could see was his bent back at the front door. *What is he doing? Oh yes, I think he is scraping the moss from the steps.*

She abandoned her haphazardly parked vehicle and ran to where Stan was working.

'Stan, Stan, I've got news, big news!' she shouted.

Stan immediately put down the trowel he was using, then attempted to straighten his aching spine.

'All right, lass, let's hear it.'

'I don't know where to start,' she said, flustered.

'Maybe the beginning would be a good place.'

Stan took her by the arm, walking her to a bench on the lawn opposite the hotel.

'Sit down, lass, and get your thoughts all together.'

Edina began. 'I got a book from the mobile library. It is a history of Pennyghael through the eyes of a local woman who lived many years ago. She and her sister both worked at Pennyghael House. There was nothing relevant in the first few chapters, and then she talked about a boy called Jeremy who lived in the cottage… my cottage, on the grounds. From what I can tell, the master of Pennyghael had an affair with a young scullery maid, which resulted in getting her pregnant. Jeremy, my ghost Jeremy, is the son from this relationship. The master of the house gave them the cottage to live in. Anyway, I'll get to the point, Stan. The maid appears to have threatened to tell everyone about the affair, and the master was furious. An argument was heard by the staff. The following day, both boy and mother were gone, apparently on a boat to Ireland. No goodbyes, no sightings of them leaving, nothing.'

Stan sighed heavily, sitting up straight against the back of the bench. 'Wow! You really have done your homework. That is quite a story, Edina.'

'I'm not finished. In one of the photos…' She rummaged in her bag to find her phone. 'Here, look, I think that is Jeremy at the tower's window. I have discovered no door into the tower, so why is there a window?'

'Good point, but eh, what is your point?'

'Last night, the boy drew a picture in my journal of a tube with a square in it. I think it's the tower. I think he has drawn the tower. I believe he and his mother, Lottie, are bricked up in the tower.'

Stan digested the information that Edina had related to him.

'What do you think, Stan?'

He turned slowly to face her. 'I say we fetch the sledgehammer, and we'll soon see if you're right. I can fix any damage.'

Her eyes widened as she stared at him in a eureka, lightbulb, penny-dropping moment, then said, 'No, not yet, Stan. I have just had the most incredible idea. I'll get back to you later about the sledgehammer!'

'I'll be waiting,' he said, as he watched her run off into the hotel.

Bursting through the main door, Edina could hardly breathe with excitement. *I need to talk to Struan. I have to tell him that everything is going to be okay.*

On her way to the dining room, she passed Suzie.

'Suzie! You look great. I'm so happy to see you up and about. How are you feeling?'

'A lot better than I did yesterday. Thanks for everything.'

'It was nothing. Listen, we'll talk later. I need to speak to Struan. Have you seen him?'

'Yes, he's in the bar. Are you going to The Shell Seekers tomorrow night?'

'Suzie, that's a dumb question,' she joked. 'Of course, what else would I be doing?'

Struan was indeed in the bar, stocking up on soft drinks.

'Struan, we really need to talk,' Edina announced with such authority that Struan immediately stopped what he was doing.

'It would take too long to explain it right now, but I think I have thought of a way to get this hotel on the map so that everyone will be talking about it. It will be a gamble, but I am so hopeful about this if you just trust me.' Her heart was thudding in her chest cavity, her hands shook.

'Edina, I don't have a clue what you're talking about.' Struan was clearly bewildered by her proposition. 'The only thing that could boost trade for us is advertising, and I'm afraid the well has run dry for any extra costs.'

'That's the whole point, Struan. I have found a way to get everyone talking about Pennyghael House Hotel. I think we could have this place full very soon. We will sit down and talk about it later. I will explain everything.'

Accompanied by her faithful friend, the industrial hoover, Edina headed upstairs to clean the two rooms that had been slept in. Business really was slow, considering it was the peak season. Still, if Edina could pull off her idea, who knew what bounty it would bring forth.

In the upstairs hallway, she passed the door to the tower room and contemplated whether or not to enter. Deep down, she was looking for confirmation, a sign of some kind, telling her she was right. *Of course, I'm right. There are too many coincidences and too many unanswered questions.*

With an air of conviction, she turned the handle, opening the door wide. Just as a precaution, she sat her industrial companion down against the door. The room would feel more comfortable with the door wedged open.

The temperature drop was the most obvious feature of something not being right. Edina wrapped her arms around herself, shivering. She moved to the centre of the room where she stood motionless, waiting. The atmosphere felt wrong, but how would she explain that in her journal.

Apart from being cold, what do I feel here? How can I describe this abnormal sensation I am feeling? Heavy, bad, repellent? Yes, all of these things.

There was complete silence around her. She walked over to the tower, placing her hands on the stone wall. The quiet stillness disappointed her. She half expected cries for help or a voice saying, 'We're here', but there was nothing.

What if I'm wrong about Jeremy being in the tower? I'm not wrong. I'm positive that I am right, I think.

'Jeremy, are you in there?' she said to the wall.

No sound returned to her, not even a rustle or a scratching.

Chapter 38

Struan told Edina she could leave early because there were no hotel residents.

'I am very interested to hear what you've got to say about getting the business booming though,' he said as she was leaving. 'Do you want to stay on and talk to me about it?'

'Struan, I'd love to, but I am going home to get the wheels in motion right now. Strike when the iron's hot, as they say. I also have a date with Tom tonight, and I have to look my best for that. I promise I won't keep you hanging on. We'll talk tomorrow.'

Back at the house, she searched through her contact details for her old friend, Pip Paterson. They had worked together on a project some years ago, which had become lucrative for both of them. *How did I meet Pip?* She tried to remember as her mind drifted back to her first contact with him.

It had been her early days as a journalist when she was always looking for a story. On this particular day, she had stopped at a large charity shop in Edinburgh which often sold designer clothes donated by the wealthy residents of the area. Whilst browsing, she was faced with what she believed was a suspicious situation. A woman wearing a tailored suit was searching purposefully through the rail of second-hand dresses. On closer inspection, Edina noticed that she chose a variety of sizes, however, the common theme of their style was short and strappy. Looking back, it had been a long shot to conjure up dubious motives for this woman's purchases. After all, the woman could have been selling them on for a lucrative price. But Edina had smelt a story and like a bloodhound, she was hungry to follow it to see where it would lead, even if it turned out to be a dead end.

At the check-out, Edina could hear that the woman spoke very little English. She made no eye contact with the assistant. Before Edina followed her in the car, she attempted to analyse why a woman approaching fifty would have bought around twenty-five skimpy, some even sparkly, dresses in sizes 8 to 14. There was no logical explanation that she could settle on, so, keeping two cars behind, she tailed her.

At around 2.30pm the woman entered a house on the outskirts of Edinburgh. Edina sat across the street in her car, watching for any unusual activity. After all, she had nothing better to do in those days.

Over the course of a week, Edina returned every day to stake out the property. She wrote down everything she saw, filling her journal with descriptions of girls in their early teens, number plates of male visitors to the establishment, and even photos of the men who seemed to be in charge. This innocent-looking house in the suburbs was a hive of comings and goings, and Edina saw it all.

Going to the police first would have been the obvious answer, but not for Edina. She had read an article in a magazine about Pip Paterson, the documentary maker. This story was too good to give up to a police raid. In short, Pip and Edina worked together on a three-part documentary which involved undercover work, secret filming, police involvement, and finally, the prosecutions. The series won three awards and was aired on national and international television stations. Pip and Edina had remained firm friends ever since.

Pip's number rang until the answering machine told Edina to leave a message.

'Hi Pip, this is Edina. As you may or may not know, I live on the Island of Mull. I have a very exciting project for you if you are interested. If you want to come on board, call me back.'

Pip will be curious, he'll call. Adrenalin ran through her veins.

I never get a buzz like this from Mr Sheen or the industrial vacuum cleaner… funny that.

Contrary to her threat to Somerled, Edina did not wear anything embarrassing for their date. Jeans, a white shirt, and a blazer were as outrageous as she would get. Her hair lay loose on her shoulders, her make-up was minimal, and after checking with the mirror that all was well with her ensemble, she sat down with a notepad and pen. With one ear listening for car tyres on the gravel outside, she began scribbling down a rough plan for her documentary proposal. Using the journal, photos from her phone, Catriona's book, footage from the CCTV cameras, and the clues from Jeremy himself, she was sure they could put together an intriguing documentary to get people talking. The last episode would be the grand reveal when the wall of the tower would be knocked through to find the remains of Jeremy and Lottie. What a finale. *That's providing Jeremy and Lottie are in there. It's an embarrassing damp squib if they're not. Stop it, Edina, think positive.*

The sound of Somerled's car arriving interrupted the room's stillness. Edina tossed her notebook to one side and rose to her feet. Her hands shook with excitement and possibly nerves. The front door was opened wide before Somerled had time to leave the car. Edina stood smiling as he walked towards her. *He is gorgeous, perhaps too gorgeous. No, you can't get too gorgeous.*

'Hello, beautiful,' he said, beaming.

'Hello, handsome,' she replied right back.

'Are you ready?'

'I was born ready,' she told him, grabbing her jacket. *Oh, that was a corny line. Stop trying too hard, Edina.*

Somerled drove through the gate onto the seriously depressed road. The wheels of his car hit one, two, three craters.

'Slow down,' Edina told him. 'Be gentle. Respect the potholes by manoeuvring around them.'

'I'm starting to wonder whether I can keep dating a girl that lives down this kind of road. It's going to end up ripping the backside out of my car. You need a moon buggy to get over this.'

'On the way back, I'll drive. I will give you a masterclass on how to handle this road. I won't hit one single pothole.'

'Okay, you're on. Let's take bets on it.'

On the way to Tobermory, Somerled gave Edina a detailed account of a fisherman's life. Never would she have imagined that she would be so captivated by his tales of the sea.

'So, you see, when the water is calm and the sun is shining, it could be described as the perfect job. I don't particularly want to be a fisherman, but somehow, when you spend a lot of time at sea, it becomes difficult to accept a job on land, if that makes sense. '

Edina was captivated. 'Do you ever see any dolphins when you are out?'

'Yes, often, but today I saw several minke whales.'

'I've never even heard of minke whales. What do they look like?' she asked, genuinely interested.

'Well, they have a really sleek shape, and their backs are grey, their underside is white. You can identify them easily by the white band on the outer part of their pectoral flippers.'

Edina laughed. 'That is a very detailed description. I will certainly recognise one if I see it.'

As they talked, Somerled reached over very naturally and took Edina's hand.

She loved it.

In the picturesque harbour in Tobermory, Somerled drove to the car park at the back of Clam Rock. Again, he reached for her hand as they walked together to the restaurant door.

Edina could not believe how bustling the town was, considering it was after seven o'clock. Memories of her first trip to Tobermory entered her head. It had been like a ghost town that Sunday when she came to do her shopping, unaware that everything closed down on the Sabbath. She marvelled at the promenade of tourists photographing the iconic, coloured houses along the street. A smile of happiness appeared unexpectedly on her lips as she felt the last rays of the evening sun on her face and heard the laughter of children from the nearby swing park. Feeling Somerled's strong hand in hers was the most wonderful thing she could ever imagine.

I don't ever want to let go. I will remember this moment forever.

The restaurant owner showed them to their table at the window. The view couldn't have been better as it overlooked the pier. The low evening sun shone on the colourful fronted houses with the deep grey of the sky behind them making a perfect backdrop. In the foreground, the yachts in the harbour swayed to the rhythm of the lapping waves. It really was the perfect scene. *I am going to store this memory away for a rainy day when I'm feeling alone.*

They were talking and laughing when their food arrived. The conversation flowed without effort. During conversation, it became apparent that they liked many of the same things. Musicians, films, comedians, countries, and foods.

Somerled suddenly put down his knife and fork saying, 'I almost forgot. I've got something for you.'

'How exciting,' she said, watching him search through the pockets of his jacket.

With his hand clasped tightly in a fist, he said, 'Shut your eyes and hold out your hand.'

Edina did as she was told.

Into the open palm of her hand, he placed a shark's tooth on a leather thong.

'I made this for you. You probably think that's a bit lame, but this tooth is rare, and it's thought to bring good luck.'

'Somerled, I don't think it's lame at all. I think it's fantastic. Where did you get it?'

'I found it in some seaweed that was caught up in our nets. Believe it or not, it is from a great white shark. I read that occasionally the gulf stream and the seal colonies can attract Great Whites out of their natural habitats and into Scottish waters.'

'I love it,' she told him, tying the leather thong around her neck. 'It's great that it will bring me good luck. I've never needed it more.'

Edina's phone rang from within her handbag on the seat next to her. Pip's name appeared on the screen.

'I am so sorry, but I have to take this. It's important,' she explained.

Accepting the call, she smiled as she said, 'Hi Pip. I had a sneaking suspicion you'd call.'

'So, you're still chasing a story then, Edina?' Pip laughed.

'Actually, no, this story chased me.'

'Sounds intriguing,' he said in an exaggerated mysterious voice . 'Are you going to tell me about it?'

'No, just come over, and I will explain everything. Trust me, Pip, this will be the best thing we've done yet.'

'I'm off for a few days a week on Monday if that's any good.'

'Perfect. Give me the details of your ferry, and I will be there to pick you up.'

'Great. Good talking to you, Edina. I've missed you.'

She didn't know quite how to answer this statement, so she settled on, 'See you next week.'

Somerled only heard Edina's side of the conversation. It had been impossible to tell whether Pip was a male or female. He decided to do a little fishing of a different kind. 'Is your friend coming to Mull?'

'Yes, he's coming over on Monday for a few days.'

She was reluctant to discuss the documentary idea with him in these early stages. It wouldn't have been right to speak of it until she had first talked it over with Struan.

Sadly for Somerled, he heard the word he had fished for. He.

By the time they left the restaurant, the stars were out and the evening had turned chilly.

Knowing that he had no right to feel pangs of jealousy, Somerled tried to reason things out in his head. The car journey home was silent, but he still reached for her hand. Deep down, he felt that she was out of his league. Why would a high-flying city girl who sang like an angel settle for an island fisherman? He could only hope that she would look beyond all of that and see him as a worthy contender for her future.

They turned left on onto the pot-holed road which led to Edina's house.

'Stop the car!' she shouted. 'Move over.'

Using her full concentration, she drove ever so cautiously, avoiding all the dents and craters. On that short journey, she managed to make the road under them feel like it had been resurfaced. Out of the corner of her eye, she could see the look of awe on Somerled's face. As she pulled into the parking space outside her house, she turned to him, saying, 'Voila.'

'Amazing!' he told her, giving her a short applause. 'In fact, quite unbelievable.'

Edina freed up the driver's seat for him to get in. As he passed her at the car door, she began insulting his driving skills. Before she knew it, she was in his arms, passionately kissing. His hand lay in the small of her back, pulling her in closer and closer to him. Had she wanted to get away, she couldn't have. He kissed deeper, exploring further with his tongue. It became obvious that he was aroused but he wasn't the only one.

'Do you want to come in?' she breathed.

'Desperately, but I am out on the boat in four hours and don't want this to be rushed. I want to sleep beside you and see your face first thing in the morning. I want it to be just right.'

She had never felt so worthy.

'I have the noisiest metal bedframe on a single bed, so you may have been a little disappointed,' she laughed, trying desperately to compose herself from the kiss.

'I could not be disappointed with anything about you.'

He hugged her tight, then left.

Chapter 39

Marnie was awakened by the click of the letter box. Glancing at the time on her phone beside her bed, she saw it was 8.45 am. It had been a late night in The Shell Seekers. A group of holidaymakers from America had been having a wonderful time in the bar, sampling all the Scottish whiskies. She had decided that it was in the bar's best interest to let them stay a little later than her licence allowed. The evening's takings had been bountiful for a weeknight and she couldn't wait to tell Struan. With a yawn and a stretch, she sat on her bed, searching with her feet for her slippers. Feeling a little groggy, she descended the stairs one step at a time.

'Oh no!' she cried aloud, recognising the letter on the floor at the door.

It was an A5 brown business envelope, the same kind as before. There was no stamp as it had been hand-delivered, as always. The first thing she did was to inhale the scent of it, exactly the way Edina had done with the last one. The odour on the letter was of aftershave, but it wasn't one that she recognised. Carefully, she slid her finger under the seal, then pulled out the piece of paper, which felt stiff with glue. It read:

I AM NEVER FAR AWAY FROM YOU. I SEE EVERYTHING
THERE IS ONLY A SHORT TIME LEFT TO MAKE IT RIGHT

Marnie stared at the blend of upper and lower case letters that had been so carefully stuck on to make the words. The reasoning behind this method baffled her. Anonymity was certainly a factor, disguising his handwriting another, but she suspected that he had seen this method of communication in a film, perhaps the story of a serial killer. Regardless of his motives, it was menacing and highly disturbing. *Where on earth could he be living? He was always so obsessive about his cleanliness, so he couldn't be sleeping rough. I don't think he knows anyone in Mull, so it would have to be a hotel, guest house, holiday home, or perhaps the caravan site.*

As far as Marnie was concerned, enough was enough, it was now time to take things into her own hands and go out looking for him. Just like they say in the movies, the hunter will become the hunted.

Ashton Brook was fairly well-known as a footballer or rather as a shamed footballer. His face had been flaunted over the front pages of countless newspapers, with the headline 'Thug'. Surely someone would have seen him in a bar or restaurant. It would be the talk of the island if there was a so-called celebrity in town.

I deleted all the photos of him from my phone, but there is bound to be one that I can get from the internet. I can take it around the tourist accommodation hotspots and ask if anyone has seen him.

The moment she lifted her phone to Google images of Ashton Brook, a revelation hit her, head on. The CCTV camera outside! Of course. It would have captured him walking up to the door and posting the letter.

Marnie sat down to view the footage. It showed a hooded figure coming out from the trees across from the bar. It was frightening to watch. Marnie braced herself. The man was well covered, and his actions were furtive. Firstly, he looked in the direction of the road to ensure the coast was clear, he then looked up at Marnie's bedroom window before walking around to the back door. When the delivery had been made, he did not return to the trees but walked casually down the road.

Marnie played the film back. The figure was wearing a dark-coloured hoodie. The hood was pulled down so far it concealed practically his whole face.

Is this guy tall enough to be Ashton?

It was very difficult to tell the height of the intruder from a film. She studied every detail closely. How chilling it was to see, on screen, the person who had caused her so much fear and anguish over the past few months. Rewinding the film several times, she hoped to catch a glimpse of a nose or chin. Ashton had chiselled features, and his profile was distinct. The truth of the matter was that there was nothing conclusive from the footage. She found herself no further forward than she had been without the cameras. There was one suspect back at the beginning and there remained one suspect now, her ex-boyfriend Ashton Brook.

I've had enough of waiting for him to pounce. He probably watched the engineers setting up the cameras. He will be laughing at me right now. I am going to end this, starting today. I'll go to the caravan site on the other side of town.

Without showering or brushing her hair, she dressed, grabbed her car keys and headed off to smoke out Ashton Brook.

Chapter 40

Suzie stood at the foot of the stairs in the echoingly empty house she had grown up in. Try as she might, she could not conjure up sadness for losing her father. He was dead, and she was glad. She was free from his temper and no longer had to endure his advances. The nightmare was over. It began when she was thirteen and continued until she was twenty-two. He was never coming back except perhaps in her darkest dreams. His revolting demise reflected the sordid nature of what his life had become.

He hadn't taken it well when she announced that she was leaving him for good. Edina had given her hope that she could be free to start a new life, which gave her the confidence to stand up to him. The idea of the council giving her a flat, far away from her abuser, was the first ray of hope she had ever known. Until that point, he had only witnessed the meek side of her nature, which was generally anaesthetised by alcohol. As expected, his first reaction was to lash out at her, but she had stared him in the eye, shouting, 'Go on, enjoy yourself because when I am gone, you will have no one left to beat on!'

Her words seemed to have an effect on him. They made him stop. To her surprise, he had flopped down in his chair, sobbing into his hands. What a pitiful sight he had been, but she did not feel the slightest grain of sympathy for him.

Suzie sat on the stairs thinking back to the dreadful day when Edina shared with her the news that it would be a long time before the council could help her. Her newfound wall of confidence began to crumble around her, stone by stone. After work that evening, she stopped at the grocers on the way home to rekindle the relationship with her confidante, Mr Smirnoff. How could she have been so gullible to believe that the council would say, 'Is your daddy not being nice to you? What a shame, here are the keys to a lovely flat of your own. Have a nice life.' The problem now facing her was that life would be even more intolerable, if that were possible. Her father would be armed with the knowledge that she had nowhere else to go. There would be no mercy shown, not that there ever was.

Standing there alone in the house filled with only unbearable memories, she forced herself to think positively.

It's not where I would choose to live, but it's mine now, and it's all I've got. I now have to get rid of all the evidence that my father ever existed. Then I can turn it into home. I'm sure I can.

There was an easy rule to follow in deciding the fate of the furniture in the house; everything must go. Keeping only her bed and the chest of drawers that housed the few items of clothing she possessed, she hurled anything she could carry onto the front grass. Her intention was to burn the bloody lot. A celebratory cremation of her father's passing. A cleansing of the house as well as his memory.

The last room she entered was her father's. Her choice would have been never to step foot through that door again as it had been the epicentre of her suffering, but some things needed to be faced. On opening the door, she was met with her father's smell. Sweat, alcohol, cigarette smoke, and an odour that she could never identify. It was simply him.

Pulling the neck of her sweatshirt up over her nose, she grimaced as she dragged the sheets from the bed, stuffing them into a black bin liner. She gagged. The mattress was a world map of stains, but she kept her eyes averted. Then taking hold of the side handle, she heaved the dead weight across the room and into the hall. At the top of the stairs, she flipped the mattress head over end down to the hallway below.

Under the criss-cross wires of the bed frame, Suzie saw a dust-covered shoebox. Afraid of what she may find within it, she decided to deal with the bed before taking a closer look. In the same manner as she had dealt with the mattress, she dragged the rickety frame to the top of the stairs before launching it overboard.

Back in the bedroom, she stared down at the shoebox, which now sat exposed on the threadbare carpet. Removing her cardigan from around her waist, she laid it on the floor to use as a mat. She sat cross-legged on it with the box in her hands, pondering what the contents could be.

To her astonishment, when she removed the lid, she saw that the box contained memorabilia of her father's life. Among the train tickets and concert programs, she found a menu card with the meal choices at his wedding to her mother. The photos were difficult to look at as Suzie saw herself in her mother's arms. Her beautiful, smiling mum, so proud.

If only she knew how things turned out after she died. He was supposed to look after me. I'm sure that he probably vowed to her that he would. We were all badly let down by him.

Digging deeper into the box, she found strips of photos from a booth. The teenage faces of her parents looked back at her. They had once been young and in love. It was difficult now to imagine. A plastic strip lay curled up in the corner of the box. Suzie reached in and unfurled it. A sharp pain stabbed at her heart when she saw that it was her mum's hospital band that must have been removed after her death.

A canvas pouch with a drawstring caught her attention. Loosening the ties, she pulled out what she could now see was a tightly packed wad of cash. She peeled off two or three notes, which all had £50 printed on them. There had to be thousands of pounds there, she realised. It was incomprehensible that her father could have saved that kind of money.

Why did he take almost all of my wages? Why was the house a rundown dump? Why was every day a struggle? What was he saving for?

Tears turned to cries, which developed into racking sobs.

The selfish old bastard.

Chapter 41

When Edina closed her eyes, she could see Somerled on his fishing boat, far out at sea. The water around the vessel was calm, like glass. Keeping her eyes shut tight, she added minke whales to her image. They were performing somersaults all around the boat, white underbelly visible.

I don't even know if minke whales can do acrobatics, but it's a nice thought, so I'll just leave them there in the image.

The smile that appeared on her lips brought with it a gleeful giggle. This man in her life was beyond her wildest expectations.

Memories of the previous night returned to her thoughts as she lay in bed contemplating getting up.

He didn't want quick sex with me last night. If truth be told, after that kiss at the front door, I would have taken any kind of sex, but I can't believe he wanted to wait until everything was perfect. No one has ever said anything like that to me before. If only he knew how low I set my bar in the past.

She lay back with her hands behind her head.

He looked so gorgeous in that shirt he wore and the smell of him. Damn it! I promised Struan I would go to the hotel early to tell him about the rescue idea.

With an exaggerated movement, she leapt out of her bed and stood for a moment in the stance of a surfer. This was done for no particular reason other than the fact that she was really happy.

Whilst drinking her tea, she grabbed her journal, Catriona MacLeod's book, and her car keys. The morning was fresh, and the air held the scent of Scots pines. She stood momentarily, inhaling the smell of summer on Mull. It was wonderful.

The car park at the hotel was deserted. Edina weighed up which parking place she should take to make the place look the busiest.

Hopefully one day soon, this carpark will be impossible to get parked in. Stan will need to build an overflow.

Struan was at the reception desk when she ran through the front door.

'It's about time!' he told her.

'Struan, I'm early, not late.'

'I know, but I was excited to hear what you've got to say for yourself. Follow me.'

Suzie appeared from the direction of the kitchen, 'Hi, Edina.'

'Hi, how are you feeling?' Edina asked her.

'Good, very good.'

Struan looked at the two of them. 'Never mind that. Suzie, could you bring us both a cup of coffee, and then you could keep an eye on the desk for me.'

Struan led Edina into the residents' lounge. He shut the door, then pointed an instruction for Edina to sit down.

'Okay, tell me your plans,' he said, leaning forward.

Edina produced from her bag the journal, her phone containing the photos and CCTV footage, and the historical novel from the mobile library.

A curious frown adorned Struan's face.

She laid her evidence out on the floor in front of her.

'Now, Struan, I'm going to take you back to the first day I arrived at Pennyghael House. Don't say a word until I'm finished. Oh, and keep an open mind.'

Struan stayed silent, hands on his knees, unsure what to expect.

When Edina was finished unfolding the story with the evidence to back it up, she read from Catriona's book, starting with the fire.

'I know this sounds extremely cheesy, but I have this notion that the boy, Jeremy, helped save the house once, and he will do it again. I am almost positive that he and his mother are bricked in behind the wall of the tower.'

'Can I interrupt for a moment?'

'Yes,' she told him reluctantly. 'Make it quick.'

'It's an incredible story, and strangely, I kind of believe it, but how does this help us?'

Edina sat back in the chair. 'I have been in touch with a good friend of mine, Pip Patterson. He is a highly acclaimed documentary maker. He is coming over with a couple of colleagues to see if the story has possibilities. If it goes how I think it will, Pennyghael House could become the most visited place in Scotland. People love stories of intrigue. No more advertising, no more promotions, we will be fully booked all year round.'

'Man, that's quite a story and a hell of a prediction. Here's me thinking you would suggest live music a couple of nights a week.'

Edina laughed.

'Wait a minute,' Struan suddenly thought. 'What if the bodies are not behind the wall?'

'Don't spoil it. Of course they are,' she told him. 'And, if Pip decides to run with it, he'll bring his whole crew. Guess where they'll be staying while they are working? Yes, here, as paying guests. So what do you think?'

Struan ran his fingers through his hair.

'I think it is an ingenious plan. I had no idea that anything like this was going on under my nose. I am questioning whether I want the hotel to be known for its haunted experiences. But then I think it's better to be fully booked for ghostly reasons than to have to shut the doors for good.'

'Don't worry, Struan, the story will reveal that the haunting mystery was solved and peace was restored. I wouldn't let them promote the hotel as a haunted house. There is a story to be told and a conclusion to be reached. It's a safe gamble, if there is such a thing.'

She smiled, as she could see Struan was almost as invested in the project as she was. Now all she had to do was to convince Pip.

Chapter 42

Marnie drove along the island's coastal road, looking for the turning to take her to the caravan site. The panoramic view of the ocean on her right was a feast to the eye, with its tiny islands floating on the water's surface. Most of her time was spent in The Shell Seekers, so taking this trip along the shoreline was something of a treat. She didn't expect to find what she was looking for, but at least she was being proactive rather than a sitting duck waiting to be caught. The large sign for 'Seaview Caravan Site' could be seen as she turned the bend. Indicating left, she drove down the one-track road to her destination.

A young girl was sitting at the reception desk, making a clickety click sound with her nail extensions on the computer keys.

'Hi,' Marnie said. 'I wonder if you can help me.'

'I'll do my best,' the girl replied, rising from her seat and heading to the counter.

Marnie brought up the photograph of her ex-boyfriend on her phone. 'I'm looking for this man and wondered if he might be staying here.'

The girl took the phone in her taloned fingers. 'That looks just like Ashton Brook, the footballer.'

'Yes, I suppose he does a bit,' Marnie agreed.

'No, we've got no one like that staying here. Trust me, I would have noticed.'

'I know you can't give out this kind of information but are there any men staying here alone… who may seem a little odd to you?' She knew it was a stupid question, but it was worth a shot.

The girl thought for a moment. 'One guy is staying in the caravan on the end of this row,' as she pointed in the direction. 'It's maybe not fair to call him strange, but let's just say that he stays out for long periods and returns late. He's not a friendly sort. He usually leaves for the day round about...' she glanced at the clock, 'now, actually.'

'Okay, great. Thanks so much for your help.'

Marnie drove down to the far end of the row of caravans to watch for him leaving.

She parked the car in a position that gave her a bird's eye view of the caravan in question. It was possible that the gentleman living there could be working for Ashton. Using the handle on the side of her seat, she reclined her position a few notches lower for discretion. If it were him, he would be able to recognise her instantly, whereas all she knew was his outline from the CCTV footage. A clear plan of action had not quite formulated in her mind, but she would start by getting a good look at him, then perhaps she could follow him to see where he went all day. It was dangerous, and she knew this because anyone who was connected to Ashton was bad news.

Her mobile phone rang, making her jump. It was Struan. She answered the call, keeping her eyes fixed on the door of the caravan.

'Hi love, where are you?' Struan asked.

'I'm just out and about, doing a little shopping,' she lied. 'How did you know I was out?'

'Because I am here at The Shell Seekers. I came to tell you some exciting, but quite incredible, news. Edina thinks she can save the hotel from closure, but you won't believe how she's planning to do it.'

'That sounds very…'

She paused as she saw the caravan door opening.

'…exciting but I have to go. I'm holding up the traffic. Bye.'

A man stepped out of the caravan. As soon as Marnie saw him, she moved her seat upright before starting up the engine of the car. This was definitely not the stalker on the CCTV, simply because he was no more than five feet tall. Instead of jeans and a hoodie, he wore a tweed, three-piece suit with a dickie bow tie. She released the handbrake and drove off in the direction of The Shell Seekers. It was back to the drawing board. Hotels, Guest Houses, and holiday lets were next on her list.

Chapter 43

Friday night was Shell Seekers night; no one was more ready for it than Freddy. He appeared at the hotel early with the intention of having a drink at the bar before Stan arrived with the bus to pick them up.

Suzie stood polishing the silver cutlery when Freddy entered through the bar's double doors.

'Hey, Freddy. You're looking good. It's early, Stan won't be here for…' she checked her watch, 'another hour.'

'Yeah, I know. There was no point in me hanging around the house. I thought I'd get a drink in here to get me in the party mood.'

Suzie laid the cutlery down on the table and headed to the bar to serve him.

Pulling the bar stool out, Freddy climbed onto it.

'What are you having?' she asked.

'Let me think.' He studied the optics behind the bar. 'I think I'll have a spiced rum and coke.'

'Bottled or draught coke?'

'Bottled.'

Taking a tall glass from the shelf below the bar, she half-filled it with ice before pouring the drink.

'I was sorry to hear that you lost your dad,' Freddy told her as he watched her manoeuvre off the lid of the Coke using the bottle opener.

'Thanks, but don't feel sorry about it because I'm not. It's time for a fresh start. Things needed to change. They couldn't go on the way they were. I've started clearing the house out. I'm chucking everything away.'

She came out from behind the bar to sit on the stool next to Freddy.

'That sounds good,' he told her. 'If you want any help, I'm free on Sunday.'

'Great, I'll take you up on that offer,' she said, smiling. 'So, how about you? What's going on in your life?'

'I leave for college on the mainland soon. I was dreading going away, but now I think it's for the best.'

'Why?' she asked.

'Long story, but do you remember Sally Crawford from school?'

Suzie furrowed her brows. 'Remember her? Her mean face is etched in my memory for life. She made things intolerable for me at school. Her nasty friends weren't much better. I endured relentless bullying day after day from those horrible girls, then got battered by my father when I went home.'

To Freddy, she made light of how things were back then, but the memory caused a stinging sensation in her eyes. She turned away to prevent Freddy from seeing that she was upset; it would have ruined the conversation.

'You haven't been seeing *her*, have you?'

'No, but I took her cousin out on a date. It was terrible. When I dropped her off at home, I said I would be in touch. Now Sally and her minions are pestering me, asking when I will call or text the girl. I don't want anything to do with her. In fact, I don't want anything to do with any of them.'

'So, just tell them that.'

'I can't face the backlash if I'm honest. I've just been stalling with a whole lot of lies until now. I said I'd hurt my foot, so now I'll have to limp when I see them. I also used the excuse that my dad had me working late every night. They will all be at The Shell Seekers tonight, ready to pounce like a pack of hyenas.'

'Freddy! Are you a man or a mouse?'

'When it comes to those bitches… squeak, squeak.'

They both laughed.

The horn toot could be heard from outside in the car park as Stan announced his arrival, he was early.

Freddy reached for his jacket before downing the remainder of his drink.

'It's been good talking to you, Suzie. I'll come round on Sunday morning to help you build a bonfire.'

'That's a plan. A bonfire is all that junk is worth. Thanks for helping me, it means a lot.'

Edina and Struan were already seated when Freddy entered the minibus.

'Are you singing at the karaoke tonight, Freddy?' Struan asked.

Freddy turned to Suzie, 'Hey Suz, how do fancy a duet?'

'I'm not very good, but I'll give it a go.'

'I might as well give the girls a really good reason to hate me.'

When they arrived at the pub, Somerled was waiting in the doorway of The Shell Seekers. Edina saw him from the window of the bus. *Why is he standing there? I hope he's not leaving.* Without waiting for the others, she headed straight over to him.

'Why are you standing there?' she asked.

'I'm waiting for you, of course.'

Wrapping her arms around his neck, she kissed him all over his face.

'I feel like a dog owner getting a warm welcome home from my St. Bernard's,' he laughed.

Struan pushed past the kissing couple to get into the bar to see Marnie.

'Hi, love,' he said, kissing her. 'I can't wait to tell you all about Edina's idea. Did you get what you were looking for at the shops yesterday?'

'No, it was a total waste of time. I'll go back out again on Monday,' she fibbed. 'Looks like it's going to be a very busy night tonight. I think everyone has come to hear Edina singing,' she told him, looking around at the crowded room.

'You are probably right. Everyone's been talking about it.'

The huddle of mean girls were at their usual table. The moment Freddy appeared through the door, they exchanged narrow eyed looks before simultaneously moving in towards each other to bitch.

Suzie saw the daggers being drawn for him. *Freddy wasn't wrong about the girls' hatred towards him. They are positively gunning for him.*

Freddy played it well. His gaze remained ahead of him as he walked confidently to the bar. Inside, his stomach churned but he silently told himself, you're a man not a mouse.

'Hi, Marnie, how you doing?' he asked, reaching for his wallet. 'A round of the usual drinks, please and one for yourself. Oh, wait a minute... Suzie, are you still on the vodka?' he shouted across to the table.

'No,' Suzie shouted back. 'I'll have a small glass of white wine.'

Freddy turned back to Marnie. 'Sorry about that. The usual for everyone but Suzie will have a small white wine, and I think I'll have a spiced rum and coke for a change.'

'So, it's not really the usual for everyone,' Marnie laughed.

'No, I don't suppose it is.'

Somerled walked over to his friends at the back table. Giving them all a wide smile, he lifted his pint saying, 'Nice knowing you guys, see ya.'

The fishermen adopted fake resentment toward him.

'I can't believe you're choosing a woman who almost killed you on the humpback bridge over us.'

'Don't think you can come crawling back when it all goes tits-up.'

'You're dead to us now, Tom.'

Somerled laughed. 'Yeah, yeah, fine by me. See you on the boat on Monday.'

With a pint in hand, he walked over to the table where Edina was waiting.

The book of available songs for the karaoke was passed from table to table. Freddy looked down the list, searching for a duet. *Islands in the Stream* was the only one available, so he wrote 'Freddy and Suzie' in the space beside it.

Edina scanned the selection of songs on offer before signing her name against one she liked. She rose from her seat to pass the selection to the next table.

'Last chance, Struan,' she announced, pointing at the book of songs. 'When it's gone, it's gone. It could be your big moment to make a name for yourself. Eh, what do you say?'

Struan shook his head. 'Go away and behave yourself, Edina.' He dismissed her with a swipe of the hand.

On her way to deliver the song book to the next table, she took a detour past the girl who was making Freddy's life miserable. Sometimes things had to be stamped out before they roared out of control and she believed that she was the very one to do it.

'Hi,' Edina said, smiling. 'You're a good friend of Freddy's, aren't you?'

'I *was* a good friend of Freddy's.'

'Have you two fallen out?' Edina asked.

'Well, he basically shit all over my cousin. He took her out, promised he'd text, then totally ignored her.'

'Oh dear. Perhaps I can shed a little light on that for you. Freddy had a date with your cousin, and he told me she was a really nice girl, but sadly, she is not the one for him.' Edina was pleasant but blunt. 'So, the fact of the matter is that you will not change his feelings by behaving badly towards him. No crime has been committed. He just doesn't want your cousin. Why don't you grow up and stop with all the bitch tactics.'

Sally stood speechless for a moment, examining Edina's face.

Edina gave her an even wider smile, patted her arm in a gesture that inferred, good girl, then turning around to speak to Marnie.

'How are you, Marnie? Have there been any more letters?' Edina asked, glancing around to see if Sally had gone. She had.

'No, nothing since the one I texted you about. Maybe he's tired of it. It can't be much fun cutting out all those little letters, gluing them into position, then sitting in the bushes for hours waiting for the right time to post the letter through the door.'

'Well, don't get too comfortable. Keep locking the door and checking the cameras. Don't forget that he is getting a real kick out of this. Remember, I'm here if you need me.'

'Thanks, Edina, I appreciate it. Are you buying a round?'

Edina looked over at the glasses in front of her friends to see if they were empty. 'Yes, same again.'

The karaoke began with an introduction, followed by an announcement that Freddy and Suzie were first up with the Kenny Rogers and Dolly Parton classic, *Islands in the Stream*. Neither of them was familiar with the song, but the choices had been limited.

Gripping their microphones a tad too tightly, they stood awkwardly in front of the words on the screen, waiting for the music to begin.

By the time they reached the chorus, Edina decided that Freddy was a pretty good singer, but Suzie was quite the reverse. Every other act from here on in could only get better.

When the song ended, Edina cheered in response. This encouraged the disengaged audience to join in. The applause they received was way more than they deserved.

Somerled moved in closer to Edina, his arm resting along the back of her chair. She could feel his fingers winding around the tips of her hair. His gentle touch caused her flesh to tingle. Being this close to him gave her a feeling of security. Love had been the last thing she would ever have imagined finding on the remote island of Mull. As they sat together listening to the good, bad, and average singers, she realised that for the first time in her life, she was actually happy, truly, completely happy.

'Look,' she whispered into his ear. Reaching into her shirt, she took out the shark tooth on the leather thong. 'I never take it off.'

He kissed her slowly on the lips before whispering back. 'You've accepted the shark's tooth. That means you are officially mine now.'

'Really?' she said, acting surprised. 'I have a feeling you tricked me into pledging myself to you.'

'It's done now. There's no getting out of it.'

She snapped her fingers, saying, 'Damn it.'

The man running the karaoke took the microphone.

'And now for the last performer of the night, let's hear it for Edina.'

The crowd cheered, and the fishermen wolf whistled. People at the back stood up to get a better view.

Edina made her way onto the makeshift stage.

The recognisable introduction started, and Edina swayed to the beat. Maxi Priest's *Close to You* had always been one of her favourite songs. She had performed it so many times that there was no need for her to look at the words on the screen. Only when the chorus came around did she focus on Somerled to sing that she wanted to get close to him, to do all the things he wanted her to. It was a polished, somewhat erotic performance. Even with the blinding spotlight in her eyes, she could see the audience swaying to the music.

Suzie leaned in to Freddy saying, 'Did you know that she could sing like that?'

'Yes, she blew us all away with her singing the last time. You were there.'

Suzie felt embarrassed. Not only did she not remember Edina singing, but she could not recall anything about any of the events on previous Friday nights in The Shell Seekers. Sitting there next to Freddy, enjoying the entertainment, had been a completely new experience for her. There and then, she made a private pledge to herself that her drinking would never become out of control again. After all, there was now a new life to look forward to. And maybe, just maybe, there was a place for Freddy in it.

Edina finished, and the room went wild. Somerled and Struan got up on their feet, clapping above their heads. Others followed suit, and it soon became a room-filled standing ovation. Even two of the mean girls were standing.

Edina was pleased, but the only thing on her mind was getting back into the arms of Somerled.

The audience kept cheering, with chants of 'encore!' Edina returned to her seat and looked around the table at her newfound friends. Struan, strong and dependable. Freddy, not the smartest boy in the world, but obliging and helpful. Suzie, a delicate creature who needed encouragement and care. Marnie, well, Marnie was an angel. Somerled... there were no words for Somerled. She had never met anyone quite like him, which made her the luckiest girl in the world.

A long time ago, she had read that 'grace' meant getting what you don't deserve. By the good grace of God, she had found Somerled. It had been weeks since she had thought about the editor, Robin, whose name was no longer too painful to say.

At the end of the night, they all gathered in the car park to discuss how they would get home. The consensus was that they would walk. Marnie came out to say goodbye and thank everyone for helping to make it a great night.

'I'd love to book you as a regular singer here at The Shell Seekers,' Marnie suggested to Edina.

'No, Marnie. That's not my thing. I just like having the odd singsong for fun. Anyway, I have a great idea,' she announced, feeling on a high. 'Why don't you all come round to my house tomorrow night for drinks and nibbles? Marnie, you get a taxi over when the bar is shut. What do you all think? Who's in?'

'It would be nice to get out for the night. Count me in!' Marnie agreed first. It had been over a year since she had been away from The Shell Seekers in the evening.

To Edina's great pleasure, they all agreed that they would love to come round to her house on Saturday night. Suggestions were given as to what everyone could bring with regard to the party food. The night would kick off at seven, and the workers could arrive when they finished their shifts.

Spirits were high as the friends began the long walk home.

Somerled laid a protective arm around Edina's shoulders, which she loved.

To break a short silence, Struan began singing *Islands in the Stream* purposely off-key. Everyone laughed, even Suzie.

'I didn't see you putting your name forward to sing. You probably couldn't do any better,' she said, giving him a shove.

All in a row, they headed down the single-track road. Suddenly they all gasped with relief as Stan's little shuttle bus made an appearance around the corner. He tooted three times before stopping to let them all on.

Edina approached Stan in the driver's seat. 'Would it be all right if you dropped Tom off? He lives at the top of the hill, next turning on the left.'

'If you just stop at the road end, please, Stan. I can walk the rest.'

'No problem, son,' Stan said, putting his headlights up to full beam to get a clear view of the turning.

Somerled sat back in the seat next to Edina. 'I was really proud of you tonight. You were brilliant. I love hearing you sing.' Then he whispered, 'I wish I was staying with you tonight. I would hold you so tight, you wouldn't be able to breathe.' He kissed her on her neck softly.

Shivers ran from the base of her spine to her scalp. *I simply cannot resist this man.* She glanced down at his athletic legs in his faded Levi jeans as she inhaled his intoxicating aftershave. *Oooooh, I can't wait to be alone with him again.*

Stan pulled over to the side of the road, releasing the lever for the concertinaed door. Somerled jumped off, then stood on the grass verge, waving the bus off.

Edina watched him from the window until he was completely out of sight.

Chapter 44

Marnie headed through to the kitchen for breakfast. Her thoughts were on the previous night in the bar. In all the years she had run The Shell Seekers, she had never experienced such an electric atmosphere. Although she hadn't counted the takings, she knew they must have been plentiful. Pennyghael House was struggling financially, but she would see to it that the bar would help to keep it open for the summer.

Once she was dressed, she headed downstairs to finish the clearing up. Normally, she would have everything in perfect shape before she went to bed, but it was late when the final stragglers left.

'Oh, no,' she said aloud when she saw the all too familiar envelope on the door mat.

As always, the first thing she did was to bring it up to her nose to smell the scent. Yes, it was the same as the previous letters. Using her finger as a paper knife, she burst through the top of the envelope. The sheet of paper inside was the same as before, cut out upper and lower case letters. She dearly wished it would all stop, but somehow, she realised it didn't quite pack the fear punch it had previously done.

She read the message aloud.

TIME IS RUNNING OUT
OPEN YOUR BLOODY EYES MARNIE

It was now becoming tiresome. She ran to fetch her phone from beside the bed. Her hands no longer shook as she clicked on the security camera, scrolling back, back, back.

There he was at 6.25am.

An early bird.

She watched as he walked up the single-track road, not from the woods, as he had done on previous occasions. The hood of his sweatshirt was up, and his hands were thrust deep into his pocket. Furtively, he turned to check the road behind him several times. At one point, before he reached the door of the pub, he took his hand from his pocket to pull his hood down over his forehead. Marnie saw that he was wearing a ring on the middle finger of his left hand. It was difficult to make out details in the film, but she believed it to be a signet ring. The other very obvious detail was the writing on his sweatshirt, New York Yankees. She may not have seen his face, but he had left identifiable clues to aid her in her quest to find him.

Chapter 45

Edina left sharply after her shift, as she knew the house was untidy, with dishes left in the sink. She had been running late that morning, so her clothes from the night before were still strewn over the bathroom floor.

Why did I invite everyone to my house?

She felt angry with herself for getting swept up in the moment.

All my worst decisions have been made when I've had a little too much to drink and I'm feeling high. I can't bear to think of that time when I invited all the bar staff at Tiger Lily's back to my apartment for a party... What a mistake that had been. Now I've gone and done it again.

Armed with a cloth and spray, she raced around the house, cleaning everywhere that her guests would visit. Living room, kitchen, bathroom. No need to do upstairs.

The hot jets of water from her almost adequate shower rejuvenated her somewhat. By the time she dried her hair and pulled on her jeans, she felt quite excited about having her friends over for the first time.

Her phone was playing background music as she lit all the candles in the living room. She poured herself a glass of prosecco and sat in the wing chair by the fireplace. It had been the first time she had sat down all day.

A loud knock on the front door gave her a fright. She sprung to her feet to answer it.

'Hi Freddy. You're first here.'

He thrust a bottle of wine and six cans of lager into her hands.

'Oh wait, give me a minute. I've got crisps and twiglets in the car.'

When he returned carrying the snacks, Edina welcomed him into her home with a hug.

'You smell nice, Freddy,' she told him.

'Aw, well, you've got to make the effort. Hey, you've made this house look nice,' he told her, looking around. 'I like your paintings.'

'Thanks. They're by a Scottish artist, Val Scott. I got them one day when Suzie took me to a big charity shop outside Tobermory. Do you want one of your own beers or a cold one from the fridge?'

'You can't beat a cold beer.'

Cans of Stella Artois were stacked up on the top shelf of her fridge. 'When do you leave for college?' she shouted from the kitchen.

'End of this month.'

There was a loud knock once again.

'Excuse me, Freddy.' She handed him the beer on the way to answer the door.

'Struan! Long time no see.'

'Yeah, it's been about an hour and a half, at least.'

He handed her a carrier bag of edibles and two bottles of wine.

'In you come,' she told him. 'You know Freddy.'

'Of course, I know Freddy. Edina, you can be quite a crazy girl at times.'

'So you've told me on several occasions. Beer?'

'No, I'll have red wine.'

From the kitchen, she shouted, 'Struan, I didn't think you'd be here so early!'

'No, me neither. My mum came in and took over. To be honest, it's good to get a break from the place.'

There was a quiet knock on the front door.

That will be Suzie.

The girl standing on the doorstep was unrecognisable as Suzie. Her black dress clung to the curves of her figure, and her stiletto heels were high. The deep red lipstick she was wearing changed her appearance completely.

'Oh, my goodness!' Edina screeched. 'Boys, wait until you see this.'

The boys rushed to the door to see what the commotion was about. They stood staring at the beautiful woman at the door, trying desperately to see their friend Suzie in her.

Suzie giggled with embarrassment, handing over her contributions to the night.

'Come in, Suzie. You look absolutely stunning.'

They all stood with their drinks, discussing the décor of Edina's house.

'Edina, you've made the house look so good, I think I'd better put the rent up,' Struan joked. 'If I'm being honest, I thought you'd stay about two weeks, then look for something better.'

The knock that Edina was eagerly waiting for came as they were talking. She left the conversation to open the front door.

Somerled stood there, smiling that adorable, mischievous smile. His white shirt gripped his arm and chest muscles. Oh boy did she love the flesh and bones of this man.

I want to tell everyone to go home. Then, I want to devour this unbelievable creature.

Somerled reached forward, taking Edina in his arms. 'I missed you,' he whispered in her ear.

They held one another for a few moments, both unwilling to let go.

'I think you'd better come in,' she finally told him.

'Here, I have food for the party,' he said, raising the carrier bag to show her.

'Follow me to the kitchen. Bring your bag with you.'

From the bag, she took out a bottle of champagne. 'Did you win this at one of the quizzes?'

'Maybe,' he said sheepishly.

She then pulled out a tin of pilchards in rich tomato sauce. 'What the hell?' she asked, holding the item in the air. 'Who brings pilchards to a party?'

'Just me, I guess.'

'I'm scared to look at the rest of the items,' she laughed. 'Do you want a beer?'

Edina instructed everyone to sit down. She checked their glasses were full before she joined them. To get the conversation flowing, she asked them all in turn to describe their most embarrassing moment. This game raised more than a few laughs as everyone in the room revealed all.

The conversation moved on to childhood memories but their hilarity was interrupted by a loud banging on the front door.

Struan rose to his feet automatically. 'Marnie's early. I didn't think she'd be here for another couple of hours.'

Edina opened the front door. Her smile disappeared from her face when she saw not Marnie standing there but two uniformed policemen. Instantly, her heart rate quickened, and her mind raced as she tried to pre-empt every possible piece of bad news that they could be bringing her.

It's Marnie. Ashton Brook has hurt her... worse, killed her.

Her stomach turned over several times before she finally said, 'Yes, can I help you?'

'We are looking for Miss Suzie Crawford. We have been given information that she is here with you at this address.'

'Yes, she's here, come in.'

Edina led them into the lounge. The company stopped laughing. Freddy instinctively removed his feet from the coffee table and sat up straight.

'Miss Suzie Crawford?' the taller of the two cops asked.

'Yes, that's me.' She was visibly trembling.

'You are under arrest for the murder of your father, Mr Hugh Crawford,' the shorter and somewhat younger policeman said before reading her rights to her.

'I didn't murder my father. He died of a heart attack or a stroke or something,' she pleaded.

'The autopsy has revealed that your father was poisoned.'

Suzie, who was now wailing her innocence, was led out to the squad car.

Edina followed them to the door, hearing the harrowing cries of the young girl she now classed as her friend. In the chill of the fast-approaching autumn night, Edina heard the police car hitting every pothole on the God-forsaken road.

Back in the house, the now party of four sat quietly, processing what had just occurred.

'She didn't do it,' Edina announced, breaking the silence. 'She hated the man, but she would never have murdered him.'

'How can you know for sure?' Freddy piped up. 'You've only known her for a few weeks.'

'Freddy's right, Edina. None of us really know Suzie. She's deep, secretive even,' Struan added. 'Anyway, if she didn't do it, then who did? The man was a complete loner.'

'I still believe that Suzie didn't do it. I just know in my heart that she is not capable of murder.'

Edina sat with the boys debating the matter for some time, thrashing out different scenarios without arriving at any plausible explanation. One absolute certainty for Edina was that Suzie was not a cold-blooded killer who could continue living a normal life after committing such a shocking crime.

The front door had been accidentally left slightly ajar after the police car left.

Marnie arrived at the cottage. On seeing the door open, she decided to sneak in to give them a fright.

Somerled had now turned the discussion to possible sentences that Suzie could be served, should they find her guilty.

At that moment, Marnie jumped through the door, shouting, 'Boo!'

Edina jumped, Freddy swore, Somerled let out a nervous scream, Struan shouted, 'Marnie! What the hell?'

By their reaction and the look on their faces, Marnie soon realised that something terrible had happened. Removing her tweed jacket and silk scarf, she threw them over the back of the sofa, sitting herself down next to Struan.

'Okay, what's happened? Where's Suzie?' Marnie asked, looking from one shocked face to the other.

Struan accurately described the events of Suzie's arrest. There had been more than enough drama for one night.

He finished by saying, 'Marnie, we've been sitting here trying to figure out how it could have happened without Suzie being involved. It's been extremely difficult to come up with a scenario that sounds logical. So, I think we should lay it to rest for now and let the police do their work.'

'I agree,' Somerled added.

'Marnie, come into the kitchen with me, and I'll get you something to drink. Is anyone hungry?'

'Starving,' Freddy shouted.

As they headed to the kitchen, Edina could hear Struan asking Somerled about life as a fisherman. She smiled to herself.

Somerled will wow them with his tales of the sea and the marine life he spotted over the years.

Opening the fridge to show the selection of wines, she asked Marnie if she would like a glass of prosecco.

'That would be lovely,' Marnie answered. 'I am still feeling pretty shocked by the news about Suzie.'

'Yes, me too, but I'm certain that they will get to the bottom of what really happened and be able to clear Suzie of any crime. Anyway, how are you? Have there been any more letters?'

Marnie nodded. 'I got another one this morning. It didn't say much. I checked the camera, and it showed him coming up the road rather than from the woods. He was wearing a New York Yankees sweatshirt, and I noticed a signet ring on his left hand. I couldn't see his face, though. He wears his hood down over his forehead.'

'What are the police saying?' Edina asked.

'I've given up all hope of the police doing anything. Don't tell Struan, but I'm doing a bit of detective work myself. I have been to the caravan site to find out if there are any single males staying there. There was one, but it was definitely not him. On Monday, I'm going to try the hotels.'

'Marnie, that's a dangerous thing you're doing. I'm not sure that it is a good idea. What are you going to do if you find him?'

'I don't think it's Ashton. I suspect he has paid a friend to frighten me. Trust me, he has a lot of dodgy friends. I simply plan to follow him, then give his details to the police. The way I figure it, he has to be staying somewhere, and he is probably here on his own. It makes me feel better knowing that I am doing something.'

Handing Marnie a flute of sparkling wine, she said, 'I get that, but please be careful.'

The crisps and nibbles were brought through, along with a couple of side plates and saucers. The crockery was sparse, to say the least. 'Help yourself, everyone,' Edina announced. 'If you need a napkin, too bad, I don't have any.'

Somerled looked at the array of savouries on the coffee table. 'Hey! Where's the pilchards?'

'I told you. No one eats pilchards at a party. I will give you them to take home with you.'

'I'll put them out myself. You watch, they'll all be eaten in no time.'

'Hey, wait a minute, did Suzie prepare any of this food?' Freddy asked warily.

'Freddy, please don't say things like that. I know what you are thinking and stop it. If we don't believe in her, then who will?'

Struan looked at the food on his plate, 'Just as a matter of interest, did she make any of it?'

'No!' Edina shouted disapprovingly.

As the small hours approached, Struan decided to call one of Mull's very few taxi firms.

'Hi,' he said. 'I'm looking for a taxi to pick us up from the Pennyghael estate cottage and drop off four people at three locations.' He wasn't keen on Marnie going into an empty house late at night. Staying over with her was the best option.

'No problem, mate. I'll be there in fifteen minutes. Can I ask you to walk to the end of the road? I don't want to wreck my motor on those potholes.'

'Sure thing.'

'Hey, Edina, the road leading to your house must be a big talking point. No one wants to drive on it,' Struan laughed.

'No one told the policemen that visited earlier. I heard them hitting every crater.'

Edina walked her friends to the front door, thanking them for coming.

Somerled slipped his hand in hers, hanging back as the others set off down the road.

'Are you busy tomorrow?' he asked her.

'No,' she told him, excited by the prospect of getting him to herself.

'I'll pick you up at one then. I want to take you somewhere special. I'm borrowing my father's motorboat, so bring a jacket. It can get quite cold out on the water.'

He then kissed her slowly, pulling her body close to his.

'I'll see you then.'

Standing alone on the doorstep, she watched him running to catch up with the others. Once he was out of sight, she went inside, locking the door behind her. The remainder of the food was still on the coffee table, and she couldn't help but smile when she saw the empty plate where the pilchards had been. *No one eats pilchards at a party. It must be a Mull thing.*

Before heading to bed, she sat in the wing chair and took a minute to reflect on the evening. In spite of the shock visit from the police, it had turned out to be a pretty good night. Her thoughts then drifted to Suzie sitting alone in a cell at the police station.

She must be so frightened. Apart from us, she has no one to turn to. I hope the police find a way to prove her innocence. Life has been intolerable enough for her.

There was something else about the evening that Edina couldn't stop thinking about. A very disturbing thing indeed.

Chapter 46

The ringtone from Edina's phone awakened her with a start. Seeing the room filled with sunlight disorientated her slightly, as it felt like she had only just gone to bed. Reaching for the phone beside her, she saw that it was Marnie calling.

'Hi, Marnie,' she answered sleepily.

'Sorry Edina, did I wake you?'

'No, it's time I was up. You did me a favour.'

'I just wanted to say thank you for a lovely night. I had a great time, although I'm still in shock about Suzie. I can't stop thinking about it.'

'Me neither. It was the last thing that any of us expected to happen.'

'I'll leave you in peace to get organised, but I also wanted to ask if you could look for my silk scarf? I left it behind last night. I didn't remember until I was in the taxi. It must have slipped down the back of the sofa. Just give it to Struan when you see him.'

Edina didn't remember seeing it when she went to bed. 'No problem, Marnie, I'll go and look for it now.'

'Sorry to make a fuss, but a close friend of mine gave it to me before I left the mainland. It's kind of special.'

'Don't worry, I'll find it. I'll see you next Friday at The Shell Seekers.'

Edina lay back on the pillow. Something was bothering her terribly, something that was her responsibility to investigate. An idea came into her head, prompting her to leap out of bed.

Downstairs, she headed past the kitchen. There would be plenty of time for tea once she checked her phone's camera.

The footage of the previous night began with Freddy arriving. Struan turned up shortly after, followed by Suzie. Somerled arrived sometime after that. She fast-forwarded the film until Marnie arrived through the door shouting boo. Edina watched closely. Marnie took off her jacket and scarf. Edina saw her laying them over the back of the sofa. She allowed the film to play at the regular speed and continued to watch everything.

She suddenly stopped the film. There it was. A moment when Freddy was alone in the lounge. She was in the kitchen with Marnie, Somerled had gone to the toilet, and Struan walked into the kitchen to fetch another glass of wine. Freddy was alone.

On the film, Freddy looked furtively towards the kitchen. He then snatched Marnie's scarf from the sofa. Holding it in both hands, he rubbed it over his face. After checking the kitchen door again, his attention returned to the scarf as he ran it through his fingers, caressing it, kneading it. It became uncomfortable to watch. A noise from somewhere outside the room made him thrust the scarf into the back pocket of his jeans. Edina watched him then untuck his shirt to hide the fact that he had stolen Marnie's property. Freddy sat back casually on the sofa. He ran his hand through his hair, giving Edina a good look at the signet ring on the middle finger of his left hand.

It had been Freddy's aftershave that had alerted Edina's suspicions. When she hugged him on his arrival, she smelt the same scent as that on the envelopes to Marnie. It had bothered her throughout the evening. Thinking back, he had told her several times that there was a girl he was in love with, but she had never noticed him in the way he wanted to be noticed. All the dots were beginning to join together in Edina's mind as she thought through previous conversations. This meant, of course, that Ashton Brooks was not stalking Marnie, nor were any of his henchmen. It was Freddy, sweet, helpful Freddy. She was pretty sure his methods of pursuing her had no malicious intentions. He was obsessed, desperate, and clearly inexperienced in the ways of love.

Chapter 47

Struan had been running the hotel on a basic skeleton staff for the previous few months. Now that Suzie had been arrested, it meant that they were a skeleton down. Struan had no option but to phone Freddy for help.

'Freddy, I will need you full-time until you leave for college. Is that possible?' Struan asked, feeling quite desperate at this stage.

'No problem at all, Struan. I need the money to go away anyway. I can work any shifts you want.'

'Honestly, I don't know what I would do without you. You're a great guy, and I'm so lucky to have you around.'

'I know it's Edina's day off, so I'm free if you want me in now. I was supposed to be helping Suzie clear her house, but that won't be happening now,' Freddy explained.

'That would be great. See you shortly.'

Struan's last resort would have been to ask Edina to come in on her day off, but Tom had mentioned to him the previous night that he was going to invite her to go out in his father's boat. He was a tough boss when he needed to be, but he would have found it difficult to ruin Edina's romantic excursion. Freddy had once again saved the day for him and he would be eternally grateful for that.

Edina was being picked up by Somerled at one o'clock.

A day at sea with Somerled. Just the two of us. I wonder if it's possible to get intimate in a motorboat. I suppose I'll just need to wait and see. Where there's a will... It occurred to her that the only time she had been on any kind of boat was the ferry crossing over to Mull. *I think I'll dress all nautical for the occasion. Jeans, a striped sweatshirt, and maybe a little red cravat tied around my neck... No, that's a bit Captain Pugwash. I'll stick with the sweatshirt and jeans.*

The morning was leaving fast and Somerled was picking her up at one, but Edina felt she simply had to tell Marnie who the stalker was. *She is going to be furious with Freddy, although it will be a relief that it is not someone dangerous like Ashton Brook. The sooner she knows, the better. It's cutting it fine for getting back for one, but I need to go.*

As she drove towards the coast, she consciously decided that she would first show Marnie the footage as proof before telling her the news. The signet ring and the smell of the aftershave would back up her evidence. There wouldn't be time to hang around discussing matters further as she needed to get back for Somerled. Perhaps leaving Marnie to process the information alone was the best option anyway.

She swung into one of the parking spaces in The Shell Seekers car park. Knowing that Marnie had been made to feel uneasy over the past few months, she decided to announce her arrival through the letter box. Peering through the metal flap, she shouted, 'Marnie, it's Edina! I've just popped over for a quick chat.'

On hearing this, Marnie ran downstairs to open the door. 'Edina, I'm so pleased to see you. Come in. I've got a pot of coffee on. Any joy finding my silk scarf?'

Ignoring the question, Edina followed her in saying, 'I'd love a cup of coffee.'

How can I say this? I think I'll just bring out my phone and show her the footage, wait, no, maybe it's best to just blurt it out. No beating about the bush. Tell her the facts, then show the film.

While deliberating how to broach the subject, Marnie spoke first, 'That's great news about Freddy, isn't it?'

'What do you mean? What news?'

'Struan phoned to say that Freddy is going to work flat out until he leaves for college. He is going to cover all of Suzie's shifts and more. What a guy! Struan doesn't know what he would do without him.'

'Yes, he is a great guy,' Edina agreed. The urgency to tell Marnie what she knew about the 'great guy' was leaving her fast.

'Struan also told me about your friend, the documentary maker, coming over tomorrow. If it all works out the way you've described it to Struan, then it could be great for the hotel and the island. It would bring tourists from all over. It's so exciting. I had no idea you had a ghost in your life. There I was, making a fuss about a few stupid letters, and you were getting haunted within an inch of your life!'

That sentence from Marnie was the answer to Edina's dilemma. A few stupid letters. That's all they had become to Marnie. Her fear had diminished, and she now saw them as a few stupid letters.

'Are you not worried about the letters anymore?' Edina asked for confirmation.

'Not really. I have seen the sender on my CCTV footage. Somehow, it has taken all the menace out of it. I'm pretty sure it's not Ashton because I researched him. Apparently, he's been signed by some football team. I thought about it rationally. If he had come to Mull to find me, then I would be in the hospital or worse, the morgue by now. His vicious temper is knee jerk, he's not a planner. Also, the sender wore a New York Yankees sweatshirt. Ashton's clothes are designer and his game is football not baseball. As for him paying someone to frighten me, it's been going on for months now, so how could he afford it? It just doesn't add up. I'm tired of being afraid, and I want to get on with my life.'

'That's a great attitude, Marnie. I have a feeling that it's all going to blow over soon. Anyway, I'd better get back. I just came to say hello. Tom is picking me up at one. He's taking me out on his father's boat.'

They walked down the stairs to the front door. Marnie gave her a hug, saying, 'Thanks for caring. Perfect weather for going sailing. Have a fabulous day.'

Edina drove back to the cottage with time to spare. It wasn't a wasted trip, as she now knew exactly what she would do about Freddy.

Chapter 48

Somewhere in the cupboard upstairs, she knew there was a backpack that would be perfect for packing some of the leftover snacks from the previous night. They were going away for the day, and there were no shops at sea, so she reckoned they may be glad of something to eat when they were out.

Rather than standing watching for Somerled, she opened the window slightly to hear the crunch of the gravel when his car drove up. Her thoughts had been so full of Freddy and the scarf, that she had forgotten all about checking the footage for Jeremy. The more film she had of him, the better the documentary would be, if Pip decided to do it. *Pip! He's arriving on the ferry tomorrow. I need to make a reservation for him at the hotel and find out what time to pick him up.*

She sent a short text to Pip Paterson.

What time do you arrive tomorrow? How many will be coming?

A text vibrated back almost immediately.

Ferry arrives in Mull at 1.30. There will be three of us. A few more if I decide to pick up the gauntlet.

Great, I'll be there to get you. Booking you into the Pennyghael House Hotel. Trust me, you will be grabbing the gauntlet.

I hope you're right. See you tomorrow.

Edina sent a message to Struan.

Pip arriving tomorrow. Can you reserve three rooms, one for him and two others?

While her phone was in her hand, she clicked on the previous night's footage. This time, she ignored Freddy and the rest of the guests, focusing only on the background. There was nothing to see until she came to the part of the evening when they all shared embarrassing stories. Everyone in the room was laughing. Behind the wing chair where she had been sitting, there was the outline of a small person. She stretched the image wider using her finger and thumb. Yes, it was him, facing the wall, head bowed. *Why has he turned away from everyone? Could he be vexed at the idea of us all having fun when he is trapped in the tower with his mother? If that is the case, it is so sad. I hope he knows that I am going to help. Yes, he must, or he would be defacing my property again or terrifying me in the night.*

When the sound of driven gravel came, Edina pressed save on her phone before running to open the door.

'Hey, Somerled!' she shouted as he stepped out of the car. 'Looking good.'

'You're mildly easy on the eye yourself. Are you ready to go?'

'I've been ready for hours,' she joked, shutting the front door behind her.

Before he drove off, he turned to say, 'You know that you're the only person who has ever called me by my real name. Even my mum and dad have never said it, and they bloody chose it.'

'Do you mind me calling you Somerled?' she asked.

'Not at all. In fact, I love it.'

They drove to the coast, where the boat was moored. Every time she asked him where they were going, his reply was, wait and see.

The small motorboat sat alone in the water. Its rope was looped over a fencepost to keep it secure. Edina took Somerled's outreached hand to steady her as she climbed aboard. The sea was just choppy enough to keep the vessel rocking back and forth, making it difficult for her to keep her balance. Once she was safely seated, she stared over the starboard side of the boat at the clear green water. The sight of hundreds of tiny fish swimming around them gave her quite a thrill. After all, until now, she had been a city girl.

'Oh my goodness, there are fish everywhere. I can't believe how many there are swimming around the boat,' she screeched, hanging over the side.

Seeing her childlike response to the minnows in the water prompted Somerled to ask, 'Have you been out on a boat before?'

'Yes, I came over on the ferry.'

'Ah, so you're pretty experienced then.' He laughed.

The boat hadn't been used in some time, so it took a few attempts for the engine to roar into action.

'Hold tight,' he told her. 'You are going to love this, I hope.'

They sped out to sea at around seven miles per hour. As the boat rose and fell, Edina was splashed by every wave. They both laughed as her face and clothes became increasingly wetter.

'Are you doing this on purpose?' she shouted above the noise of the engine.

'Yes!' he joked. 'Look! See that island in the distance?'

She nodded, water dripping from her chin.

'That's where we are going,' he hollered.

Edina stared in amazement at the flat-topped island made up of hexagonal columns. It was like nothing she had ever seen before; in fact, it resembled something that was man-made.

What a relief when the engine of the boat was switched off. No more splashing, just smooth coasting on the surface of the sea. The choking calls of the herring gulls overhead were the only sounds to be heard. To Edina, it felt like they were the only two people left alive on the earth.

'This is the Island of Staffa,' he told her. 'It is uninhabited. These tall structures that make up the island are made of basalt.' He pulled the boat around to the large cavern at the front.

'This is Fingal's Cave,' he told her. 'It is known for its natural acoustics. A famous composer called Felix Mendelssohn once visited the cave, and he was so inspired by it that he wrote a piece of music called Hebrides Overture. I will let you hear it when we get back. I think you'll like it now that you've seen what he was writing about.'

They sat in the bobbing boat at the mouth of the cave, just looking. Edina reached into her backpack, pulling out crisps and biscuits.

'Have you got any pilchards in a rich tomato sauce?' he asked, with an earnest face.

'Of course I don't. You are the only sad individual that eats that nonsense.'

The snacks from Edina's bag were long gone, but they still sat in the little boat beside the opening of Fingal's Cave, listening to the sound of the water lapping against the rock.

'Just give me the nod when you've had enough,' he told her.

'I could sit here with you for ten years and still not have had enough.'

Being careful not to overturn the boat, he leaned forward, kissing her with restrained urgency on her lips.

It was with great difficulty that she controlled her needful desire to be intimate with this man who she had fallen flat on her face for. It had been such a short time that they had known each other, and yet, it felt like a lifetime.

He pulled her over to the bench seat where he sat. It had been an ill-thought-through decision as the boat became top-heavy. The fear of the vessel capsizing soon made him push her back onto her own seat.

'Oops,' he said. 'I thought we were going to end up in the water there. I didn't mean to shove you quite so hard.'

She laughed.

'Have you visited all of the islands around here?' she asked him, attempting to diffuse the sexual tension that had left them both with a craving for the other.

'Most of them. Next week I will take you to Iona. It's only about a mile away from Mull. There is an ancient abbey on it, which is really worth seeing. The island is often used as a spiritual retreat. I don't know if I'm just imagining it, but there seems to be a feeling of peace and calm about it.'

'Is it uninhabited too?' she asked.

'No, there are about a hundred and twenty-five people on it. It makes Mull look like a bustling city. It would be too cut off for me.'

'Where would you like to settle?' she asked him.

'I'm glad you asked that,' he replied rather mysteriously. 'That's our next stop. Ready?'

'Definitely! You've made me very curious now.'

He steered the boat away from the mouth of Fingal's Cave, heading back in the direction of Mull.

Edina stared up at the cloudless sky, feeling the spray from the sea on her cheeks. *I am going to remember this day always.* She stole a glance at Somerled's muscular, tanned arm as he steered the boat towards land.

The boat arrived alongside the shoreline. It was on the island's far side from where they had set out. Edina looked all around her for the intended target of their visit. A coastline flanked by sand dunes was all she could see in every direction.

The engine stopped, and Somerled climbed out of the boat first. He held out a steadying hand to Edina.

'Okay, sweet girl, there is a bit of a walk next, but I promise it's worth it.'

'Lead the way,' she told him, firmly holding his hand.

Edina needed help as they hiked up the sand dune steeper than it appeared from the boat. Two steps up the white sandy hill, and she slipped three back down. It was not an easy climb. Then came the dense, spiky tufts of the grasses covering the dunes. *I am so glad I didn't wear a skirt.* Edina felt the razor-sharp blades whipping her legs.

To give her a little encouragement, he turned, shouting, 'Not far to go now.' He was almost dragging her along by the hand. 'Just up this hill.'

Mercy! she thought, as they began the steep climb. *Please show me some mercy.*

'Are you okay there, Edina?'

'Of course. Why wouldn't I be?' she replied, breathing heavy, armpits moist with sweat.

They finally reached the top of the hill. 'Well, what do you think?' he asked, spreading his arms out for her to look in every direction.

'I think it's beautiful, but what about it?'

'I've bought it, and I have planning permission for a four-bedroom house to be built on it. The work starts next spring.'

'Wow, you are full of surprises. Will you have to do that trek every day to get in and out to the shops and civilisation?'

'No, don't be ridiculous. The main road is five minutes down that way,' he told her, laughing, pointing down the hill at the road on the opposite side. 'I could have brought you that way, but this way is much more interesting.'

Somerled walked her through every room-to-be in the future house. He described the lounge in great detail with the full-length picture window looking straight across the sea.

'This is the kitchen, which will open out into the garden. Decking will go all around here. I want unusual, possibly tropical, trees and plants growing at the front and back of the house.'

Listening intently to his animated plans for the future, she started to wonder. *Am I part of this house? Will I live here with you, Somerled?*

Facing the sea, she closed her eyes and pictured herself in the kitchen, looking out the window at Somerled working in the garden. *Oh, my goodness. I can see us here, and we have a little son.* Joy welled within her at the sight of a possible future to come.

Somerled was still walking around, describing the planned features of the house.

Edina walked up behind him, turning him to face her. She kissed him with great passion, like her life depended on it.

Pulling her tight, he pressed hard against her. The desire within him was overpowering. His hands reached under her sweatshirt. The small, firm breasts that he found there were just as he liked. Caressing them gently, then with more force, he heard her cry out with pleasure. This was a turn-on that he could hardly deal with. He knew there would be no stopping now as he opened the button and zip of his jeans.

As soon as Edina realised what Somerled was doing, she did the same with her jeans, using great haste.

With his powerful arms, he lifted her up, laying her down on the grass. In less than a moment, he was inside her. It was ecstasy mixed with relief. The tension had been building since they first met. Now, they could both let go, satisfying their own needs.

Afterwards, they lay on the grass together, staring up at the feathery clouds above. For Edina, it had been the most erotic moment of her life.

Somerled turned to her, saying, 'It wasn't the way I had planned it, but I just couldn't wait.'

'I wouldn't have had it any other way. It was perfect,' she told him.

The trek back was all downhill, and, conveniently, they had trodden down a path to follow through the reedy grasses. Edina's thoughts were of the magical moment they had just shared on the site of, what she had visualised was, their future house. *It's funny how I imagined a son. I didn't even know I wanted children.* Edina had this thought as she ran down the sand embankment. *With Somerled, I want absolutely everything.*

An early evening coolness arrived as the boat sped back across the water. The cold sea spray caused Edina's teeth to chatter. She wrapped her arms tightly around herself to control her shivers.

Somerled noticed how cold she looked. 'How do you fancy fish and chips with salt and vinegar?'

'I think that would be the perfect end to a perfect day,' she told him, through the uncontrollable chatters from her teeth.

In the car home from Tobermory, Somerled casually commented, 'You will be looking forward to your friend, Pip, arriving tomorrow?'

'Yes, I can't wait. We have a very exciting project to discuss, and I will tell you all about it when we've sealed the deal.'

'Sounds a bit too exciting,' he said. 'You had better not forget about me.'

She laughed heartily. 'I could never in a million years forget about you. Pip has only ever been a good friend of mine, just in case you thought otherwise. We've worked together on a couple of successful projects, and if this works out the way I hope it will, it will benefit a lot of people… dead and alive.'

'Did you just say *dead* and alive?'

'Yes, but I will tell you more the next time I see you.'

Somerled drove with caution over the cratered road, pulling up outside Edina's cottage.

'Why don't you come in and stay the night?' she asked before getting out of the car.

'Honestly, I would love to, but I am out on the boat at 4am. I will stay the next time I have a free morning. Thanks for coming today. I have really loved spending time with you.'

Wrapping her arms tightly around his neck, she was reluctant to let him go.

When Tom finally drove off, Edina stood in the silence for a moment before returning to the house. It had been a wonderful day that she would never forget.

She splashed her face in the bathroom with cold water as her skin felt taut. She noticed that the sun had brought her freckles out in droves, and her nose was burnt. It hadn't felt terribly hot, but presumably the sun had been stronger out at sea. She had no idea why.

Feeling at a loose end, she slumped into her armchair and lifted her journal and pen which lay beside her on the sideboard. She decided to write a few lines before heading upstairs. *Jeremy, tomorrow I put the wheels in motion. I will do everything I can to find you.*

She stood under the shower, washing the salt from her skin and hair. The thoughts that filled her head were of the wonderful day she had just spent with Somerled.

Before plugging her phone in to charge beside her bed, she sent one last text message.

Goodnight sweet prince. Visit me in my dreams. E xx

A text came straight back.
Good night my angel. You are the only one for me. S x

She lay on her side in the rickety bed, staring up at the star-filled sky, whispering, 'Good night, Mum. I think you would be happy if you could see how my life has turned out.'

Chapter 49

Struan was quite obviously excited when Edina bounded through the doors of the hotel. She stood statue-still at the reception desk for a few seconds, then gave a royal wave.

'We're not back at that again, are we? Stop acting crazy and tell me what time your friend is coming.'

She laughed. 'You can be so grumpy at times, Struan. You really need to chill out, you know. Did you get my message about booking three rooms?'

'Yes, it's done. What time are they arriving?'

'I'm picking him up from the 1.30 ferry, so if it's okay with you, I'll sneak away at one. That can be my lunch hour.'

When the front door opened, Edina turned around to see Freddy walking in. He was wearing his New York Yankees sweatshirt. She seethed at the sight of him.

'Freddy,' Struan announced. 'If I had an employee of the month, it would be you.'

'No problem, I'm due to leave next Thursday, but I'm happy to stay on until Sunday just to help out, if you like.'

'That would be great. We actually have some residents in the hotel tonight, and according to Edina's crystal ball, it's going to get even busier.' Struan looked to Edina to join the conversation. She remained silent.

'Upwards and onwards,' Freddy told them, heading to the kitchen. Edina followed closely behind.

In the doorway to the kitchen, she watched Freddy gathering the old newspapers from the recycling bin.

'Are you collecting these newspapers for anything special, Freddy?' she asked casually.

Freddy was startled. 'No, I'm just taking them home for my father to use when he lights a fire.'

'Did you know that some creep has been pestering Marnie with letters? She's terrified. In fact, she has been so frightened that Struan has set up CCTV cameras at the front and back of The Shell Seekers.' For a few moments, she just watched him squirm. 'It's quite a coincidence because when Marnie played the film back, the intruder was wearing a hoodie, just like the one you have on today.'

The newspapers were ceremoniously dumped back into the bin before Freddy took a seat at the table. His gaze was fixed on the Formica top, his hands were clasped together under the table.

'Struan has involved the police. They are searching through the film footage at this very moment. I just worry about what Struan will do to the guy when he catches him.' Standing over him, she stared as he nervously picked away at a small split in the edging of the table.

'What are you saying, Edina?' he asked, avoiding her eyes.

'I'm saying that you have stalked and terrorised a really nice girl because you have a crush on her. Did you really think she was going to read your creepy letters, realise that it's you she wants, then fall into your arms? I mean, what did you really think was going to happen here?'

Freddy broke down. 'I didn't know what else to do. I love her. I've always loved her. How else was I going to get her attention?'

'You certainly got her attention all right!' she snapped.

'Are you going to tell Marnie and Struan?' he said, sobs escaping from him.

'I should tell them. I owe it to them.'

A lengthy, uncomfortable pause was left hanging in the air.

Freddy scanned her face through his tears, desperately looking for clues as to her decision.

'I have thought long and hard about how to approach this unpleasant situation.' A modicum of sympathy kicked in as she looked at him. An unexpected and generous sigh expelled from her, taking with it the anger she felt towards this socially inexperienced boy. Planting herself down on the chair beside him, she sat shaking her head at the situation she had found herself in.

'I have decided not to tell them.'

Freddy's body slumped with relief. 'Thank you.'

'Don't thank me. I decided this because I don't think your letters were malicious, although they did look pretty sinister. I don't think you intended to frighten Marnie, but just for the record, you did.' Her eyes bored into him as she delivered her speech.

He glanced up at her when he realised he was being given another chance.

'Listen Freddy, Marnie loves Struan. They want to get married. Get that knowledge into your head and look for a girl who feels the same as you. All the stalking and letters have to stop, now.'

'I promise I'll never do it again. I don't know why I did it. Once I started, I just couldn't stop. It became like a habit, you know, something I had to do every day. When no one suspected it was me, I just kept going.' Hanging his head in shame, he cried into his hands.

Edina looked upon the pitiful sight and wanted to make things better, for everyone. There was nothing worse than having a spotlight shone on your transgressions. She knew that feeling only too well.

'I am going to get you to do something as a penance. I won't say a word to another living soul, but in return for a squeaky-clean slate, you have to do something good for someone else.'

'I'm listening,' he said.

'I don't believe that Suzie is guilty of the crime she is being accused of. I think she will be home soon. I would like you to go to Suzie's house and clear all the furniture and carpets from her front garden. You can burn some of it, but you will need to transport the rest to the dump. I know you are working for Struan now, but you can find the time after your shifts. I want to see the garden completely cleared, and perhaps you could mow the lawn. Do we have a deal?' she asked, putting her hand out to shake.

'Definitely.' He vigorously returned her handshake. 'Thank you so much, Edina.'

'Don't thank me. I don't even know if I'm doing the right thing here. We are both betraying Struan and Marnie.'

'I will begin the work at Suzie's tonight.'

Chapter 50

The ferry, on course for Mull, could be seen in the distance. Edina was parked in the space she had used all those weeks ago when she first arrived. It felt like a lifetime had passed since the CalMac ferry had dropped her at the terminal in Craignure. Now, she was waiting exactly where she had sat, reading the instructions about how to find her cottage. *I was so depressed back then. I think I came to a remote island partly to punish myself. It's difficult to analyse my thinking back then, but I had done such a terrible thing in Edinburgh, I thought that I deserved a terrible life away from civilisation.* She gave a wry smile. *I suppose, in a way, it was just like the convicts getting sent to Australia. If I hadn't taken the job here, I would never have met Somerled. Somerled, Somerled, what is it about that name that makes my knees feel weak?*

The ferry grew larger as it neared the terminal. Edina's thoughts switched to Pip and the project ahead. The final episode of the documentary could possibly turn out to be one of the most powerful scenes on television. Solving an age-old murder and finding the remains of a ghost that had led her to his resting place. Now, that was really something worth seeing. Unless of course, no remains were found, and it turned out to be the biggest anti-climax on television. *I have to shake off these negative thoughts. I am about to sell this idea to Pip, so I have to believe in my own instincts.*

Only when the ferry docked did Edina get out of the car. She walked over to the gaping mouth of the vessel, searching the crowd for Pip. *There he is. I can recognise that cocky swagger anywhere.*

'Pip! Pip!' she shouted, waving frantically.

A huge smile graced his face as he headed over towards her.

He began speaking before he reached her. 'Hey, girl! This had better be good.'

Edina hugged him tightly, 'Have a little faith, will you?'

'I'm here, am I not?' Reaching for her hand, he told her to lead the way.

Pip sat in the front seat of the car with Edina. His two companions took the back. All three visitors had brought only a holdall each.

'Buckle up, men, it will take us about half an hour to get to the hotel in Pennyghael,' she said, pulling on her seatbelt. 'When we get there, you'll get a chance to meet Struan. He's the owner.'

She stopped herself from saying that Struan was also her boss. Today, she wanted to wear her journalist hat, rather than the headwear of a chambermaid, waitress, dishwasher, or barmaid. Pip was an influential documentary maker who had come to Mull at her request. Working in the hotel was fine, but boy, it felt good to investigate a story, just like in the old days.

Edina led her visitors through the doors of Pennyghael House Hotel. She knew beyond all doubt that Struan was waiting like a child for Christmas for their arrival.

'Struan, this is Pip Patterson and his assistants, Daniel and Cal.'

Struan walked round from the reception desk. 'Hi, it's good to meet you all. I hope you enjoy your stay with us.' He gave a short but firm handshake to all three men.

Watching Struan talking to the men, Edina could see he was nervous. In fact, she had never seen him behave so formally with the guests. Pip's confidence and even his expensive taste in clothes could be a little intimidating. Edina had seen it before. Over the years, she discovered that the first impression you glimpse of Pip, was not the man he truly was.

'This is some place you have here, Struan,' Pip told him, looking at the décor around him.

'Thanks. It wasn't like this when we bought it.' Struan laughed.

Pip then turned to Edina. 'I've come to hear your proposition, so should we get started?'

'Come this way,' Struan said, taking the lead. He led them into the residents' lounge, where he pulled over an extra seat to a table of four. Turning to Edina, he then said, 'Over to you, Edina, this is your pitch.'

Armed with her bank of evidence, Edina began to slowly unfold Jeremy's story. It began with her first day on Mull when she stopped by to see her new place of work. Each stage of the story was backed up with evidence she had collected from photos, footage, her journal and Catriona MacLeod's book.

The men listened to the remarkable, quite frankly, unbelievable story. They may have doubted every word if Edina had not shown the actual physical evidence.

'So this brings me to the documentary opportunity I think is way too big to pass up. The filming could take place at my cottage and in this hotel. You could start by interviewing me, giving me the chance to tell the story. I also have an old gentleman called Stan who I am sure would be willing to share some information given to him by his elderly mother who worked with the children of Pennyghael House many years ago.'

Pip sat silently, nodding.

Unsure of what he was thinking, she continued to sell the idea. 'The last episode would take place in the tower room, the one I told you about. I thought we could get Stan to take a sledgehammer to the wall of the tower, where I believe we will find Jeremy and his mother, Lottie.'

'How do you know for sure that they will be there?' Pip asked.

'Because I am almost certain that Jeremy has led me to the tower. I think the master of the house murdered Lottie and her son because she was threatening to tell everyone that he was the father of her son. He got rid of them, telling everyone at Pennyghael that they had left on a boat for Ireland.'

'You realise, Edina, that there could be a lot of time and money spent only to find out that they are not there.'

'Yes, I do realise that,' she agreed. 'But, the story stands alone, for the evidence is remarkable. People love a ghost story. If Lottie and Jeremy are not behind the wall of the tower, then it paves the way for a second documentary when I do find them. I have to find them. My life won't be worth living if I don't. Jeremy won't stop pestering me.'

Pip was non-committal about the idea. 'You have to let me discuss it with Daniel and Cal. We can talk pros, cons and cost. Could we have some time alone?'

Struan rose to his feet. 'Come on, Edina, you've said all there is to say.'

Chapter 51

Freddy drove straight over to Suzie's house after his shift. Making things nice for Suzie's return didn't feel like a punishment. He was more than happy to help her. In the beginning, he had doubted her innocence, but Edina had been so adamant about it he started to believe her. It would take more than one visit to the house to even make a dent in the work to be done, but he had no better plans lined up. In fact, he was happy to keep a low profile.

Surveying the state of the garden for a moment, he decided to separate the old pieces of furniture into two heaps. Bonfire and dump. The metal bedframe and carpets were definitely destined for the dump. The sideboard and wardrobes could be burned.

It was dark by the time Freddy had everything in order with the furniture. Using his foot, he managed to break apart the wardrobe and bookcase by kicking it fiercely. He was about to call it a night when he noticed the peeling paint on the front door. *If I could scrape most of that off tonight, I could buy paint tomorrow and give it a couple of coats. There's bound to be a scraper in that old garage. There may even be a hammer and some petrol in there.*

The garage door was padlocked, but on closer inspection, Freddy saw that the screws that held the lock were rotten with rust. He gave a quick scan around the driveway looking for a suitable rock to break it open.

One blow and the perished lock was left in pieces on the ground. Freddy entered the musty space, looking on the wall for a light switch. An old strip light buzzed into action, giving off an adequate flickering glow.

The smell of cat urine was overpowering. Freddy pulled his New York Yankees sweatshirt over his nose and mouth to prevent himself from retching. He searched the home-made shelves against the wall. Everything was tarnished with age and dampness. A cupboard below the shelves contained nothing but old car parts and rusty screws. Freddy presumed that Suzie's father thought they would come in handy one day. Bending down onto his knees to search further, he noticed a paper bag and reached for it. The top of the bag was rolled up tight, the words 'Brodie's Hardware Store' was written in bold letters on both sides. Curiosity got the better of him, so he unrolled the top of the bag. Peering inside, he saw an opened box that displayed an image of a black rat on the front. Resting on top of the box contents, he saw a blue plastic scoop with a powder residue on it. At the bottom of the bag, there was a till receipt. He knew he wasn't the sharpest tool in the toolbox, but he was smart enough to know that he may have found something important. Without touching any of the contents, he rolled the bag back up at the top and carried it to the boot of his car.

Chapter 52

Pip was in on the project from the moment he heard the word ghost. Daniel and Cal, who would be investing in the documentary, were also sold on the idea. Mysterious events like these didn't happen daily, and Pip knew that Edina was right when she said everyone loved a ghost story.

It was Pip's intention to start filming as soon as possible. Before he left the mainland, he had tentatively booked a film crew to join him. They were on standby, waiting to hear if they were needed. Pip would be directing as well as producing the project, alongside Daniel and Cal. The sound mixer he always used for productions such as this was an older gentleman named Otis Blake. Otis had worked on many highly acclaimed documentaries over the years, making him a specialist in his craft. Such was the respect that Pip had for Otis, he had only ever called him Sir.

Eli was a videographer and a lifelong friend of Pip's. Before they began any collaboration, they would sit down together to map out a plan for the documentary. Eli liked to know exactly how Pip would be editing the story. That way, he could record the perfect material for a smooth process. Eli and Otis would both be bringing an assistant, along with Liz Fairhurst, a young woman Pip generally brought on board for research purposes.

The crew members would be arriving on the six o'clock ferry. This was great news for Struan as eight rooms would now be occupied for the foreseeable future. Pip had already hinted to him that his crew would be eating all meals in the hotel for convenience. Struan now needed more staff urgently as he would be losing Edina during the making of the documentary. He intended to spend the day putting out feelers for new staff who could start immediately.

The crew arrived in two cars just before seven. Pip had supplied them with directions to the hotel, which they followed easily.

Struan saw them all to their rooms before going down to the kitchen to help the chef prepare dinner. He instructed Freddy to cover the bar, then deal with dishes at the end of the night.

Edina headed home just before the crew arrived. Pip told her that they would be having a meeting the following morning, and he wanted her there. They were going to sit down in the lounge area to outline the documentary's format. While Edina was involved with the project, Struan's mum would take over her duties at the hotel until he could find some temporary staff.

Although Edina was incredibly excited about Pip and the crew being there, Somerled was coming over for the evening and that outtrumped the project hands down. If she could, she would chose to spend every moment of the rest of her life with him. He was her world.

They indulged in passionate sex the moment he arrived at the house. He was barely through the front door. They laughed afterwards at the frenzied urgency of how it had happened.

'Can I come in and sit down now?' he asked. 'I'm beginning to feel like nothing more than a sexual plaything for you.'

'Well, if the cap fits, wear it,' she joked back. 'Glass of wine?'

Somerled rested his arm along the back of the sofa, twirling the ends of Edina's hair with his fingers.

'Is it good having your friend Pip over to visit?' he asked.

'I wondered when you were going to bring up Pip. I think you're a little bit jealous of Pip.'

'Pip!' he scoffed. 'What kind of a name is Pip? It sounds like a little elf in a green felt hat with a feather in it.'

'Now, don't be nasty,' she laughed. 'I can now tell you why Pip is here on Mull. We have a project together.'

While they sat on the sofa, Edina unravelled the story of Jeremy and his visitations. She told Somerled all the information she had gleaned about the boy's past and disappearance. She then explained that Pip Patterson was a documentary maker and that the story would be told over three parts, ending with the knocking down of the tower wall.

'I'll show you the photos I took on the first day I arrived in Mull. Do you remember my first day when I gave you a cheap thrill on the humpback bridge?'

'I needed therapy to help me forget it,' he laughed.

Somerled was baffled by the photos of the hotel with Jeremy in the background. There was no logical explanation for any of the events Edina had described to him. However, he felt great relief to hear that Pip Patterson was no more than an old friend and work colleague. The idea of sharing Edina's affections with anyone else was unbearable to think about.

'What happens to the documentary when Pip has finished making it?' Somerled asked.

'Pip has so many contacts now with TV networks, streamers, and agencies. He will send a pitch to every company and go with the highest bidder. His reputation is so good that he won't have to wait long before getting an offer. In fact, if I know Pip, he'll have already been in contact with some of the big fish before the crew even got here.'

'Mr Make it Happen, eh!' Somerled said, with more than a hint of sarcasm.

'Yep, that's Pip Patterson, Mr Make it Happen.'

The hour was late and Edina knew that both she and Somerled had an early rise in the morning. Reluctant to let him leave, she instigated intimacy between them.

Somerled was more than willing to engage in her flirtations before he left.

Chapter 53

Rays of early morning sunshine streamed through the window, landing on Edina's cheek. Her eyes flickered open, and thoughts of Somerled instantly flooded into her head. She smiled. *I can't believe how easy it is to get up early when the sun is shining, and I have Somerled in my life. He makes the world such an exciting place to live in.*

Flipping her legs over the top of the duvet, she propelled herself up and out of the bed to the high pitched screech, 'Laaaah.'

Since she had a meeting with Pip and his crew, she decided to wear the black trouser suit that she had brought to Mull but had not yet worn. It occurred to her that when the documentary was finished, and the crew had returned home, she may find it difficult to reacquaint herself with the duster and industrial hoover. This small flavour of her previous journalistic life tasted oh so sweet.

Perhaps when this is all over, I could apply to The Mull Courier for a job or even write freelance articles. It's a thought for the future. I won't leave Struan until business is booming, and I am never leaving the Island of Mull, as long as I live.

When she arrived at the hotel, the crew, excluding Pip and Cal, were sitting in the dining room having breakfast. She gave them a wave, then headed to the reception to speak to Struan.

At full speed, Freddy ran down the staircase, two steps at a time.

'Edina, Edina! I need to speak to you in private. It's urgent.'

'Okay, let's go to the kitchen,' she told him, leading the way.

The front door opened, and in walked the flushed, sweating faces of Pip and Cal, wearing their jogging clothes.

'Ah! You're here, Edina. Good, let's get started. I'll round up the rest of the team.'

Freddy stood waiting for Edina. 'Can we talk, please?'

'Freddy, I'm sorry, I can't. There is a meeting scheduled for right now. I have to be there.' She noticed a look of frustration on his face. 'I promise as soon as it's over, we'll talk.'

In the far corner of the lounge, Pip dragged the chairs into a circular formation. He beckoned the team over, indicating for them to take a seat. When he saw Edina, he patted the chair next to him for her sit on. Before he opened the meeting with introductions, he nodded to Eli. Reaching into his briefcase, Eli took out a small taping device. He switched it on before laying it on the middle of the table.

'Thanks for coming, everyone. I value your expertise on every project that I do. You are probably wondering what we are doing on the beautiful, though somewhat remote, island of Mull.'

There were a few nods from the company.

Otis raised his hand to speak.

'Yes, sir.' Pip asked.

'Apologies for interrupting, but I wanted to say I had my honeymoon here on Mull forty-two years ago. This is the first time I've been back.'

Everyone made their own small response to the news that Otis shared.

Pip smiled. 'Thank you for that. You'll need to plan a visit here with your wife, on your 50th anniversary. Back to business, I am going to hand you over to Edina, who will explain some quite extraordinary events that we think would be of great interest to the public. Edina, just start at the beginning.'

With her evidence laid out on the table before her, Edina began by describing her first day on Mull.

The meeting in the lounge did not wrap up until early afternoon. After the crew had perused the lunch menu, Edina wrote down everyone's preferred option. She then headed down to the kitchen to give the orders to the chef.

'Finally!' Freddy exclaimed when she walked through the door.

'Okay, I'm all yours,' she told him, pulling out a chair from the table.

The truth was, she had completely forgotten all about him.

'Just wait there,' he told her, 'I have to go and get something from my locker.'

He returned minutes later.

Edina's curiosity was now fully aroused.

He sat back down at the table, clutching the bag by the rolled-up top.

'This may be nothing, but it may be something, something big, very big.'

'Just get on with it,' she snapped.

'Last night, I went to Suzie's house. I piled up the furniture into two bundles. I then looked at the front door and saw that it was peeling. I broke into the garage... It wasn't difficult because of the lock—'

'Freddy, get to the point.'

'Anyway, at the back of a cupboard in the garage, I found this bag.' He unfurled the top. 'Here, look in, but don't touch anything.'

Peeking into the bag, Edina saw the box of rat poison. She made eye contact with him, unsure of the relevance of the contents.

'Let me explain,' he told her, wrapping the bag back up at the top. 'There is a box of rat poison in that bag which is opened. There is also a little plastic scoop for measuring. But, the most important thing is that there is a till receipt for the hardware shop, at the bottom of the bag. So, I was thinking that if the police checked the scoop for fingerprints, they may not find Suzie's on it. They may find that it was her father who took the poison himself. Suzie did say that he had been really down since he found out she was going to be moving out. The receipt should tell the cops who actually bought the poison, if the person used a bank card.' He looked at Edina for a response.

'Freddy, you may be sitting there with a key piece of evidence in a murder inquiry. You are a genius for thinking that through. I can't believe it.'

'Edina, no one has ever called me a genius before. Thank you. Should I take it down to the cop shop?'

Edina smiled. 'Definitely. Would you like me to phone ahead to explain things?'

'No, thank you. I can do that myself. I'm a genius, remember!'

Chapter 54

'How do you think that went?' Edina asked Pip, after being interviewed by him in her cottage. 'Did I manage to lay the groundwork without giving away too much?'

'Yes, it was spot on,' Pip told her. 'You gave the viewers enough titbits to keep them watching. It's got to be a slow unravelling. Eli and I will check over it tonight to see if anything needs to be added or cut. You came over very well. You're a natural.'

'It's a bit unnerving having a film crew in my house. Have you any idea how much cleaning I had to do before you arrived?' she joked. 'What have you got on this afternoon?'

'I have arranged to meet Stan and his mother. I may need directions to the house. Fancy coming?' Pip asked.

'Okay, but I need to be back by early evening. Every Friday, we all go out to a bar called The Shell Seekers. It's a great night. Bring the crew along if you like. It would be a good way to unwind for the weekend. You guys have been working flat out.'

'Yeah, we might just do that.'

For the duration of the car journey to Stan's mother's home, Pip chatted enthusiastically about ideas for the documentary.

With a smile on her face, Edina listened, marvelling at the extent to which he had bought into the idea. She loved the fact that whenever he was focused on a project, nothing would railroad him off it. The ideas he had formulated were highly original, ground-breaking even, but Edina's mind was on Somerled. It was becoming more and more difficult to be separated from him, even for a short time. The thought of seeing him in The Shell Seekers, waiting for her, smelling as good as he looked, was the only thing on her mind.

'I have decided that Stan should be the man to knock the tower wall down at the end of the last episode. Mainly because he has a history with Pennyghael House and he is the hotel handyman. So, it's important the audience get to know him as a person throughout the series. I can almost hear the viewers rooting for him as he takes swing after swing at the wall. 'Come on Stan, you can do it,' they'll shout from their armchairs.'

Catching only the tail of Pip's conversation, Edina laughed. 'Pip, you don't half get carried away sometimes. Stop on the left at the foot of the street. It's the house with the navy blue door,' she told him, pointing in the direction.

It was difficult to say whether Stan spoke more than his mother or the reverse. Between them they recounted many stories and personal experiences of life in Pennyghael. Pip was aware that most of their conversation was completely irrelevant to his purpose, but he enjoyed the flavour of island life they shared with him.

'Life on Mull has always been more restricted from that on the mainland,' Stan's mother explained in her singsong, island accent. 'The church made the rules, and they had to be obeyed. My mother received a visit from the minister when a report was brought to him that she had hung out washing on the Sabbath. The Reverend Malcolm MacKay let her off with a severe warning. She had to give a solemn promise that it would never happen again. It never did.'

'Oh, and if a baby were conceived out of wedlock! Phew!' Stan added, 'It would bring shame on the whole family. Young girls were often sent away to avoid anyone knowing.'

Everything that was discussed was recorded with permission. Later, when Pip was to return to the hotel with the recording, he and Eli would listen over it, tweezing out the information they could plan an interview around.

Edina sat next to Pip on the sofa, listening to the mother and son discussing a life so alien from her own. Hearing about this simplistic existence that the family had lived for generations was wonderful to them. They regaled their colourful memories with such fondness. Edina realised that her life, until now, had been all about striving for more, then even more, stepping on anyone who got in her way. It was a past filled with shameful regrets. Hearing Stan and his mother reminisce with laughter cemented her decision to remain on the island forever.

Chapter 55

The film crew were in high spirits as they climbed aboard Stan's bus. Before taking his seat, Pip exchanged a few words with Stan about their afternoon at his mother's house. A time was arranged between the two to develop things further regarding a filmed interview. At this meeting, Pip would put the idea to Stan about knocking down the wall in the tower room.

'Is that all aboard that's coming aboard!' Stan shouted at the top of his voice.

'Yes,' Struan shouted back. 'Take it away.'

The Shell Seekers was packed with people. The warm evening had brought the customers spilling out of the door, holding their drinks. Edina could think only of seeing Somerled as she scanned the crowd for his face. *He must be inside.* She stepped off the bus and glanced around. In her excitement, she hardly felt Pip's arm sliding around her shoulder.

'This was a great idea,' he said as they walked towards the door. 'It's just what the crew needed.'

His arm remained around her.

From his table at the back of the room, Somerled saw Edina entering the bar. The familiarity between Pip and her caused him a certain degree of discomfort.

Edina looked towards the usual table that The Fisherman's Friends frequented. Her eyes suddenly fixed on her beloved Somerled, inspiring her to push her way through the crowds to be with him.

Scooping her up into his arms, he whispered, 'I missed you, sweet girl.'

'I missed you, handsome boy,' she replied, kissing his cheeks and forehead. 'Are you coming over to our table?'
Somerled threw a glance at his friends. They returned a look of 'don't you dare', but he ignored this, saying, 'See you later, guys.'

Two tables were pushed together to accommodate the Pennyghael staff and the film crew. Edina pulled her chair in tightly next to Somerled's. Using the tips of her fingers, she massaged his neck and shoulders. Across the table, she noticed Freddy turning around to look at Marnie. Edina delivered a swift kick to his shin, shaking her head when he glanced over.

The sheets of paper and pens were passed from table to table for all those participating in the quiz. The volume of the music was lowered to an almost soundless level, allowing the quiz master to take to the microphone to explain the rules.

With the added knowledge of Pip's crew, and in particular, Otis Blake, Edina's team managed to answer all of the questions. She, along with her teammates, were pretty confident that this was the week that they would walk away with the prize of a bottle of champagne. How they were going to share it among them all was anyone's guess.

Marnie turned the sound of the music up. She knew that this would act as a trigger for people to approach the bar for refills. Everyone knew that they had approximately twenty minutes to get the drinks in before the quiz master would be back with the results.

Pip's assistant, Daniel, began to recap over the questions.

'Hey guys, I've been thinking about the sport question, how many caps did Kenny Dalglish get for Scotland. What did we answer?'

Struan piped up, 'We said it was 101, why?'

'It's not 101, it's 102. I've just realised.'

The men continued going over every answer that they gave for every question. As they did so, Somerled leaned in close to Edina, whispering in her ear. 'I wish we were sitting together in my newly built house.'

Edina turned to look at him. This comment, which had come out of nowhere, touched her deeply. 'Me too. We could look out across the sea and watch the sunset.'

He pulled her in tight, holding her like he was never going to see her again.

'Bloody hell,' Freddy shouted, on hearing that the Fisherman's Friends had won the quiz. 'Not again. I thought we were in with a shout there.'

'Hey pal, what are you talking about? You didn't answer one single question,' Cal heckled.

The company laughed, embarrassing Freddy.

There was no bus in the car park waiting for them at the end of the night. For some reason, Stan had not returned.

'Does anyone know any taxi numbers?' Pip asked.

Struan laughed. 'The few taxis on Mull are booked well in advance on a Friday night, I'm afraid. Walking is the only other option.'

The large group headed down the single-track road, in the direction of Pennyghael. Pip walked alongside Edina and Somerled.

'So, what kind of things do you do for entertainment here?' Pip asked the couple.

'Last weekend, we went in Tom's father's boat to the island of Staffa.'

Somerled was her private name for him. She had no intention of sharing it with Pip, or anyone else for that matter.

'Really!' Pip laughed. 'Tom, have you any idea what a party girl Edina is?'

Edina stiffened.

'I'm sure she was,' Somerled answered through slightly gritted teeth.

'Barmen were forever telling her to stop dancing on the tables,' Pip laughed. 'I always thought she was untameable. I never thought she would settle for just one man. A fisherman at that!' He continued laughing.

Somerled seethed but stayed dignified.

Edina shouted, 'Shut up, Pip! I'll excuse you because you are drunk, but I don't appreciate your insults.'

Pip drunkenly put his hand over his mouth, pretending to stop himself laughing. 'Oh! Miss Pure and Innocent now, eh? I bet you haven't told Tom the half of it!' he said, poking the stick further through the bars.

Somerled stopped walking. He walked towards Pip saying, 'You are such an arse!'

He then rolled his hand into a fist before effortlessly jabbing a fast punch into Pip's nose. It bled instantly. Reaching for Edina's hand, he led her away from the groaning Pip, who was nursing his injury in both hands.

'I'm sorry, Edina, but that guy has been begging for that all night,' he told her, while looking straight ahead, quickening the pace.

'You did what you had to do. I totally understand.'

Everyone continued on down the road. No one spoke. Amidst the silence around them, an engine whirring could be heard in the distance. It was Stan in his wonderful little shuttle bus.

Chapter 56

The following morning, when Edina arrived at the hotel, a bruised and somewhat sheepish Pip was standing on the steps waiting for her.

'I'm sorry,' he said. 'I deserved everything I got. I am a loose cannon with alcohol. Everyone tells me that.'

'Just forget it,' she said, walking past him. 'You really embarrassed me. Please don't do that again.'

She left him standing alone on the stairs.

'Ah, Edina,' Struan said when he saw her. 'There's a surprise in the kitchen. Go and see.'

Narrowing her eyes at him, she asked if it was a joke.

'No, it's not a joke. Go on, take a look.'

She walked towards the kitchen, squinting back at Struan to check if he was laughing. Not knowing what to expect, she pushed the kitchen door open. 'Suzie! You're here!' she screeched.

Suzie rose to her feet, throwing her arms around Edina's neck. 'Was it you who found the rat poison with my dad's fingerprints on it?'

'No, it was Freddy.'

'It bought me my freedom,' she told Edina. 'Who cleared the house, cut the grass, and painted the front door?'

'Freddy.'

Suzie cried. 'I am the luckiest girl in the world.'

Wiping away tears of her own, Edina hugged her young friend. *This girl has had the toughest life I have ever known, and now she thinks she is the luckiest girl in the world.* Edina felt incredibly humbled.

'I told the taxi to stop at the grocery store on the way home from the police station. I bought vodka, but when I saw my house all neat from the outside and completely cleared inside, I just took the lid off the bottle and poured the contents down the sink.'

Edina squeezed her again. 'I am so happy that you did that. This is a fresh start for you. Now, wait till you hear what's been going on here at the hotel. I have so much to tell you, Suzie. '

The hotel had quietened down for the afternoon on account of the crew filming outdoor shots of Mull. Pip's research assistant, Liz Fairhurst, called him to meet her at The General Register Office in Tobermory, where they held all records of births, deaths, and marriages. She told him that she may have found something that could be useful for the documentary. Pip left Eli and Otis filming scenes around the island while he drove straight to the Registrar's office.

Liz was sitting at a table situated at the back of the office. She was studying a document using a magnifying glass.

'Anything interesting?' Pip asked, sneaking up behind her.

'Not a huge discovery, but I had come here to find out if Lottie named the father of her baby on the birth certificate.'

'And had she?' Pip asked, feeling curious.

'Yes, she named Angus Robertson as the father. His occupation was listed as a stable boy. Now look at this.'

She reached into her handbag, taking out Catriona MacLeod's book. Turning to the folded-down page, she read aloud the section which documented the events of the fire. It talked of Lottie and her son Jeremy helping to put out the fire. Pushing her glasses onto her head, she skipped to a chapter addressing the mammoth task of clearing up after the fire. 'Listen to this... Seventeen-year-old Angus Robertson, the stable boy, was given the task of scrubbing down the whitewashed walls...'

Liz removed her glasses once again, looking up at Pip.

'Yes, so what?' Pip said with confusion.

'Catriona describes Jeremy as a six-year-old boy. If Angus were his father, he would have been eleven when he conceived him. I don't think that could possibly be correct. I believe that Lottie put his name on the birth certificate because she couldn't put the Lord of Pennyghael; she had to put someone. This shows she had something to hide about the baby's father.'

Pip nodded, 'Yes, I see what you mean. Good work, Liz. It's another small piece of evidence to back up the story.'

This project captivated Pip more than any other story he had covered in the past. Now that it was almost time to knock through the tower wall, he could feel the adrenaline flowing with excitement and a touch of trepidation.

Chapter 57

At precisely 7pm, Edina's front door was knocked on loudly.

A smile spread across her face. *He is never late. I love that.*

Snatching open the front door, she was, as always, thrilled by the sight of Somerled. For a moment, she stood admiring him before inviting him in.

'Pick a hand,' he told her, hiding both arms behind his back.

'That one.'

He brought the chosen hand to the front, showing that it held nothing. 'No luck. Try again.'

'Okay, that one,' she laughed.

'Oh, look what you've won.'

From behind his back, he pulled out a bunch of orange chrysanthemums.

'These are… eh, nice,' she lied.

'I was trying to make them a bit more exciting by turning it into a game. I know they're horrible, but it was all I could get at the garage.'

'Here's a crazy idea you might want to consider in the future. There is a place called a florist that has flowers of every type for sale, not just the old lady kind.'

Taking the flowers, she kissed him on the cheeks, lips, and forehead, as she always did.

'Come in and sit down. I'll put this exceptional bouquet in a vase.'

'Any more of your ingratitude, and I will never buy you chrysanthemums again.'

She feigned a look of disappointment. 'Do you promise?'

After they had made love on the sofa, Edina rustled them up toasted cheese sandwiches in the frying pan. She no longer hid the fact that she couldn't cook. After all, everyone had their limitations and she couldn't possibly be good at everything.

The absence of a dining table meant that she had to set the coffee table with cutlery, table mats, and glasses. The vase of chrysanthemums sat between them. A bottle of red wine she had uncorked earlier was for Somerled to help himself. Having arrived by car, she knew that he wouldn't touch the alcohol unless he had intended to spend the night. *I hope he pours himself a glass of wine to the brim.* Edina tried not to be too obvious that she was watching.

'Edina, could you do me a big favour?' he asked seriously.

'Of course, anything.'

'Could you move these bloody flowers off the table? They're putting me off my food.'

Later, she cleared the table, leaving the dirty dishes in the sink for the following morning. As far as she was concerned, a few minutes of washing up was valuable time away from Somerled.

They sat together, discussing the documentary and its latest developments. Edina made sure she didn't mention Pip's name, as it was now pretty obvious that Somerled did not approve of him.

While they were talking, Somerled twirled the ends of Edina's hair around his fingers. He then turned to face her, looking straight into her eyes. She wondered what was coming.

'Edina,' he said softly. 'I can't see you for the next few days. According to the forecast, we have four calm days ahead before high winds and storm conditions move in. My father wants us to go further out to sea to get our full month's catch quota in that time. The weather determines everything for a fisherman. If it's unsafe, we can't go out. I'll miss you, though,' he added, pulling her in close to him.

In the past few weeks, Edina had seen him almost every day. The thought of being away from him, for any length of time, filled her with panic.

'That's terrible news,' she told him. 'I don't think I can manage without you for that long.'

'We can make a pact to look up to the stars at the same time every night. The connection we have is so strong that we will be able to communicate telepathically. I will send you a message every night in my mind, and I want you to write it down. When I get home, we'll compare notes. Agreed?'

'Yes, that sounds fun. Imagine if we really do manage to read each other's minds. It will be amazing.' This idea brightened Edina's mood. 'Hey, I might even make a documentary about it.'

'Oh, here we go again,' he told her, rolling his eyes, laughing.

'Guess what? You'll miss the big climax of the project. The director has decided to film the ending tomorrow so that he can shape the documentary around the outcome. Stan's going to be smashing through the wall in the tower to reveal what we hope will be Jeremy and Lottie.'

'You can telepathically tell me all about it, then I can watch it when the documentary is released.' He took both of her hands in his and, looking sternly into her face, he said, 'I have something really important to ask you when I get back home. No, before you think it, I am not going to propose... yet, but it is in connection with the future.'

She furrowed her brow and narrowed her eyes. 'That's not fair, ask me now.'

'No, I want to ask you when the time is right. There will be a lot to think about. Four days, you can surely wait four days. When I get back, I will take you away for a couple of nights to a really nice hotel on one of the other islands.'

Squealing with excitement, she performed tiny hand claps at this idea.

He laughed at how adorably childlike she could be at times. After all, the first time he had met her, she had been trying to get a funny feeling in her tummy on a humpback bridge.

'Do me one favour while I'm away.'

'I'd do anything for you.'

'Don't let that arse Pip come sniffing around you when I'm gone. He really fancies you, you know.'

She laughed at his request. 'He doesn't fancy me, and I would never let him sniff anywhere near me.'

Chapter 58

Being cut off from Somerled was not easy for Edina, but she immersed herself in the project. Struan needed an extra pair of hands around the hotel, and she was happy to help. Staying busy was key to passing the time. She had suggested to Pip that they could film a few re-enactment scenes using a local boy from the village. By doing a little research through the night, she had found a costume resembling the clothes worn by Jeremy in the photos and a courier company was willing to deliver it to the island the following day.

Pip was on board with the idea, as he had used this method in a previous documentary. The fire scene would make a perfect re-enactment, although he knew it would push the costs up even further. The most important issue for him was finding out what was behind the wall. Filming the ending of a story early was not unusual when it came to documentary-making. The scenes were always filmed in no particular order. If mother and son were there, he had decided that they would extend the budget of the production and stay for a further few weeks at the hotel.

Large spotlights on tripod stands were set up in the tower room, facing the wall. Pip wanted camera shots from two different angles as well as a handheld for moving to the faces of the people who would be present. This had been Edina's story, her ghost. So he wanted clear shots of her reaction to the wall coming down. Whether her response was that of relief or disappointment, it didn't matter. The tension for the viewers would be tangible.

The crew were called to the tower room by Pip. Struan had been invited in to witness the scene, as was Liz Fairhurst, Edina and Stan.

As Edina walked through the door, she instantly felt the drop in temperature. There was an uncomfortable chill in the air, which came from something other than the cold. Looking around at those in the room, she could see Liz with her cardigan pulled tightly around her. Struan rubbed vigorously at his arms to generate heat in his body. This was a supernatural phenomenon, and it was real. They all felt it.

Edina sat on a stool in the middle of the room, spotlights blinding her. Pip had asked her to recap the events leading to this moment. Earlier that day, she had written and learned the words she wanted to share with viewers. She talked about how Jeremy had stopped at nothing to get her attention, and with her being an investigative journalist, she found it impossible to ignore him.

'We are now here to find out if Jeremy did indeed lead me to the place where his life was cut short to simply cover up a scandal.'

She lingered a poignant look into the camera before carrying off the stool to clear the way for Stan to take the stage.

Stan's hands trembled as he walked forward with the sledgehammer. Opening a grave was a terrible sin in his eyes, but there was comfort in the knowledge that this was what the boy wanted and that it could lead to a Christian burial.

He feared that his strength might fail. He was not as young as he used to be. With everyone standing silently around him, he took a deep breath before lifting the heavy sledgehammer. Drawing it back as far as he could, he swung with all of his might. A small dent appeared on the wall. This was going to be a long process.

Cracks in the plaster had appeared, but Pip noticed that Stan's strength was, indeed, failing. The last thing he wanted was for him to have a heart attack on the set.

'Cut!' Pip shouted, surprising everyone in the room. 'Stan, take a rest. Cal, you work out at the gym, don't you?'

'Yes, when I can.'

'Come and take several swings at this wall. Get the bricks nice and loose for Stan to finish the job.'

This was a chance for Cal to show off his strength. Raising the sledgehammer above his head, he let out a roar as he smashed it against the wall. A few flakes of plaster fell to the ground. He repeated the action several times with minimal results.

'Struan,' Pip asked. 'Do you have a drill here at the hotel?'

Stan stood up from where he was sitting on the floor at the back of the room. 'I've got one in my tool cupboard downstairs in the basement. I'll fetch it.'

'No, you save your strength. Struan, could you go and find it?'

Nodding, Struan ran off to find the drill.

'Why did they have to make the walls three feet thick back then? It's so inconvenient,' Pip mumbled.

The enormity of what was happening was really hitting Edina hard at this point. Her limbs began to ache with the nervous tension she was experiencing. All she wanted was to know the truth. Were they there or not? Had she read the signs correctly? It was almost too much to bear. Her mind raced with visions of what she might see when they finally broke through.

The drill was plugged into the extension cable and Cal began to work on the plaster between the bricks. It was working. There was movement in the wall. He continued until he believed that Stan would be able to take over with the sledgehammer.

As he rolled up the cable of the drill, he shouted, 'We are in business, Pip.'

'Okay, Stan, take over. We are about to find out if two souls are behind the wall.'

Pip's terminology caused a shiver to run across Edina's scalp and down her back.

The cameras rolled as Stan took the wall down in two heavy swings. Clearing away the debris, he peered furtively into the cylindrical space.

'Holy Mother of God,' he said, crossing himself.

It was with great trepidation that Edina took several steps forward. The handheld camera focused on her face. She was unaware of this. She moved Stan gently to one side to clear a space for herself. As the dusty stoor settled, she could clearly see the skeletal remains of an adult and a child. They were locked in an embrace. She sobbed unashamedly for Jeremy and Lottie, falling onto her knees with grief. The camera caught her full reaction.

The camera moved around the tearful faces of everyone present. No one was unaffected by this tragedy.

It was more than Edina could stand, and she left the room to be alone. From out in the hallway, she heard Pip give an emotional dramatic monologue about the gruesome discovery. It had been a dream ending for him and his crew.

'Rest in peace, Jeremy,' she muttered as she walked out of the front door of the hotel. *I am so sorry that your life ended the way it did. You were a good boy.*

As soon as she reached into her handbag for her car key, Edina suddenly froze. Large splashes of rain whacked against her windscreen. The trees swayed wildly in the wind. *The storm's not due to arrive for another two days. It's supposed to be calm. Bad weather's very bad for fishermen. Somerled, where are you? Are you safe? Oh God, please take care of my precious Somerled, please.*

Chapter 59

The downpour turned torrential, and Edina's windscreen wipers struggled against the weight of the excessive water. The fierce gale rocked the car from side to side. She made a split-second decision not to travel back to her cottage but to head to Somerled's family home. She needed to know if there had been any contact from the boat.

As she drove, her breathing became erratic, speaking her desperate thoughts aloud.

'Maybe they got back before the storm hit. Right now, Somerled could even be sitting in an armchair with a blanket around his shoulders and a cup of hot chocolate in his hands. But, if he's not back, the boat will not survive these conditions.'

The car wipers worked overtime, fighting against the deluge of rain. It became impossible to see the road ahead. Using her memory to guide her, she travelled in the direction that she knew to be correct. Fortunately for her, the roads were deserted.

The turning for Somerled's house was somewhere on the left. She slowed the car to see it. Flooded areas had deepened on the road, escalating the treachery of the conditions. Seeing the left turn ahead, she took the road wide to round the corner safely. The house was situated at the top of the hill, and she could see the lights on. That was a good sign. The climb was not easy with the force of what had now become a river against her wheels. The car struggled, jerking and spluttering against the full force of nature.

The car was left abandoned in the driveway as Edina ran to the front door of the house. Soaked through to the skin, she shivered uncontrollably. The doorbell made a pleasant tune. Edina thought that it was not appropriate for such an occasion.

She rang it again. *That tune is so, so wrong. Sombre church bells would be more suitable. How can the bell sound so flippant when my Somerled may be lost at sea?*

Her thoughts were unreasonable, and she knew it, but hysteria had left her thinking irrationally.

On the third ring of the cheerful bell, she could see a woman, possibly Somerled's mum through the glass on the door. Under different circumstances, she may have been nervous about meeting her potential mother-in-law, but her state of distress, the overwhelming need for news was all she could focus on.

The blonde, striking-looking woman stood at the door. Edina could see the tear tracks on her face.

'Hello, my name is Edina,' she babbled breathlessly. 'I had to come. Is there any news of the boat?'

The storm raged behind her, water dripping from her drenched clothes.

'Come in, Edina. I know all about you. I'm sitting, waiting for them to get in touch. I'll be glad of your company. Just go straight through.'

Removing her shoes at the front door, Edina dripped her way across the wooden floor, down the hallway to the kitchen.

'I'm Kate, by the way. I'll put the kettle on and fetch you some dry clothes.'

A tall cupboard stood behind the kitchen door. Kate opened it and reached for a towel from the neatly folded supply on the shelf.

'Take a seat on the bar stool. Give your hair a good rub with this. I'll go and find something to fit you.' Laying her hand softly on Edina's shoulder, she spoke in no more than a whisper. 'All we can do is wait and have faith that they got to shore in time.'

Edina was soothed by Kate's calming manner. She saw so much of Somerled in her. Her thoughts were muddled as she sat alone in the kitchen. There was no strength left within her to dry her hair with the towel; she didn't care enough to even try. *Oh God, please, please let him come back safely to me. I will do anything if you just bring him back to shore.*

Kate returned carrying a grey tracksuit. She told Edina to get changed in the downstairs bathroom.

'It's just across the hall. I'll make you a cup of sugary tea. You'll feel better after it.'

The two women sat in the kitchen together. Kate explained that her husband, Ralph, had made a call from the boat in the afternoon. Their trip had been successful, with almost a full month's quota caught within the first three days. Not until she turned on the radio did she hear about the unexpected storm moving in from the west.

'I tried to get in touch with the boat, but there was just nothing. That's not unusual at sea, though, so I'm still hopeful. I've contacted the coastguard, and they are doing all they can. They will call me back when they have news.'

In the early hours of the morning, Kate took a call from the coastguard. With great reserve, she relayed the conversation to Edina exactly as it had been told to her.

'Three hours ago, the coastguard discovered the wreck of the fishing boat. No souls were found aboard. A helicopter has been searching the surrounding seas for the six missing fishermen, but as yet, they have been unsuccessful. They plan to call off the search as the chance of finding any survivors is slim, considering the weather conditions of the previous night.'

Chapter 60

Driving along the wet roads, Edina couldn't think. She could barely breathe. Nothing had sunk in. Nothing made sense, just a jumble of upsetting information she could not process. She turned into the single-track road that led to her house. Her wheels landed in every pothole. She didn't care. Nothing mattered anymore. Life as she knew it, was over.

She pulled the suitcase out from under her bed and threw some of her clothes inside. She didn't care what she was packing, she just felt that it was something she should do. After dragging the case downstairs, she left through the front door, shutting it behind her for the final time. The heart and the soul of the cottage had gone. It meant nothing to her.

Her next stop was Pennyghael House. She had no interest in saying goodbye to anyone but felt that it was something she should do. The skin on her body felt cold and numb. No tears were in her eyes. The world around her was unfamiliar, hostile even. She no longer fitted into it.

Struan outstretched his arms when he saw her walking through the door.

She stopped without accepting his embrace. Her flesh hurt way too much.

'I am leaving on the ferry tonight, Struan. I can't function. I feel like I have crawled into a dark tunnel with no light at the end to go towards. I'm sorry, I can't discuss anything further.'

Struan cried to see her behaving in this way. He saw that her bright, shining light had simply extinguished.

'Thanks for everything. You saved our hotel and touched a lot of people along the way. I'll never forget you, and I live in hope that you will one day walk through these doors again. You're one of life's special people, Edina.'

Chapter 61

A loud knocking awoke Marnie with a start. It had been a late night at The Shell Seekers, with a little bit of trouble from some locals who had been out celebrating all day. Running down the stairs, she slipped on her dressing gown, tying the belt tightly around her waist. The key unlocked the door, but there were two bolts that Struan had fitted for extra safety. Drawing back the final bolt, she opened the door but quickly shut it again. It was jammed. Glancing down, she saw a foot had been wedged in to block its closure.

'You ruined my fucking life!' Ashton Brook shouted in her face, spraying saliva on her cheek. 'You didn't honestly think that I would leave you alone? Fuck no, it's payback time.'

Chapter 62

The storm that was officially forecast blew in over Mull. A raging tempest swelled the sea, and the darkened sky blackened its colour. Edina held onto the railings of the ferry. She felt hollow and broken. There was nothing nature's vicious onslaught could do to her that would cause more pain.

Just take me. Take me down to the deepest depths where you took Somerled. Take me to him.

Torrents of rain whipped at her flesh, and the wind beckoned her overboard, tugging at her clothes. Her foot stepped onto the first rung of the railings, and the other foot followed. Balancing precariously, she climbed another rung.

'Where are you, Somerled?' she shouted into the bubbling cauldron below. 'I want to come in and save you.'

'Excuse me, miss,' a voice came from behind. 'I think you should come down from there before something serious happens.'

A guiding arm coaxed her down.

Something serious? Something serious? Something serious has already happened, you fool.

The ferry worker led her below deck, where all the other passengers had taken cover from the storm.

She said nothing as he guided her into a seat near the window.

'You'll be able to get tea, coffee, hot chocolate over there if you want it.'

Her unresponsive manner told him he should leave her alone. His duty of care was over.

After driving off the ferry into the town of Oban, she had no idea which direction to travel in. How she wished that her mum was alive to help soothe her agony. Edinburgh was no longer home. The welcome she would receive would not be warm. She was too fragile to deal with any harsh judgements from former colleagues and friends. Tears blurred her vision as she took the road ahead.

I'll keep driving. I won't turn. I'll drive until my petrol runs out. I don't know what to do. I don't know where to go. I don't want to be alive. I'll never start a new life. I don't want a new life. I want the life that I had.

The low-fuel petrol light illuminated the dashboard. Edina looked out both side windows. Through the darkness outside, she could see that she was surrounded by the countryside. A sign indicating that there was a layby ahead caught her eye. There were no other traffic headlights anywhere in the distance. She drove into the small designated pathway. Reclining her seat back fully, she pulled her wet jacket from the backseat to cover herself. Sobs began to burst from deep within her; she gave herself up to them until she slept.

A light tapping on her driver's side window awoke her. Sitting upright, she lowered her window slightly when she saw an elderly gentleman with a golden retriever.

'Are you all right?' he asked. 'Have you broken down?'

'No. I'm fine, just resting my eyes. What town is that?' she asked, pointing at a town that could be seen just over the hill.

'It's Peebles.'
'Thank you.'
She closed the window.
She rubbed her tired, crusted eyes, realising that she had slept in the car all night. Her neck hurt, and her stomach growled with a scraping hunger.

I have a cousin in Peebles. We used to be close when we were young. I wonder if I could find her house. It has been so long since I've been there.

A much-needed petrol station stood on the outskirts of the town centre. Indicating left, she turned in to fill her tank.

On entering the town, she could see that there had been many changes over the years. The housing estate on the right had not been there on her last visit nor had the shopping mall which loomed ahead of her. She drove on until she arrived at the picturesque main street with all of its colourful, independent shops. This was the Peebles she remembered but where her cousin lived from here, she had no idea.

She lives near the river. Rivers don't change. They always remain in the same place. I'll follow the river through the town.

The sight of the Tweed Bridge was a soothing comfort to Edina. It waved a green flag, telling her that she was on the right road. The road to someone she knew, someone who would take her in and care for her. Once over the bridge, she saw a row of identical bungalows, one of which she was certain belonged to her cousin

I'm sure that it is on the left, about halfway up. I'll park here until I see something I recognise.

In her painful state of distress, it was strangely reassuring to know that, somewhere in the vicinity, she had someone who was family. All she had to do was find her.

It wasn't long before a car drove past, pulling into the space in front of where Edina was parked. A woman, who Edina recognised immediately, stepped out before reaching into the back for her shopping bags. Tears stung Edina's eyes. She climbed out of the car and stood on the pavement.

'June!' she shouted.

The raven-haired woman not much older than Edina, turned to look at her. It took a few moments before she saw who was calling her.

'Edina!'

She walked with pace towards her.

'Edina, what's happened?'

The girl that stood before June was a shadow of the vibrant cousin she remembered.

'June, I'm not coping very well.'

Two loving arms wrapped tightly around her. Her legs trembled as she was led into the bungalow that she hadn't given a thought to in years. Now, it was her refuge and lighthouse in the most in most tempestuous storm of her life.

'I don't know what's happened to you, Edina, but you're safe now. I'll run you a bath and make you some breakfast.'

Chapter 63

Forty miles from the island of Mull, near the shallow waters of the Island of Tiree, a small fishing vessel spotted something in the water. As it neared the object, they saw a man draped over a piece of driftwood. Three burly fishermen hauled him onto the boat. It was obvious that he was confused and suffering from dehydration.
'Who are you?' one of the fishermen asked. 'What's your name?'
The answer was barely audible as he slipped in and out of consciousness. 'I am summer led,' was his reply.
'Yes, but what's your name?' he asked again.
'I am summer led.'

The third and final part of the Mull trilogy

CoralMac

Available from September 2024 on Amazon

Also by this author and available on Amazon:

Exitum: A Classic Disappearance
Easy Live and Quiet Die

Printed in Great Britain
by Amazon